THE MAIDEN LANE MURDERS

THE MURDER BLOG MYSTERIES
BOOK 6

PAMELA FROST DENNIS

To my number one fan and partner in life.
My husband, Mike.

PROLOGUE

"Better start saying your prayers," she said, her voice low and cold.

"Why are you doing this?" My voice cracked as tears streamed down my face. "I've never done anything to you."

And that's when it hit me—I wasn't getting out of this alive.

———

CHAPTER ONE

WELCOME TO MY BLOG

A quick introduction to my life for my new blog followers. I'm thirty-two, 5'9" with auburn hair. I'd love to lose ten pounds, but let's be honest—life's too short to skip chocolate. Especially dark chocolate.

I'm happily divorced and financially stable thanks to a stash of gold coins I found in my attic. Long story.

No children yet, but I've got my two furry kids. Daisy, my brave yellow Labrador, saved me from a frying-pan-wielding lunatic—true story. Then there's Tabitha, my sweet gray tabby cat.

Until recently, I was in a serious relationship with my next-door neighbor, Josh Draper. That ship has sailed—and I missed the boat.

I live in Santa Lucia, a charming California coastal college town. My parents, Kurt and Marybeth, live nearby in the home I grew up in. Mom's a hairstylist; Pop (my stepdad) was a cop until a bullet forced early retirement—now he fixes appliances for fun and not much profit. My younger half-sister Emily lives in Santa Monica with her partner, Dawn.

My biological father, Bert McKenna, is a successful plastic surgeon in Palm Springs. He mostly mailed in fatherhood via child support. We're on friendly terms, but not close. He has a toddler named Baldwin with his much-younger wife. I visited last week—mainly for little Baldy.

My best friend since elementary school, Samantha Drummond, lives nearby with her husband, Spencer, their teenage daughter, Chelsea, and their young son, Casey.

And then there's Ruby, my fabulous fashionista grandma on my mom's side, who is my other best friend.

CHAPTER TWO

SUNDAY • AUGUST 23
Posted by Katy McKenna

It's been a couple of weeks since my last post. Usually, that means I've had some horrendous near-death experience, but not this time!

I've been on a few dates with a forest ranger I met at that fundraiser Sam and I attended at Beaver Lake. Let me introduce you to Kyle Cruise. Tall, dark, and ruggedly handsome. Generous, thoughtful, romantic—basically a real-life Hallmark Prince Charming. He's thirty-five, never married (no baggage!), and has a great relationship with his folks in Montana. Loves kids and is a vegetarian like me.

If you've been following my blog, you already know about his voice. Imagine fingernails on a chalkboard, but worse. I thought I could get used to it, but after two dates, I was ready to move on. Yet, he's so darn sexy when he keeps his mouth shut. At restaurants, I see women drooling over him, then glance at me, probably wondering how I snagged such a catch—until they hear him laugh like a braying donkey.

Last night, I dreaded telling him it was over, so I polished off half a bottle of pinot grigio at dinner to muster the courage. When we pulled up in front of my house, I was feeling woozy-good, and he was looking really good. When he leaned in for a kiss, I practically dragged him into the house.

Picture this: We're inside. I'm leaning against the front door, and Kyle is closing in, his soulful brown eyes devouring me, leaving me weak in the knees. He sets one hand against the door and runs his fingertips down my bare arm, sending lusty tingles up my spine. Then he whispered in my ear, "Before I met you, I never knew what it was like to smile for no particular reason." He chuckled. "Now I smile all the time." And then, with his voice in full throttle, he said, "My friends keep asking me if I'm drunk."

Suddenly cold sober and no longer tingling, I slid to the side and stepped away.

His brows crinkled, looking perplexed. "What's wrong? Am I moving too fast?"

"It's not you. It's me."

"Oh." He shook his head. "Like I haven't heard that before. I thought we had a real connection."

"We do. It's just that—" I set my hand on his forearm and gently squeezed. "I told you about Josh."

"I thought that was over."

"It is." I sighed heavily. "But I don't think I'm over it."

"We can go slow," he said. "One day at a time. You're worth waiting for, Katy."

"That wouldn't be fair to you." I opened the door and moved out of the way. "I'm so sorry. You're everything I could wish for in a man, but I'm not ready. You deserve so much more than I can give you."

At that moment, Daisy barreled through the laundry dog door from the backyard, barking her head off.

"I need to close the door, Kyle. Daisy hates men. She might bite you."

As I shut the door, he hollered, "I thought you said she loves everyone!"

Sagging against the door, I slowly slid to the floor and cuddled my girl. "Oh, Daisy. Why is he so almost perfect? Why can't I get past the voice thing?"

"I heard that!" yelled Kyle. "And you're right. I deserve more."

CHAPTER THREE

MONDAY · AUGUST 24
Posted by Katy McKenna

Ruby called while I was in the shower this morning. I got concerned when the phone rang again immediately after the first call.

Oh God. Who died? —That was my first thought. I got out and dribbled to my phone on the counter. As I reached for it, it started ringing again—her name and smiling face flashing on the screen.

"It's about damn time you answered," she barked.

"What's wrong? Is it Mom? Pop? Ben?"

Ben is Ruby's sweetheart—a former hotshot LA attorney. He had a thriving career but eventually had enough of defending spoiled, and often guilty, celebrities. He retired but kept his license active to work the occasional pro bono case in our town.

"No," she said.

"BeeGee?" Her beloved little malti-poo.

"She's fine. It's—"

"Did you fall and can't get up?"

8

"No!" she yelled. "Everyone is fine. I'm at work, and we're on a time crunch."

Ruby works at a temporary job agency called Nothing Lasts Forever.

"What's that got to do with me? I don't work there anymore." A while back, I worked at the agency for half a day and then handed my job over to Ruby. "Hold on." I wrapped a towel around my dripping body and perched on the toilet seat. "Okay. I'm listening."

"A job just popped up that I think might be right up your alley, given all your crime escapades over the last couple of years. It's with a private investigation firm here in town. They're looking for a receptionist—someone who can start immediately. It's part-time for now, but there's potential for it to turn into something permanent if you play your cards right. You've often said you were interested in being a private investigator, so this would be a great way to see if it's a good fit."

"What happened to their receptionist?"

"I have no idea. The agency has an A-plus rating with the Better Business Bureau and no nasty comments on Yelp or Google. What do you think?"

"Give me a minute."

My graphic arts career is kaput, and I've thought about taking PI classes online. Plus, I've solved a few local crimes. Okay, stumbled into them—but still, the bad guys are behind bars thanks to me.

"Katy, I don't have all day. Are you in? Or do I call someone else? The clock is ticking."

"What are the job requirements? I don't have a lot of secretarial skills, you know."

"It's probably not much different from what you did here."

"Ruby, I worked there for approximately four hours and did nothing except learn where the coffee machine was—then gave the job to you. How's Paul, by the way?"

Paul is the agency's owner. He's a nice guy who loves to play poker online. Now he plays with Ruby. If they were playing for money, he'd be bankrupt.

"He's fine," she said. "The job requires answering phones. Basic computer skills. Nothing you can't handle or learn. Remember, it's temporary until a permanent person is hired. So? Are you in?"

What the heck? This could be fun, I thought. "Okay. I'm in."

"Good. Come by my office before lunch and we'll do the paperwork. You start tomorrow, 8:30 a.m."

———

I signed the final document and slid it across the desk to Ruby. She straightened the stack, tucked it into a folder, and smiled.

"All right, my dear. You are now officially employed by Nothing Lasts Forever."

"I am? No, I'm not."

"I meant you are now a skilled professional contract temp worker. Therefore, you work for us." She gave me a critical once-over. "You won't be wearing that tomorrow, will you?"

I was dressed in my usual go-to ensemble: jeans, a T-shirt, a cardigan, and sandals.

"No. I promise to be office appropriate. What is that these days, anyway?"

My grandmother stood and did a spin to show off her chic outfit: a knee-length tan wool pencil skirt, a warm tan leather belt, black stilettos, a black square-neck top, gold chunky necklace, and a black blazer.

"That is so not business casual," I said. "That's more like corporate-dressed-to-kill on one of those lawyer TV shows."

She glanced at her gold watch. "You hungry?"

I nodded. "I could eat. There's a new vegan place I've wanted to try."

"Vegan? Oh, goodie. Twigs and leaves." She made a frowny face that reminded me of Casey, my best friend's six-year-old, when served a vegetable of any variety. He doesn't discriminate—he hates them all.

————

The Happy Vegan Bistro is bright and airy, with a farmhouse vibe. Even Ruby gave a nod of approval when she saw the décor, but when she saw the menu, she was less than impressed.

"Yeesh." She wrinkled her nose. "Quinoa, chickpeas, lentils, kale, tempeh? What the heck is tempeh?"

I scanned the menu. "It's nice to have so many options for a non-meat eater."

"But you still eat fish, right?"

I shook my head. "Casey has a new goldfish he named Winky. When he introduced me to the little guy, I swear we had a moment. It winked at me, and I knew we were simpatico. So, no more fish for me."

Ruby rolled her eyes. "Yeah, we'll see how long that lasts." She returned to the menu with a sigh. "Fine. I'll try the Karma Asada tacos with vegan carne asada—how delightful. And cashew cream instead of cheese. Yum."

"I'm having the black bean veggie burger and fries."

I ordered our meals at the counter and returned with a number for our table.

"So, what's new with you?" I asked. "Anything exciting?"

"Actually, yes." Ruby leaned forward, resting her elbows on the rustic wood table. "I'm starting a new project and need your help."

My first thought was, *Oh no, not another pyramid scheme.* "I'll help if I can. My new job might keep me pretty busy."

"Don't worry. It's not another multilevel marketing disaster

like E-Z Lip Stencils. I'm going to be"— she paused dramatically
—"a social influencer. A glam-granfluencer."

"A what?"

"You always call me your glamorous Grammy. I keep up with
the trends, so why not share my expertise?"

"Cool. I can dig it."

"Oh, eat my shorts!"

"Yes, dear Grandma. You're a very hip chick."

Our lunch arrived, looking quite appetizing. As the server
topped off our waters, Ruby pointed at her plate.

"Like this. I'm about to eat a vegan meal. Isn't plant-based
eating all the rage now?"

I stifled a laugh. "I've been eating like this for years."

Ruby took a big bite of her taco, chewing thoughtfully. "You
know what? It isn't terrible. Even the fake cheese is almost
edible."

"Who, exactly, do you plan to influence?"

"Obviously not you millennials," she replied with a snarky
tone.

"Well, excuse me for not being a hip Boomer."

I watched her scroll through her phone. "What're you looking
for?"

"I bookmarked the generation list." She kept scrolling. "Here
it is. The oldest Gen Zers, also known as Zoomers, are now in
their twenties. Then there's you, Ms. Millennial—also known as
Generation Y. Next are Gen Xers, from 1965 to 1980. Good grief,
they're already in their forties and fifties."

"That's Mom and Pop's generation."

"Yep. Then my peeps, Boomers, born from 1946 to 1964.
After that, it's Post-War, also known as the Silent Generation,
from 1928 to 1945."

"And what's before that? Dinosaurs?" I dipped a fry in the
housemade ketchup. "So, what's your target group?"

"Boomers and the younger Silent Generation—maybe older Gen Xers. God, I feel old."

"What will your influence specialty be?"

She stole a fry off my plate. "Style, makeup, hair, health, nutrition."

I raised an eyebrow. "You've never been exactly...health conscious."

"True. But I don't have to practice what I preach. Who's gonna know?"

I slathered my burger with ketchup, cut it in half, and set a piece on her plate. "Try this."

"Then you get one of my tacos." In the exchange, half the taco's contents spilled onto the table.

"What kind of help do you need from me?"

"Not that much." As she counted on her fingers, she said, "Help me set up a YouTube channel for my vlog, a website, Instagram, WhatsApp, Snapchat, Pinterest, LinkedIn, TikTok, a Facebook page, and a blog." She shrugged with an impish grin, as if it was nothing.

"Is that all? I don't have a YouTube channel or a website. How would I know how to do it?"

"But you have a blog. The rest we'll learn together. Won't that be fun? A grandmother–granddaughter project. Oh! I'll need you to be my videographer, too."

"Sounds like a lot of work, Ruby. A lot of work for me."

"Oh, don't be a poop. Someday, you'll look back on this as a treasured memory of time spent with your dear departed grandmother."

"You're not dying anytime soon. I forbid it, so quit with the guilt trip." I took a bite of the half-empty taco. Not bad. "We might as well start right now."

"Don't talk with your mouth full. And what do you mean by 'right now'?"

"You're going to need a lot of content." I took my phone out of my purse, set the camera app to portrait mode, and snapped several photos of our remaining, messy food. "Now, a few shots of you eating."

Ruby sat up straighter. "How's my makeup?"

"There's a smudge of mascara under your left eye."

She unsmudged, then fluffed her blonde weave.

"Okay," I said, lining up the shot. "Big smile, like you're thrilled about your trendy plant-based meal." I snapped a few photos. "Now let's do a video. Say something clever, then take a bite and look orgasmic, like it's the best thing you've ever eaten. Ready, set, action!"

Ruby cleared her throat and sat up straighter. "Hi there, fellow Boomer babes! Ready-Set-Ruby here! And I'm ready to help you set foot on your path of action in our golden years." She sagely shook her head. "Golden years! Pish-posh! This is merely a new, exciting chapter in our lives. So, let's embrace it. We'll be talking about our health and ways to improve it. And, more important," she said with a wink, "how to look good doing it."

She paused for a breath, and I put the phone down.

"Why'd you stop filming?" she asked.

"Because everything you just said should be the introduction to your YouTube channel and website. It was almost perfect. I like the *Ready-Set-Ruby* thing. We'll film it for real once we figure out where you'll be doing most of your videos. But for now, let's pretend you've been making videos for a long time, and this is just one of many."

"Oh. Got ya. We're creating"—she air quoted— "content."

"Yes. And we—I mean you—will need a lot of it." I picked up my cell phone. "And...action!"

"Hi there! Ready-Set-Ruby here. I'm so happy you could join me for lunch at one of my favorite vegan restaurants on the sunny California Central Coast. Yes, I know—vegan. Crazy, right? But I gotta tell you, I'm having a delicious and healthy meal—the best of both worlds." She picked up the taco and chomped into it, rolling her eyes. "Yummy for my tummy!"

CHAPTER FOUR

TUESDAY · AUGUST 25
Posted by Katy McKenna

My first day as a "skilled professional contract temp worker!"

———

The Diligent Detective Agency is tucked into a well-maintained strip mall near the university. I parked under a shade tree and surveyed the other businesses: dry cleaner, donut shop, laundromat, hair salon, nail salon, and a reflexology foot massage parlor. There was also a Verizon store, Babette's Boutique, a 7-Eleven knock-off, and a couple of vacant storefronts.

This was not what I'd pictured. A detective agency should be in a decrepit old building with dark-paneled hallways, frosted glass doors with the agency's name in gold letters, and the lingering scent of cigars. You know, like Sam Spade's office in *The Maltese Falcon*.

Oh well. It wasn't like I was dolled up in a skirted suit, seamed silk stockings, heels, and a smart little veiled hat. I was business casual, which can be just about anything these days. For me, it's navy-blue pants that require dry cleaning, ballerina flats, a blouse (which I would inevitably spill coffee on), and a lightweight, one-button, uncomfortable tan blazer that I do not love. If this job were going to last a while, I'd have to invest in some work clothes.

At 8:25, I pushed through the glass door into the reception area. The cheerful, contemporary office had white walls adorned with splashy, colorful abstracts. A chenille teal sofa faced a glass-topped coffee table flanked by two Scandinavian-style orange chairs. I assumed the desk in the corner would be my head-quarters.

I stood there waiting to be discovered, then finally called out, "Helloooo?"

"Hold your horses," yelled a feminine voice from another room. "We don't open until nine."

"No rush. I'm from the temp agency."

"Oh! Be right there!" A moment later, a rosy-cheeked, slightly pudgy woman—perhaps in her early to mid-sixties—with a cute, silver, longish pixie cut and smiling hazel eyes, entered the room. "I guess I forgot to lock the door when I came in."

One look at her baggy, flared jeans, sandals, and yellow peasant blouse assured me I wouldn't have to purchase new clothes. She held out her hand and gripped mine with assurance.

"I'm Maxine Baker. Call me Maxie."

"I'm Katy McKenna. Nice to meet you."

"Ditto. The agency sent over all your information. From your job history, I gather this will be a new experience for you. You used to own the Bookcase Bistro. I loved that shop. I was disappointed when it closed." She shrugged. "Along with every other small bookstore in the county."

"That happened after I was out of the business. My husband and I divorced—he got the store, I got the house, and I went back to being a freelance graphic artist."

"Not always easy working with your spouse."

"Especially when he is a dirty, rotten, two-timing, cheating bastard," I said with a sweet, cherubic smile.

"Oh, gotcha, girl. My husband and I started this agency over thirty years ago. We had our petty differences, sure, but we made a good team. Tim passed about ten years ago, and here I am—still at it." She gave a little chuckle. "I always say my funeral will be my retirement party. My son keeps pestering me to retire and move in with him and his young family in Boise." She shrugged again. "And do what?"

I shook my head. "I don't know...shovel snow? Babysit?"

She laughed. "Bingo! Don't get me wrong but living with my son and his wife and their three adorable little rugrats, all under the age of eight, and being a five-day-a-week daycare, is not how I plan to spend my golden years. Maybe I'll move out there when the kids are in high school, but not now. You got kids?"

"No. I'm single. I live with a sweet yellow Lab named Daisy and a cat named Tabitha."

"I love dogs. Don't have one at the moment, but if Daisy's good with people, feel free to bring her to the office. I'm trying to keep up with the times, and I hear that's a thing businesses do now."

"My understanding is this is just temporary until you find the right person."

"Who knows?" She arched a brow, looking sneaky. "You might be that person."

"May I ask what happened to your last receptionist?"

"His boyfriend's job transferred him to Paris." She gave me a wry smile. "Jonathan was with me for several years, like family. But who can compete with love and gay *Paree*?" Maxie chuckled. "No pun intended."

She glanced at her watch and stepped to the desk. "This is your domain. The chair is new—one of those special posture chairs. The computer is a few years old. A Mac. At least it's not a Commodore, right?"

I laughed, not getting the joke. "I'm a Mac girl. Although I must admit, I'm not a whiz with programs like Excel."

"No problem. I have a bookkeeper. You'll mainly answer the phone, type up some letters, and make appointments. You do type, right?"

"Oh, sure."

"Your most important duty is keeping the coffeepot full," she said, motioning toward a coffee station on a teak bureau. A mini fridge was tucked underneath. "I'm a caffeine addict by day, wino by night."

"I can relate. Coffee in the morning and afternoon, wine in the evening—a perfectly balanced diet."

Maxie grinned. "Want a cup? I'm due for one. Then again, I'm always due for one."

"Sure."

She poured coffee into two ceramic mugs, then opened the fridge. "Cream?"

"Yes, please." I reached for the carton, added a generous splash, then dumped in three heaping spoons of sugar.

"A girl after my own heart," she said as she doctored her brew. "Let's sit."

She grabbed a file folder from her office, and we settled on the comfortable couch. I took a sip of coffee, then set my mug on a coaster on the coffee table. I was really starting to like this office —and Maxie.

"Your main gig here is babysitting the occasional client in the waiting room," she said. "I try to space out appointments so nobody's left stewing too long. Some folks are emotional, some are jittery, and some are just plain cranky. Most are fine, though. But let's be honest—they're not here for fun. They've got problems, and we're the ones they're hoping can fix them."

She flipped open the file. "You'll also help with case research from time to time. Ever heard of the dark web?"

"I've heard of it, but I've never dared to explore it."

"Smart. We mostly stay away from it, too, but it can come in handy now and then, when we're deep into a case." She laughed. "I keep saying *we* when it's just me."

"What kind of cases do you handle most often?"

"I'd love to say it's hunting down Russian spies, solving murders, breaking up drug cartels, and steamy run-ins with James Bond." She grinned. "But no, our bread and butter is divorce work—cheating spouses, mostly. Girl, the stories I could tell... People never cease to amaze me."

She leaned back, her smile softening. "I always told my husband he'd be the first to know if I was interested in another fella because I'd pack my bags and file for divorce first." Then, gently, she placed a hand on my arm. "I'm sorry. That was thoughtless."

"No worries. I am so over it. Life goes on."

She smiled softly. "Don't worry, Katy—there's someone out there for you."

Josh flickered through my mind, and I forced a smile. "I know. Can't wait to meet him."

Maxie opened the folder and pulled out a sheet of paper. "The agency sent over your references." She scanned the page. "I see our police chief, Angela Yaeger, is one of them. Care to elaborate?"

"We've worked together on a few cases. The most recent involved my elderly neighbor, who was abducted and held captive—"

Maxie slapped her knee. "Yes! The cabin case! That's why you look familiar—I saw you on the news. Your neighbor was lucky to have you as a friend."

Something outside the window caught her attention, and I followed her gaze.

"Our 9:00 is here," she said. "Nice woman, but wow, does she have a history. This'll be her eighth divorce. She's in her late seventies. You'd think she'd have thrown in the towel by now, but nope—she hates being alone, so she marries the next guy who gives her the time of day. Then ends up paying alimony to these bozos. Good thing she's got money. I keep trying to convince her to move into a senior community—you know, where there's plenty to do and lots of potential friends." She leaned forward and whispered, "I've heard those places have a lot of spicy flings going on."

"My grandmother lives at Shady Acres."

Maxie's eyes widened. "Oh, good grief! I keep putting my foot in it, don't I?"

I laughed. "It's fine. She has a wonderful boyfriend."

This evening, I called everyone to share the news about my new temp job. Mom's thrilled that I'll finally be getting out of the house. Pop said Maxine has a solid reputation. Samantha's excited for me and already looking forward to hearing some crazy stories. My sister said it'll be a great inspiration for her writing—a mash-up of several genres all in one book: fairytale, fantasy, and murder mystery.

Later, I looked up Commodore computers. The Commodore 64 was released in 1982, making home computing more affordable for the general public. It was introduced in January 1982 at a price of $595, equivalent to approximately $1,972 in today's dollars. By May 1983, the price had dropped to $250. The company went bankrupt in 1994.

CHAPTER FIVE

WEDNESDAY · AUGUST 26
Posted by Katy McKenna

I woke up with a mixed bag of emotions—pumped, nervous, and ready to dive into my new temporary career. If it doesn't work out, Maxine will hire the right person for the job, and I'll move on to the next adventure. I am so thankful for the gold coins I found in my attic, but I don't want to spend all that money. I want to save it for my golden years.

Daisy, my ever-faithful friend, was less enthusiastic about me leaving. She's gotten used to me being around 24/7. Daisy's idea of a hard day's work is napping in my garden shed office while I wrestle with graphic design projects—although it's been a while since I've had one. Now she's going to be a "latchkey canine," at least for a while. At some point, maybe I will take her to the office with me.

At 8:10, I backed out of the garage, giving a wave to Randy and Earl across the street. They were on their porch, engulfed in a cloud of sage smoke, sipping on their morning matchas.

Simon, my neighbor to the left, was likely holed up in his upstairs office, deep into his latest project. He's working on a how-to book about living off-grid in suburbia.

My neighbor—and ex-boyfriend—Josh, now lives down south in Marina Del Rey, caring for his ex-wife, who claims to have stage four colon cancer. I believe she's sick, but I'm not convinced it's that advanced. I think she's using the diagnosis to win Josh back —and it seems to be working. He and I were exclusive and getting serious when she told me she still loved him and wanted another chance. I can't really blame her, but it still hurts. That said, I truly hope she makes a full recovery. In the meantime, Josh's younger cousin is living in his house.

I cruised by my former neighbor Nina's once-lovely home, which her niece, Donna, recently destroyed, inside and out. Nina's whimsical English garden, which had won many awards over the years, is now a ripped-up, bulldozed, weedy disaster zone, thanks to Donna. There's a For Sale sign out front. Someone will get a good deal on the house, but their work will be cut out for them.

If you've been following my blog, you're up to speed on the saga of Nina and her mystery-writer niece, Donna, from Ketchikan, Alaska. It's a heartbreaking story that could make a great book. Donna is currently in prison, serving a seven-year sentence—though she'll likely be out in three or four.

As for Nina, she's thriving in her new two-bedroom at Shady Acres, where she's found a fresh start—and possibly a new beau named Frank. At eighty-seven, Nina's got more of a social life than I do!

I pulled into the parking lot of the Diligent Detective Agency with twelve minutes to spare. Before heading inside, I checked my messages. The vet had sent a reminder about Daisy's annual checkup, and the only other message was obvious spam. Evidently, I owe a massive toll fee for crossing London Bridge. Delete.

As I rapped on the locked office door, a noisy old blue VW bug rumbled into the lot. Maxine rolled down the car window and shouted, "Hi there, newbie! Sorry you had to wait." A minute later, she joined me at the entrance. "I'll give you a key to the door. There's an alarm system to disable, too. Follow me."

The alarm was already beeping, but she didn't rush. I watched as she tapped in the code next to the bathroom door. "T-I-M-5-6," she said. "That was my husband's age when he passed."

I offered a sympathetic smile, feeling a pang of sorrow for her loss. "I'm so sorry."

"I'm thankful for all the happy years we shared. Many never get that. It took a while, but I'm in a good place now."

"I'm glad."

Maxie turned away, and I asked, "Is it okay if I put the code on my phone so I remember? Although I doubt I will forget it."

"Sure. Are you familiar with alarms?"

"Yes. I have one at home that I usually forget to set."

"First thing, let's make coffee," she said. "Then we can discuss the day ahead. We have a full calendar."

She opened a cabinet above the coffee station, took out a bag of dark roast beans, and measured them into the grinder. As the rich aroma filled the office, she checked the voicemail on speaker.

"Hi. It's Candace," a shaky voice said. "I'm canceling our appointment. John has stopped drinking, and he promised things will be better now. Thank you for everything, Maxie. Please send me a bill." Click.

Maxie leaned her backside against the desk, folding her arms. "Damn it. That woman needs my help. Her husband is an abusive drunk. This isn't the first time she's canceled. One of these days, he's going to kill her, and there isn't a damn thing I can do about it."

"Has she talked to a therapist?"

"I tried to get her to do that, but..." Maxie shook her head. "I can't help her until she's ready. I just hope it won't be too late. She's stayed at the battered women's shelter in the past, and this time, I had a safe apartment lined up for her. The first three months paid by a local organization. I hoped this would help her get on her feet and make a new life."

"My grandmother's boyfriend is a retired attorney and volunteers at the shelter."

"He wouldn't, by any chance, be Ben Burnett, would he? Kind of looks like Richard Dreyfuss?"

"Yes," I said. "Do you know him?"

She nodded. "Ben has helped me a few times with cases like Candace and given me legal advice. He's a good guy. Your grandma is a lucky lady."

"I agree. He's a great addition to our family." I added that in case she was harboring any interest in Ben. Is that catty?

"Ready to get to work?"

I sat at the desk and folded my hands. "Ready, boss!"

Maxie stood beside me. "First thing every day, check the voicemail and emails and handle any follow-up. Today, we've got two new client appointments." She flipped open a red spiral-bound calendar. "Is it Wednesday already? Where does the time go? Anyway, have them fill out this new-client form." She placed a clipboard on the desk. "I have to warn you; I'm not very tech-savvy. Most of my records are old-school, in paper files. I trust paper more than I do cloud storage. If it was good enough for the Egyptians, it's good enough for me."

"Works for me," I said.

The phone rang, and she answered. "Diligent Detective Agency. How may I help you?" She paused. "Yes, this call is confidential." She listened for a long minute. "No, I'm sorry, but I can't do that. It's illegal."

Still listening, Maxie settled on the sofa and propped her sandaled feet on the coffee table.

"Sir, may I interrupt? You're asking my agency to perform an illegal act that could put us all in prison." She paused, listening again. "The thing is, this is real life. Whatever you've seen on TV or read in a book is make-believe, written by writers who don't know a darn thing about the law. It's not real life. A private investigator's license does not give me the freedom to do whatever I want. That means I do not break into people's homes and search their drawers. If you think your lady friend is cheating on you, ask her. Or you can hire us to follow her." She waited. "Well, sir, that is up to you, but you will get the same answer from every reputable private investigator in town." She disconnected and dropped the phone on her lap, gazing at me with a weary smile. "We get lots of calls like that."

"I don't know the first thing about this profession, so what do I say?"

"In your top desk drawer, there's a script for you to follow, more or less."

I set it on the blotter and did a quick once-over. "Okay. I get their name and phone number and a brief rundown of their needs."

"Right. Then, tell them I will return their call by the end of the day. Unless it's already near the end of the day, then say tomorrow—end of day, unless it's Friday. I usually return calls ASAP. However, if they ask for something you know to be illegal, then say I am out of town on a case for the unforeseeable future."

"How will I know it's illegal?"

"Trust me, you'll know." She put her feet on the floor. "I want you to lock the entry door when I'm not here. People will occasionally drop by without an appointment, and I don't want you alone with them. You never know."

She walked to the glass door and drew down an opaque gray

shade. "So no one sees you. We have a sign that says we're out on a call and has the office phone number on it." She took a letter-sized sign from a drawer in a bookcase that also housed vintage mystery novels. The sign had suction cups on it. "I'm serious about this, Katy."

"You're making me a little nervous."

"I don't care what the business is. A restaurant. The library. An office. No employee should ever be alone unless the door is locked. There are too many dangerous people out there. Better safe than sorry."

"What if one comes in when both of us are here? How do two women fight them off?"

"I have a system in place. First—a little story. A couple of years ago, a fella walked into the office. Let's call him Fred. Fred wanted me to locate a woman he'd met in a chat room. He said they'd made a real connection. He'd fallen in love and proposed to her, without ever meeting her. Now she was ghosting him, and he wanted me to find her so he could surprise her with a ring."

"That's creepy," I said. "No wonder she ghosted him. What did you tell him?"

"I said it was time to move on. Get his friends to introduce him to a nice local girl."

"What did he say to that?"

"He said he had no friends. At that point, I was getting nervous." Maxie motioned for me to follow her into her office. "I want to show you something."

She bent down and pointed to a buzzer underneath the ledge of her old oak desk.

"I have a deal with the dry cleaners next door. This is a wire-less remote doorbell that rings in their shop. If I press it once, a couple of burly guys will come over and say they have an appointment. Two rings, and they bring baseball bats."

"Have you done that?"

"A few times. So far, just one ring, though. I did it for desperate and dateless Fred. One look at those dudes walking in the door, and he split."

"Do you pay them for this service?"

"Yup." She grinned. "A big box of donuts from the shop here in the center. Word of advice—never eat their donuts. They are so damn good, and the reason," she squished her waist between her fingers, "I'm lugging around this donut-tire."

"So, what if there's no time to buzz for help? I mean, if they're psycho. I watch the news and—"

"Hold that thought." Maxie opened a desk drawer. "In over thirty years of business, I've only had to pull this out once." She set a shiny revolver on the blotter.

I stepped back, swallowing hard. "Whoa. Is that thing loaded?"

Maxie snickered, shaking her head. "Not much use if it isn't. But don't worry. The safety is on."

"Did you shoot someone?"

She nodded. "I did. Years ago, I was sitting alone at my desk, and, like an idiot, I hadn't locked the door. A big, nasty thug stormed in, demanding I find someone for him. I asked him what his intentions were, and he bluntly told me he was going to kill, pardon my language, the motherfucker. Turned out the dude had just been released from prison that very morning and had a long rap sheet of violent crimes."

"Oh my God. What did you say to him?"

"I told him I couldn't help him. He didn't like that answer and decided to kill me instead. Whipped a switchblade out of his back pocket, clicked it open, and came at me, slashing the air and screaming like a madman." She sighed and patted the deadly weapon lying peacefully on the desk. "I grabbed Betsy and shot him just as he was lunging over the desk at me. End of story."

"Wow." I was seeing Maxie in a whole new light. "Did he survive?"

"Unfortunately, yes. Get this—he tried to sue us from behind bars. Claimed I'd disabled him. Said I damaged his rotator cuff."

"That makes it harder to stab people, you know," I said.

She laughed. "I like you, Katy. Anyway, it looked like he might win the case...until he strangled a prison guard." Maxie caught my horrified expression. "That was over twenty years ago. Nothing like it has happened since." She stood. "I need coffee."

She kept talking as she walked to the coffeemaker. "Had dinner with Angela Yaeger last night. Let me tell you—Angie thinks highly of you. She told me about your adventures—like the petition campaign that nearly got you killed." She waved the coffeepot. "Want one?"

"No, I'm good."

"Then there's your cousin who left you for dead in the attic, and your misadventures in England." Maxie shook her head, chuckling. "This job is a cakewalk compared to what you've been doing. And it pays."

———

I was organizing my workstation when our first client of the day walked in. I put on a smile, determined to mask the nervous energy bubbling inside me. "Good morning. I'm Katy. Are you Phyllis Kaplan?"

The woman paused at the door, clutching a large manila envelope. She gave a small, hesitant nod.

I joined her. "Is this your first visit? I ask because I'm new here. First day."

"Yes," she murmured.

"How about you take a seat? I have some paperwork for you." I led her to a chair. "Would you like something to drink? Coffee?"

"No. Tea would be nice if it's not too much trouble."

I handed her a pen and clipboard with a form attached, then rummaged through the coffee station drawers and found some

Lipton bags. I filled the plug-in pot and made small talk while it heated. After commenting on the lovely weather, I poured the boiling water into a mug and dipped the tea bag in. "Sugar?"

"No, thank you." Her layered, short russet hair framed her gentle hazel eyes, and although she looked weary, her face brightened when she smiled, revealing a natural beauty untouched by makeup.

I placed the tea on the coffee table and went down the short hall to Maxie's office. "Phyllis Kaplan is here. I made her some tea. She's filling out her paperwork."

"Oh, good. We'll need a retainer fee. I'll show you how that's done." She walked out to the woman. "Hi there, Ms. Kaplan. I'm Maxine Baker. While you're filling out your paperwork, we'll take care of our retainer fee. How would you like to pay for it? Cash or credit?"

The lady reached into her purse and pulled out a wallet. "You said twenty-five hundred. Would you prefer a check or credit card?"

"Check," said Maxie. "The credit card fees are killing us."

Once our client finished her paperwork, Maxine took the clipboard, steered the woman into her office, and closed the door.

Clueless about what to do now, I dusted the furniture and rearranged the old magazines. *AARP*, *Good Housekeeping*, *People*, *Travel and Leisure*, *Health*. Next, I checked the coffeepot. Half full. Or was it half empty?

Finally, Maxie's door opened, and the women emerged. Ms. Kaplan's eyes were red, but she seemed calmer than when she arrived.

My boss said, "As soon as I have something, I'll contact you, Phyllis."

The woman smiled at me, turned toward the exit, and then spun back around. "I'll bring by those old photos of Graham tomorrow. I should have thought of that before I came today.

Who knows how he's aged, though? He's five years older than me, so he'd be sixty-eight now."

I watched the woman walk to her car, then asked my boss, "Everything okay?"

"Sit," said Maxie.

"Did I overstep? Oh, God. I did, didn't I?"

"No. Katy," she said with a reassuring smile. "Not at all. You'll be helping me on cases, so I'm glad you're interested."

"I will?"

"You betcha." She gazed out the window at Phyllis's blue Prius backing out of her parking space. "Her adult son desperately needs a kidney, and so far, no matches. He was exposed to toxic chemicals while serving in the Middle East. His missing father might be his last hope. She's tried all the regular online searches. It's like he doesn't exist. For all we know, he's been dead for years."

"How old is her son?"

"Thirty-eight. He's an elementary school teacher named Alex Brownstadt. He lives here in town and is happily married with a baby on the way. But he's been on dialysis for a long time, and he's deteriorating."

"So, Phyllis must have remarried at some point since her name is Kaplan."

Maxie nodded. "She's widowed."

"Do you think you can find Alex's father?"

Maxie shook her head. "I'm not holding my breath. He walked out over thirty-five years ago when Alex was just a toddler."

"I have a question about payment," I said. "Why do you prefer a check? Hardly anyone takes checks these days."

"I have to pay a 2 percent fee for every credit card transaction. It adds up fast. I'll take a check any day over a credit card. In fact, I'm thinking of charging a credit card fee. A lot of shops and restaurants are doing that now."

———

I did the math on the credit card fee that Maxie would pay for $2,500. Fifty bucks! I had no idea.

CHAPTER SIX

Posted by Katy McKenna

Maxie had a court date this morning, so I didn't need to go to the office until after lunch. I briefly considered vacuuming the house but was saved by the bell when Ruby called to invite herself over for coffee. Of course, she had an ulterior motive.

———

"Have you checked your Thirty-Something dating profile lately?"

Quick FYI: Ruby signed me up for a dating app three months ago—without asking me first. I haven't checked it, and I have no plans to. Ever. So not my thing.

She looked like she was about to burst with excitement, so I leaned back against the kitchen counter, crossed my arms, and took my sweet time responding.

"Hmmm. Let...me...think." I dragged out each word, adding a

long, dramatic sigh while tapping my cheek thoughtfully. "When was the laaaast time I—"

"Oh, for God's sake! Have you, or haven't you?"

"Haven't. But I'm guessing you have."

"Well, yes. As a matter of fact, I have. Somebody's gotta keep an eye on the ball, ya know."

"Or balls," I said.

"Don't be naughty!"

"Sorry."

"No, you're not," Ruby said, rolling her eyes. "Anyway, a couple of promising, non-creepy men have left messages. Both in your age range, too."

"Want a cup of coffee?" I asked.

"Changing the subject won't work. And yes, I'll take a cup."

Ruby sat at the kitchen table and, with a flourish, pulled a folded sheet of paper from her purse and slapped it onto the table like she was revealing a winning lottery ticket. "I printed this from the site last night. Eric is a high school science teacher. Divorced, no kids." She tapped a finger on the next prospect. "And then there's Mark—a hunky personal trainer. Never married. Three cats."

I sat next to her and peered at the printout. "Wanna cookie?"

"No." She sipped her French roast. "What say we take a little look-see on your laptop and see what else pops up? And on second thought, I'll take a cookie."

I set a bag of snickerdoodles on the table, then went to get my laptop. Back at the table, I opened the computer and got online. Just as the dating app opened, loud shouting outside caught our attention.

"Let's go see what's going on." I dashed for the front door with Ruby on my heels. "Maybe someone needs help."

The commotion was coming from Simon's house next door. He was standing in his front yard, hands on hips, next to a tall, hefty, bald guy waving his hands to guide a big white truck backing into the yard. The truck bed held a large, shiny red machine.

"Now, what's he up to?" I mumbled.

Hefty Guy signaled the truck driver to stop, then lowered the tailgate.

"Oh, for crying out loud. Look at the sign on the truck," said Ruby.

It said, "Lucia Drilling and Water Supply."

She continued, "Is he planning to dig a well or drill for oil?"

"I guess this is the next chapter of his suburban off-grid project." I strolled over to Simon and tapped his shoulder. He turned, and his grim countenance bloomed into a sunny grin.

"Hey, Simon. I thought you were installing a water harvester in your backyard that converts humidity into water."

"I am," he said, smiling at Ruby. "But it's on backorder in the UK, so I'm drilling a well. It's the best of both worlds. Backups to each other, and no water bill."

"You can dig a well in this neighborhood?" I said. "I thought you had to live in the countryside to have a well."

"I have a permit that says I can."

"Good luck with that," said Ruby. "We've been in a drought for years, so you probably won't get anything but sand." She grabbed my hand. "Come on, Katy. I don't have all day. I have to get to work, and I want to check out those men on the dating site before I go."

He cocked an eyebrow at us. "Men? Dating? Ruby, did you break up with Ben?"

"No. They're good," I said. "A while back, my dear grand-mother, bless her meddling heart, signed me up on a dating website."

His other brow shot up. "Really? How's that working for you?"

Granny huffed from behind me, arms crossed like a drill sergeant. "We'd know if she stopped dragging her feet and replied to anyone."

———

Back at the kitchen table, Ruby said, "Why in the hell aren't you dating Simon? Not only is he a dish and a nice guy, but he's loaded, too. The total package."

Simon Prichard comes from a wealthy blue-blood family in upstate New York. However, the guy doesn't just live off his trust fund—he made his fortune by developing a GPS tracking system called Wandering Angels, designed for people with Alzheimer's and dementia.

"So why aren't you two an item?" she asked. "This is like a Hallmark movie waiting to happen."

"I've told you this a few times already. Simon and I both know that dating your neighbor is a bad idea," I said. "Look what happened with Josh."

Ruby, clearly unimpressed by my lack of Hallmark-worthy romantic spirit, sighed. "You're probably right." She pointed at the laptop screen. "Let's see what's on the site today. Just for funsies."

The first guy to pop up looked like he could've babysat King Tut.

"Not ready to date a great-great-grandpa just yet," I said.

"Moving on." Ruby leaned closer to the laptop screen. "This one looks promising."

One glance and a sick lump jammed my throat. "Oh, God. That's Kyle."

"Oh. The ranger." Ruby pushed her cheaters up her nose. "When you said he was good-looking, you forgot to mention that he's a Greek god. He could be a movie star. Maybe he could get a voice operation." She shrugged. "If there is such a thing."

"There is. I checked. But how would I broach that subject? 'Hey, Kyle, have you ever considered getting voice masculinization surgery?' "

She shook her head. "What a waste." She took one last look at him before scrolling on. "Here's the high school teacher on the printout. Eric."

A pleasant-looking, trim man with thick, curly dark hair and a bushy beard sat under an oak tree with his arm curled around a multi-colored Australian Shepherd named Dundee. Both were grinning broadly at the camera.

Ruby said, "The dog's color is called blue merle. I looked it up."

I read his brief bio. "Okay, as you said, he's divorced, no kids. Thirty-seven, so in my age range. Loves animals and is seeking a life partner who shares a desire for a family someday. He teaches at the high school in Cala Grande and lives there too, so he's close by, but not too close."

Her eyes widened with giddy expectation, practically bouncing in her seat. "Does that mean what I think it means?"

I sighed wearily, like the weight of the world was on my shoulders. "Yeah, what the heck. Nothing ventured, nothing gained. I mean, how much trouble can I get into, meeting for a cup of coffee?"

I now have a date for coffee with Eric on Saturday afternoon at a local coffeehouse. What have I done?

———

I arrived at work at 1 p.m. to find Phyllis Kaplan waiting at the locked door.

"Hi, Ms. Kaplan. I didn't realize we had an appointment."

"We don't, and please call me Phyllis. I brought some photos of my ex." She pressed her lips tight like she was holding back tears.

"Anything else going on?"

"I'm just so worried I can't think straight. My son, Alex, wound up in the hospital last night. I thought we would lose him, but he's stabilized now and will probably go home tomorrow."

I unlocked the door, set my grocery bag on the desk, and hurried to turn off the alarm, thinking, *TIM56, TIM56.*

"Sorry about that. It's my first time with the alarm." I gestured to the couch. "Please, have a seat."

She smiled, slipping off her navy cardigan. "I know I'm pinning my hopes on you, but until my appointment yesterday, I was feeling completely hopeless."

"Now you're feeling hopeful?"

She nodded slightly. "Yes, a little. I know it's a long shot, but as long as I'm doing something productive, I can keep going."

I checked my watch. 1:22. "I wonder where Maxie is?"

As if on cue, we heard Maxie's decrepit blue VW bug rumble into the parking lot.

"There she is," I said. "Perfect timing."

"I should scoot," said Phyllis. "I'm sure you have appointments lined up."

"I haven't looked at the calendar yet." I went to my desk and flipped open the book. "No, we're good. No need to rush out."

Maxie entered the office, toting a stuffed grocery bag. "Sorry I'm late. I stopped at the store for a couple of things and got carried away and lost track of time." Her eyes landed on our client. "Oh, dear. Did I forget an appointment?"

Phyllis stood, shaking her head. "No. I just stopped by to drop off some photos."

I told Maxie about the medical emergency last night.

She dumped her tote bag on my desk. "Let me see what you have, Phyllis."

I glanced over her shoulder as she looked at the four photos. A wedding closeup, yellowing with age—Graham and Phyllis's wedding photo.

Her husband was dressed in a military uniform. "He looks like a young—"

"I know," said Phyllis. "He was in the army. He served in Vietnam. Got drafted right out of high school."

In the following picture, the young Tom Hanks doppelgänger was grinning like a proud papa, holding his toddler son on his lap. A family Thanksgiving photo with Dad carving the turkey. And a picture of a pregnant Phyllis with her husband's hand on her tummy, while little Alex stood in front, thumb in his mouth, finger curled around his nose.

"Oh, you have two children?" I said.

"No," Phyllis replied, her voice faltering. "We lost the baby in the fifth month. I had a bad fall." She lowered her head, wringing her hands. "But that's not the full story. Graham had a drinking problem."

"Was he abusive?" Maxie asked gently.

"No. Never." She sighed. "One night, Alex had a bad dream. I was rushing to him and didn't see Graham passed out cold in the dark hallway. I tripped over him and landed hard." She paused, biting her trembling lip. "I lost the baby. Graham blamed himself, and I let him. I blamed him, too. He swore he would stop drinking, but instead, he drank more. Lost his job. Our friends gave up on us. Finally, I took Alex and went to my parents. Before I left, I told my husband that if he didn't get himself cleaned up and sober, we were done. That was the last time I saw him."

Phyllis reached for her sweater and slung it over her arm. "I'm not expecting miracles, but you are both so..." she hesitated. "Caring. Not what I expected from a detective agency, and after last night's scare, I needed to see your kind faces." She inhaled deeply. "I also need a nap before going back to the hospital."

After our client pushed through the door, Maxie dashed to the bathroom, and I peeked into the grocery bag. Cookies, York peppermint patties, tea, half-and-half, ground low-acid decaf, TP, and air freshener.

Maxie eventually returned, looking serious. "I need to tell you something," she said, collapsing onto the couch. "It's personal, but since we share a bathroom, there's no hiding it from you."

I sat on my red, rolling desk chair, wondering what she was going to share.

"I'll be spending a lot of time in there." She nodded toward the bathroom door in the short hallway between the front office and her office. "I have ulcerative colitis."

I'd seen lots of TV commercials about drugs for it, but that's about all I knew. "Is it like Crohn's?"

"Yes. And no. Simply put, they are both inflammatory bowel diseases but claim different intestinal territories. Both are no fun. At the moment, I'm in what we call a flare. I've had this since middle school, and oh boy, I could tell you some embarrassing stories." She gave a dry laugh. "In fact, at some point, I'm sure I will. I mean, ya gotta laugh. However, looking back at my age now, it's way easier to see the humor than it was when I was a mortified teenager."

"When you say you're in a flare, what does that mean?"

"Diarrhea. A lot. Cramping, too. However, the pain was worse when I was young. For the last couple of years, I was doing so well. Food was fun again, and I was normal." She air quoted. "But I guess I reached my limit, and now I'm paying the price. One thing I have to stop right now is the caffeine. And dairy, dammit. So, I bought some decaf that'll probably set me off, and some Starbucks instant coffee for you. However, you are welcome to drink my boring," she air quoted again, "so-called coffee."

"I'm sorry you have to deal with this."

"I've been dealing with it for over fifty years, so I'm used to it. But you needed to know—not just because it may indispose me a lot, but I may need your help."

"In the bathroom?"

That threw her into a laughing fit, and she rushed to the toilet again. When she returned, still giggling, she said, "Oh, my God! The look on your face! I meant that I might ask you to cover for me on some stakeouts. If I'm running to the bathroom every few minutes, I can't sit in a car or follow someone. I hope you're okay with that."

"I definitely am." *Wow,* I thought. *I'll be doing real investigative work!*

At the coffee machine, I picked up the pot of hot caffeine. "We won't be needing this." As a show of solidarity, I didn't pour myself a cup before dumping it down the jasmine-scented bathroom sink. I returned and prepared a pot of decaf.

"I hate you so much right now," muttered my employer.

CHAPTER SEVEN

FRIDAY • AUGUST 28
Posted by Katy McKenna

My life has certainly taken an exciting turn in the last couple of days. I'm practically a detective—"PI Katy" at your service—and I have a date with a stranger tomorrow. That's why I'm wide awake at 3 a.m. and blogging.

I've seen my fair share of *Dateline* episodes. You know those true crime stories they feature? Absolutely terrifying. The last thing I want is to go on a date with someone who moonlights as an axe murderer. I have no interest in being the next headline. That's why it's so much safer when a trusted friend introduces you to a potential boyfriend. After all, they wouldn't set you up with a potential serial killer, right?

Long pause here as I reflect on this dating situation. You can hum the *Jeopardy* tune while I ponder.

Okay. I've made a decision. One new thing on my plate is probably enough for now. I need to concentrate on my career, give it my full attention, and leave dating for later.

I'll contact Eric and tell him—tell him what? You know what? I don't need to tell him anything other than it's not happening.

———

I burst through the office glass door, announcing, "I come bearing gifts from that fancy new coffee shop down the street!"

"The Dirty Dog?" hollered Maxie from her office.

"Yup! One cup of low-acid decaf, extra-bold French roast for you, and a matcha tea latte for yours truly." I pulled a little brown bag out of my purse. "I also got you a warm oatmeal cookie, and—"

I heard her chair screech across the plastic mat under her desk. She snatched the bag and took a deep sniff. "Ahhhh. I shouldn't, but I will. I started back on a prescription for my tummy troubles this morning, so I deserve a cookie." She enjoyed a big bite, then returned the cookie to the bag. "That's all for now. You know what Oscar Wilde said about temptation?"

"Strangely enough, I do not."

"The only way to get rid of temptation is to yield to it." Maxie opened the bag and took another bite. She patted her little pot belly. "Thank goodness for these comfy yoga pants. Okay, change of subject. Do you know anything about photo enhancing? Our client's pictures are a bit fuzzy, and the colors have faded. Is there an app for that?"

"I would think so. These days, there seems to be an app for everything except one to magically clean my house." I sat at my desk and fired up the desktop.

"Oh, and see if you can find something that does age progression," she added, her eyes suddenly darting toward the glass door. "Oh no. Not today. Lord, give me strength."

I glanced up, concerned. "What's wrong?"

"You'll see," she muttered, and from her tone, I wasn't sure if I wanted to.

I followed her gaze to a tall, stooped, elderly man dressed in baggy khakis, a plaid shirt, and a baseball cap. He was locked in a wrestling match with a walker, trying to extract it from the trunk of a shiny, cherry-red classic car.

I started to the door. "I should go help him."

"No! Just leave him be."

"But he's having a hard time."

She shook her head. "Do what you gotta do, but don't say I didn't warn you."

I dashed outside wearing my best Good Samaritan smile. "Hi there! Need a hand with that?"

"You do, and I'll chop it off," he growled. "I am perfectly capable of taking care of myself, missy."

I took a step back, feeling crushed. Then plastered my smile back on and tried again. "Wow, love your car. What is it?"

"It's a damn car. What do you think it is?"

"A super nice classic car," I murmured.

"For your information, it's a 1960 Chevrolet Impala. Goes by the name of Roddy. One owner: me. The last thing I need is you scratching the original paint job."

"Why would I do that?"

He shook his head in exasperation. "No respect! You and your generation have no respect for the classics. Damn Gen Xers!"

"Whoa! I'm not Gen X. I'm a millennial."

"Well, la-de-da for you! Drivin' your hybrids and electric cars and thinking you're saving the planet. Bah!"

I pointed at Veronica, my 1976 orange Volvo wagon. "Hey, I'll have you know that's my car!"

"I'm supposed to be impressed that you drive a gas guzzler?"

"Uh," I stammered, scrambling for a good comeback. "Well, so do you!" Infuriated, I shoved through the entrance door, letting it slam into the cranky old fart's walker.

"Oh, my God!" laughed Maxie. "That was so hilarious. You just made Uncle Walter's day."

Leaning against the door, still fuming, I couldn't help but smile as Walter banged on the glass, yelling at me to open up or else. "Wait, what? He's your uncle?"

She eased me aside and opened the door. "Shame on you, Uncle Walter."

"I see ya got a new gal." He chuckled as he trundled inside.

"I do, and thanks for breaking her in. If she quits, you get her job because I need help."

Uncle Walter shot me a dentured grin. "Ahh, you can take it, right?"

"Do I have a choice?" I grumbled.

"Katy," said Maxie, "meet Walter Hoffman. My husband's uncle, and mine by default."

He extended a big, bony hand and gave me a firm handshake. "No hard feelings, right, Katy?"

I narrowed my eyes. "I'm not letting you off the hook that easily, Walter."

"Atta girl," he said. "Don't suffer fools like me. We're gonna be good friends."

"Uncle Walter, why are you here?" asked Maxie. "Usually, you're at the Veterans Hall for brunch and bingo on Friday mornings."

Walter winked at me conspiratorially. "They're hosting a 'Sensitivity Awareness' seminar today. About fifteen minutes in, most of us made a break for it. These days, everything's off-limits because there's always someone looking to get offended."

After settling his tush on the sofa with a grunt, it was time for me to get to work. "I'll search for an app that may help enhance Phyllis's photos, Maxie."

"Thanks. But before you do that, what's on the calendar?"

I flipped it open, and we scanned the day. "Injury insurance fraud. Peggy Prendergast versus—oh my gosh—my favorite vegetarian restaurant. Suzy Q's."

Walter groaned. "A millennial vegetarian. Who could've guessed?"

In a snotty tone, I said, "I'm thinking about going vegan."

"Oh, God. It figures," he muttered.

"Hey! You're offending me." I thumbed my nose at him, which he seemed to appreciate.

Maxie ignored our antics, tapping the calendar. "This Prendergast woman is suing Suzy because she slipped in the bathroom. Says there was water on the floor, and it was slippery. Which was baloney. Suzy heard Prendergast hollering in the bathroom and found her sprawled on the floor, groaning like a drama queen. When the woman asked to be helped up, Suzy said, 'No. We must make sure you are all right first.' She immediately called an ambulance and took photos of the scene, particularly the bone-dry floor. She's been down this road before. Now, poor Peggy is apparently too injured to work and is suffering from PTSD."

"How much is she suing for?" I said.

"Five million for permanent disability and three mil for trauma. It looks like you got your first stakeout this afternoon, Katy."

"What do I need to do?"

"Get photos and videos of her that prove she's fine. The insurance company wants to settle." She shook her head. "So typical. But Suzy wants to fight it because she knows it's a scam. Plus, her insurance payments will skyrocket otherwise."

"What did the hospital examination say?" asked Walter.

Maxie joined him on the couch. "The woman had bruises on her hip and elbow that could've been from earlier in the day, and she said her neck hurt. The X-rays showed no internal damage, but she might have pulled a muscle." She shrugged. "If this Prendergast woman really did fall—which I seriously doubt—it wasn't at Suzy's. She doesn't have health insurance, and maybe this was her way of getting a free exam and an early retirement plan. A win-win."

Walter snickered. "How old is she?"

"Fifty-six. The 'accident' happened a few weeks ago. I only heard about it the other day when I bumped into Suzy at a chamber meeting. Suzy and I go way back—home ec class in middle school. She wants to pay for our services, but I struck a mutually beneficial deal. We trade our detective work for food."

Maxie headed to her office, adding with a wink, "I've got all the pertinent information in a file on my desk. Photos, addresses, place of employment...even her favorite reality show, if you're interested." She returned and handed the file to me.

"Addresses?" I asked.

"Yeah. Her latest residence is a house near downtown. An old Victorian."

I gazed at the woman's photo. Overly bleached blonde, pudgy face, heavy black eye makeup, and according to her stats, tall. Not ugly, but not a head-turner.

"I pulled that from her Facebook profile," said Maxie. "She doesn't post much, but I think it's pretty current."

I picked up the photo and file folder. "Would you mind if I scanned this all into the computer, made a folder, and then sent myself the information and photos?"

Maxie shrugged. "Knock yourself out."

"When do you want me to leave?"

She checked her watch. "After you scan those papers."

"While I'm sitting in my car surveilling, I can hunt for an app on my phone to enhance Graham Brownstadt's photos."

Walter piped up. "What's this about enhancing photos?"

Maxie filled him in on Brownstadt's disappearance and his sick son.

"Well, hell," he said, scratching his thin, obviously dyed black hair. "I know someone in the DIA who could help with that."

"What's that?" I asked.

"The Defense Intelligence Agency in DC—defense and military intelligence. The DIA produces about a quarter of all intelligence content that goes into the President's daily brief."

"And you know these people how?" said Maxie, narrowing her eyes. "Were you in the DIA and kept it a secret all these years? The Uncle Walter I know was a cop."

He sniffed. "Once a cop, always a cop, although these days you couldn't pay me enough to go out there and put my life on the line in one of those big cities."

Maxie's brows furrowed. "Walter? This is hardly a big government case, and besides, who would you know in the DIA?"

"My buddy Bob's grandson is a career military man. He's in the Navy. Commander Phil Kowalski. Little Philly. Who knew that little rabble-rouser would grow up to be a naval officer? He's on special assignment for a year at the DUI."

And there it was. The man was delusional.

"Ha!" he chortled. "Did I say DUI? I meant DIA. Anyway, I can ask Bob to call him on the horn and see what he says. I think the age progression idea would be helpful."

"It certainly could be," said Maxie.

I made the copies and then scanned the file into the computer. "I'll start a special folder for it later. Do you have cloud storage, Maxie?"

"Nope, I back everything up to USB drives and lock them in the safe in my office. I don't trust that so-called cloud," she said, using air quotes. "If the grid goes down, then poof! Clear skies— no cloud."

Peggy Prendergast works at a title company. I assumed she wouldn't be working right now, but before heading out of the office, I called anyway to hear what they would say. A woman answered in a monotone voice. "Central-Western Title Company. Please listen to the following options."

I tapped a drum solo on my desk while listening to the umpteen options. Finally, a live person answered. "May I help you?"

"Hi. Is Peggy Prendergast available?"

The woman's tone morphed to phony-sounding concern. "Ooo. Sorry. No."

I put the call on speaker, and Walter shimmied to the edge of the couch, ears perked.

"When's a good time to call back?"

"Well," she said, lowering her voice like she was about to divulge top-secret information, "she's on sick leave. Had a terrible accident and can't work."

"Oh, no! What happened?" I gasped while giving Walter a wink.

"She fell. At a local restaurant and suffered horrific, life-changing injuries."

"How awful."

"I heard she might be paralyzed. Or even quadriplegic." She paused and cleared her throat. "May I take your name and number and have someone else call you back?"

"No. Not right now. It wasn't that important compared to what poor Peggy is going through."

———

Peggy Prendergast's old Victorian on Maple Avenue is not far from my cozy, yellow and white three-bedroom 1930s bungalow on Sycamore Avenue. Peggy's house is probably thirty years older and is tastefully painted an olive green with maroon and cream trim. A low, wrought-iron fence lines the front yard with a rose-covered arbor over the gate. A For Sale sign sits in the middle of the small lawn. Her single detached garage is set back on the lot but still visible from the street. Mature sycamores and maples line the avenue, creating a shady tunnel.

The big question was where to park my orange Volvo without looking like a creepy stalker. The answer was I couldn't, at least not for any length of time. As I cruised the street, I spied doorbell cams on nearly every entry, ready to catch me in the act of doing nothing, no matter where I parked. However, it wasn't as if I was going to commit a crime, so I decided not to worry about it. What other choice did I have?

First, I headed to a nearby café to grab a to-go lunch: a grilled cheese sandwich, sweet potato fries, and iced tea. Then I returned to the neighborhood and parked across from her house, two doors down. My cover story for anyone who might ask why I was hanging out was that my hubby and I are thinking about buying in the area and wanted to get a feel for it. You know, is it safe for the little ones?

I enjoyed my lunch while monitoring Peggy's house and watching the third episode of the original 1980s *Magnum PI* series with Tom Selleck. Ruby got me going on it, and I have to say, she was right. He was dreamy.

It was a hot day, and I had the front windows rolled down, hoping for a breeze but just getting more hot air. Luckily, my spot was shady. But I was still melting. I checked the local weather, and it was supposedly 81 degrees, but I wasn't buying it.

Just as I was about to call it, a new, shiny red Porsche 911 Carrera convertible cruised by and turned into Peggy's driveway, stopping in front of the garage door. Suddenly feeling pumped, I started snapping photos. A tall man climbed out and went to the mailbox at the curb, and I zoomed in on him. Longish, wavy black hair. Olive skin. Sexy five-o'clock shadow. Maybe late twenties or early thirties. Tight black T-shirt stretched over beautifully sculpted muscles. The man looked like he should be on the cover of a steamy romance novel.

After smoothing out his expensive-looking, snug dove-gray slacks, he grabbed a wad of mail from the mailbox and disappeared into the house through a side door.

Naturally, I sent a couple of photos to Samantha—one close-up and one full-body shot—and texted, I'm on a stakeout.

Seconds later, she answered: OMG. Be still my heart!! What a hottie!

I popped the last cold fry into my mouth and checked the time—2:35. How long had the Adonis been in the house? It had to be at least an hour by now.

"Dammit. I should keep notes," I muttered to myself.

I started pecking in my phone's Notes app, thinking how much easier an actual notebook and pen would be. Sweat trickled down my forehead while my underwire bra gathered puddles. I decided to call it quits at 4:10 p.m. Tomorrow, I'd be better prepared for the stakeout.

———

At home, I took a quick cool shower and threw on some baggy, lightweight cotton clothes. We don't get many hot days here, so I don't have air conditioning. Then, with a notebook under my arm, a pencil tucked behind my ear, a tumbler of ice water in one hand, and a bag of Ruffles in the other, Daisy and I went out to sit on the shady front porch.

I started jotting down a list of necessary spy gear for tomorrow's mission, and then remembered tomorrow is Saturday. I'm supposed to help Ruby start her new career as a social media sensation, and I still have that coffee date with Eric that I'd forgotten to cancel.

"We do not have time for that, do we, Daisy?" I rubbed Daisy's ear. "Ruby's project will take all day and then some, so I'll text him right now."

My phone rang. Ruby's perfectly made-up face graced the screen.

"Hey, Granny. What time do you want me over tomorrow?"

"That's what I'm calling about. We need to postpone. Ben got us matinee tickets to *Moulin Rouge! The Musical* down in LA. We're leaving in the morning and will spend the night."

"Oh, you are so lucky! And why aren't you taking me? You know I love musicals."

"Don't I know it! Sorry to let you down."

"Make sure to take lots of photos for social media!"

"I'm influencing makeup and diet. Things like that. Not Broadway musicals."

"No, you are influencing a lifestyle for millions of wannabe-trendy senior ladies and branding yourself. We're going to need tons of content. Snap photos of everything and make sure Ben is looking sharp."

"A three-piece suit?"

"No. Cool-vibe business casual is for mature men. You two need to look like a hip-happening couple living the life seniors dream of."

Ruby let out a snort. "Whatever that is. I need to study up on this."

After she hung up, I had to laugh. It's not like I was feeling let down not to be working on her new business project. Truth be told, I don't have a clue about "branding" oneself. But I sure do wish I were going to the musical.

I started texting Eric and stopped mid-sentence. "Oh, what the heck? It's just coffee."

CHAPTER EIGHT

SATURDAY • AUGUST 29
Posted by Katy McKenna

According to Sam's sixteen-year-old daughter, Chelsea, I'm officially a dinosaur—a full-blown, thirty-two-year-old relic from the ancient past.

The little darling was over for breakfast to interview me for a school assignment about crime in our community, since I now work for a detective agency and have solved a few mysteries. We were sitting at the kitchen table, enjoying bowls of oatmeal with fresh peaches, when her eyes zeroed in on the basket of newspapers by the kitchen door.

"Are those real newspapers?" she asked, sounding incredulous.

"Yup. Newspapers that I need to take out to recycling."

She gingerly picked one up, as if it were an ancient artifact, and set it on the table. "I thought only old people read newspapers."

"I'm twice your age, so I suppose I qualify." I did a little finger math. "When I'm ninety-five, you'll be seventy-nine."

She wrinkled her cute pug nose. "That's old."

"Don't tell Ruby. She's just four years shy."

"Yeah, but she doesn't act old." She tapped the paper. "Why do you read these? There's news on TV and online, you know."

"True. However, this is a tradition for me that dates back to ancient times, when I was a wee child, younger than you are now. My folks read the newspaper at breakfast on the weekends. If anything was interesting—and appropriate for my innocent ears—they'd read it aloud to me. And they gave me the funny pages, which were even funnier once I learned how to read."

I chuckled at my hilarity. Chelsea did not.

"Funny pages? What's that?"

"Seriously? You don't know what a funny page is? It's a page—or pages—in the newspaper with comic strips, like *Peanuts* and *Garfield*. On Sundays, there are even more comic strips. In color! Like a comic book. Or a graphic novel."

Chelsea ruffled the newspaper pages. "Does this one have those?"

"Give it to me." I opened the paper, laid it flat on the table, and flipped through until I found the comics. "Here ya go."

Chelsea tucked her shoulder-length, blonde hair behind her ears and started reading. "*Peanuts* is funny!" she said with a giggle. "I thought it was just those old TV holiday cartoon shows."

While she got lost in the funnies, I reread the front page. I had forgotten that the lead story reported a homeless person found dead in Maiden Lane Park.

Not too long ago, the park was a lovely, safe place. Old shady, wide-spreading oaks, towering redwoods, Monterey pines, a colorful heirloom rose garden, and a community vegetable garden. A large gazebo, built in the 1920s, hosted band concerts. There's a playground, picnic tables, barbecues, and an expansive grassy area where people played badminton and Frisbee or enjoyed Sunday concerts in the summer. I spent many happy afternoons there with my parents.

But in the blink of an eye, it's been taken over by destitute street people. Ragtag tents, tarps, shopping carts, and piles of junk are scattered everywhere. Dogs, cats, and rats scavenge like it's a third-world country—just a few blocks from my front door.

"I never thought this would happen in my community."

Chelsea glanced up from her cartoons. "Huh?"

"Oh, sorry. Didn't realize I was talking out loud. I was thinking about what a mess Maiden Lane Park has become."

"Oh, yeah. Dad and I drove by last weekend. It's really bad. Last summer we went to a concert there. It was a cover band playing old-time rock music from way back, like 2005. Have you ever heard of a band called—" she narrowed her eyes. "I think it was Cold Day?"

"Coldplay," I said.

She waved her spoon. "Yeah, that's it. Coldplay. It was pretty good. Anyway, no concerts this summer, that's for sure." She scooped a drippy spoonful of oatmeal into her mouth and went back to the funnies.

I turned to the second page. "Here's one you might like," I said, tapping a story. "Teachers are threatening a strike."

Sounding breathlessly elated, she asked, "Does that mean no school?"

"We shall see. The school district is asking voters to pass a $425 million bond. Maybe that means they'll give the teachers a raise. Wouldn't that be nice."

She slumped in her chair. "There goes the strike. Darn it."

"Sorry, kid. You know it won't be long before the Santa Lucia newspaper stops printing. It's available digitally now, but I still prefer the real thing."

Chelsea reverently ran her hand across the funny page. "My kids will never see one of these."

"Yes, they will." I dumped the basket of newspapers destined for recycling into a grocery bag. "Here you go. A little bit of history for your someday kids."

"Seriously? Wow, thanks, Auntie Katy!"

From the look on her face, you'd think I'd given her a $500 gift certificate to Ulta.

———

I wasn't sure how to dress for a date with a stranger, so I wore my usual daily ensemble—jeans, sandals, and a T-shirt—and I go nowhere without makeup. Ever. Like grandmother, like mother, like daughter.

Eric, looking relaxed in baggy blue board shorts and a T-shirt, was waiting outside the Dirty Dog Coffee Shop with his Australian Shepherd, Dundee. I recognized the dog before I recognized the guy. He'd shaved off his beard and looked cuter in person than in his dating site photo.

Feeling nervous and shy, I leaned over and said, "Hey, Dundee." Then I glanced up at Eric and smiled, noticing his dark brown eyes and warm, tawny skin. He was taller than me by several inches, making me feel petite—a rare experience.

"May I pet your dog?"

"Sure. He loves everyone." Eric patted the dog's side. "Don't ya, boy?"

Dundee's tail wagged while I ruffled his furry neck, and he gave that funny doggy grin when I hit the sweet spot. "Does that feel good? Yes, it does, huh?"

When I was done bonding with Dundee, Eric extended his hand. "I'm Eric Diaz. And since we don't put last names on the dating site, you are...?"

"Katy McKenna," I said, shaking his hand. "Pleased to meet you, Eric."

He led the way to a metal patio table, where we sat. Dundee nuzzled my hands in my lap, encouraging me to keep petting him, so I did.

"I don't think they have table service," I said. "So, how about I get our coffees while you stay with Dundee?"

His cheeks tinged with a bit of embarrassment. "I probably should've left him home, but he misses me during the week while I'm at work. Plus, he's a great icebreaker."

"I get it. I'm also under the rule of a dog and a cat. They basically run my life."

"You've got a yellow Lab, don't you? I remember seeing your photo on the site. Her name's Dana?"

"Daisy. Almost every other yellow female Lab is named Daisy, so I should've renamed her Gertrude or Harriet after my two great grandmothers. Dana would have been good, too. But Daisy was the name they gave her at the pound, so I kept it." I scratched behind Dundee's ears. "You smell Daisy, don't ya?"

"Looks like he's got a new friend." Eric stood and handed me Dundee's leash. "What would you like? My treat."

"Oh, okay. A small coffee with three raw sugars and half-and-half."

"I take it black, then add three or four sugars." He patted his nearly flat belly. "Which I shouldn't."

"Make mine four, too. Let's live dangerously."

After he went inside, I noticed a few fellow patrons smiling at Dundee. But one exception—a surly-looking woman—clearly wasn't in the mood for canine cuteness. She caught my eye and, with a sour voice that could curdle milk, snapped, "You do know that dogs aren't allowed in restaurants, right?"

I flashed her a cheerful grin. "Yes. That's why we're on the patio. In California, it's up to the business owner to decide if pets are allowed outside." She kept scowling, so I added, "I was going to bring my cow, Tiffany, but she's not a coffee drinker. She's more of a French bistro kind of gal."

That got me a round of chuckles from the other patrons just as Eric returned to our table. He set our coffees and a paper bag down, then sat with his back to the cranky lady, shielding me from her death glare.

"I caught the last part about Tiffany. Too funny. Is she still staring at us?"

I took a quick peek. "Yup."

"Is what you said about California allowing dogs on patios true? I've always assumed but never checked."

"It's true. At least in our area. My father's a retired cop, so we do everything by the book in our family."

"That's good to know." He opened the bag, revealing two chocolate chip cookies and two oatmeal.

I snagged a chocolate chip and, after a bite, said, "You shaved your beard. I didn't recognize you at first, but I recognized Dundee."

He ran a hand over his smooth face. "My grandmother said I looked like a vagabundo. So I shaved it in honor of her upcoming ninety-eighth birthday party. All her friends are going to be there." He shrugged with a sweet smile. "I have to look sharp."

" 'Vagabundo'? What does that mean?"

"Bum. Vagabond."

"That was nice of you," I said.

"More like self-preservation. You haven't met my grandmother."

We chit-chatted for about twenty minutes and seemed to be on the same wavelength about life in general. You know, the important things like "Is it okay to eat breakfast for dinner?" (yes) and "Is pineapple on a pizza a crime against humanity?" (yes, for me, no for him).

I was starting to think I wouldn't mind going on a real date with Eric when his phone rang.

He pulled it from his back pocket. "Sorry. I have this thing on Do Not Disturb except for emergencies and Mom." He glanced at the screen. "Yep. It's Mom. I have to take it."

"Of course." I expected him to leave the table, but he stayed.

"Hey, Mom." Eric's tone softened, gentle and patient, like someone speaking to a small child. "No, it's okay that you called."

He glanced at me. "I'm having coffee with a friend. Remember? I told you that. Then I'll be home." He paused, listening and nodding. "Yes, I'll get your favorite ice cream and fix the car." Another pause. "Set the timer for one hour. When it rings, I'll be there, okay?" Eric ended the call and set his phone on the table. "Mom. I'm living with her now because she has Alzheimer's."

"I don't want to be too nosy, but isn't your mom a little young for that?" I was thinking about my folks. They're in their fifties. I couldn't imagine this happening to them.

"She's seventy-seven, but it was early onset. My parents were in their forties when I came along. They'd given up trying by then, so I was a surprise."

He hadn't mentioned his father, so I asked.

"He passed several years ago. Heart attack. Died while he was giving an economics lecture at Stanford. I guess that's one lecture those students will never forget. He was a great guy, but honestly, I'm glad he's not here to see Mom's decline."

"And your grandmother. She's not your mother's mother, right?"

"Right. Dad's mother. Nearly ninety-eight and healthy as a horse." He shook his head. "Anyway, Mom's on a waiting list for a care facility. During the week, she has a caregiver while I'm at work, but I don't have much of a social life these days. Probably shouldn't have gone on that dating site. I mean, who wants to get involved with a guy taking care of his mother with Alzheimer's?" He shrugged, looking apologetic. "My grandma pushed me into it."

I laughed. "My grandmother pushed me into it, too. You said you'd fix the car. Does your mother still drive?"

"Hell, no. I took the keys away a couple years ago. I tried to explain why she couldn't drive anymore, but she kept searching for them and getting very riled up. So, I put them in her purse and took the battery out of the car. She tries to fire up the old Camry several times a week, and the darn thing won't start for some strange reason. I'm always working on the car, but I can't figure out the problem."

Eric was growing on me. He had his priorities straight, a good heart, and a sense of humor.

I gave him a synopsis of my family and showed him photos of Daisy and Tabitha like a proud mom.

"Your grandmother Ruby sounds like a lot of fun." He checked his watch. "I hate to cut this short, but—"

"You gotta get that ice cream. What's her favorite flavor?"

"Mint chocolate chip."

"A girl after my own heart. My fave, too."

We hugged awkwardly and simultaneously said, "Let's do this again."

———

"And that's it?" said Sam. "All you said was, 'Let's do this again?'"

I was sitting in my car in the grocery store parking lot, giving her the rundown of my coffee date before heading in to shop.

"What did you expect to happen? Jump his bones in the parking lot?"

"I don't know. Are you going to call him? Or text? I've been married so long I have no clue what the protocol is with you young folks these days."

"Text. And I will. Maybe tonight. You know, something like, 'I enjoyed meeting you and Dundee.' Then see what happens."

"But you do like him. Right?"

"Yeah. I guess I do."

CHAPTER NINE

MONDAY • AUGUST 31
Posted by Katy McKenna

Today marked the start of my first full week at the Diligent Detective Agency. I was excited to get to work and ready for another stakeout at Peggy Prendergast's house. The weather report had us back in our normal comfort zone—mid-seventies. I wore black yoga pants—more comfortable for a long sit in the car —and a loose, printed top. My phone and tablet were fully charged, and I even brought a portable power bank, just in case the stakeout turned into a marathon. I'd packed a lunch, snacks, water, a thermos of coffee, a notebook, and pens.

Last night, I downloaded several episodes of *Moonlighting*, one of my mom's favorite 1980s detective shows. Cybill Shepherd (who played Maddie Hayes) and Bruce Willis (who played David Addison) ran the Blue Moon Detective Agency. I'd already watched the first episode and loved it. Bruce was in his early thirties—so darn cute with that smirky smile.

I rolled into the office parking lot before 8:30 and found the old curmudgeon waiting at the door, leaning on his walker and looking like he'd just sucked a lemon.

"About damn time you got here," Walter grumped. "Some of us got work to do."

"According to my watch, I'm five minutes early."

"In my day, if you were five minutes early, you were already fifteen minutes late."

"You sound like my dad." I unlocked the door and while rushing to disarm the alarm, hollered over my shoulder, "Anyway, looks like we both beat the boss!"

Uncle Walter rattled his walker through the door. After he collapsed on the sofa with a loud "oomph" and a follow-up fart, I said, "I'm starting a pot of decaf for Maxie. You want a cup?"

"Decaf is for sissies. What's the point?"

"Would you prefer Starbucks Instant Dark Roast—fully caffeinated?"

"Caffeinated—the way nature intended."

Just as the coffee maker started chugging and the water pot started boiling, Maxie arrived. She stopped in the doorway, sniffing the air. "Ahhhh." Then, "I love you."

Walter said, "I love you, too."

"I was talking to the coffee machine, old man." She dumped her huge, embroidered cloth purse on a chair. "I filled my gas tank on the way in. Back in the day, it cost me six bucks to fill my Bug. Now it's sixty! Hell, the old heap isn't even worth sixty bucks."

"Used to cost me two bucks," said Walter.

"I thought everything cost a nickel back in your day." I grinned at his scowl. "Cream in your coffee?"

He grunted. I took that as a yes, then sat at my desk and listened to voicemails. Three robocalls and one message from Suzy at Suzy Q's: "Just checking in. Let me know if anything exciting happens." I scanned the calendar. Looked like it was going to be a quiet day.

Maxie doctored her decaf and sat next to Walter.

I watched her take a sip and scowl. "I made it extra strong to compensate for it being—"

"I know. Wannabe coffee. But thanks for trying. At least it tastes halfway decent." She yawned and hollered, "God, I need caffeine!" She downed half the cup and cleared her throat. "Katy? You up for another stakeout?"

"I sure am. Totally. Whenever you want."

Maxie turned to Walter. "Did you get a chance to talk to your friend at the DIA?"

"I got his number from my buddy." He glanced at his watch. "I'll call right now before it's lunchtime in DC."

I was antsy to go hunting for Peggy Prendergast. "Shall I head out now, boss?"

"Hold your horses, cowboy. Let's see if Walter gets to talk to this guy."

After several rounds of being transferred, he finally said, "It's about damn time!"

Maxie whispered, "Tone, Uncle Walter. Vinegar or honey?"

He nodded. "Am I speaking to Commander Phil Hoffman?" A pause, then a smile. He listened for a moment. "I'm an old friend of your grandfather. I remember you when you were just a little guy. Anyway, I hope it's all right that he gave me your number." Another pause. "Oh, he gave you a heads-up. That's great. I guess you're aware we've got a situation here in Santa Lucia, California, that you may be able to help us with—and maybe save a man's life."

I listened as Walter explained the dilemma. His speech was surprisingly compassionate. The commander must have thought so too, because he gave Walter an email address to send our photos to and said it would get top priority.

I'd already scanned the photos the other day, so I emailed them immediately.

"Fingers crossed the age progression will help find Graham Brownstadt," I said.

"If he's still on this planet," said Maxie. "Which I seriously doubt."

———

Before heading to my stakeout near Peggy's house, I swung by Mom's beauty shop, Cut 'n Caboodles. Pop's Fixit Shop is right next door, and they both park in the back alley. I didn't think sitting in my conspicuous orange car so soon after my last stakeout was a great idea, so I was hoping to borrow one of theirs for a few hours.

Mom's car is a late-model white Honda CR-V. Pop's is a green Dodge minivan he got when I was a kid. Both were perfect for my espionage.

After assuring Mom I wouldn't be in danger, I handed over the keys to Veronica. She dug her keys out of her purse and, before handing them to me, said, "Promise me again. You'll be careful. No high-speed chases or anything like that."

I hugged her. "Cross my heart, hope to die."

"No! Don't say that! It's bad luck!"

"I swear I'll be fine, Mom. I'm just going to sit in the car, eat lunch, and watch your *Moonlighting* show." I pried her key fob from her clenched hand. "If I see the perp, I'm only going to shoot some photos and take notes."

"The perp? That sounds dangerous."

"It's just detective lingo, Mom."

"You will be the death of me yet," she whimpered.

———

It was just a few minutes past ten, but my stomach was already growling. I unwrapped my peanut butter and marmalade sand-wich, thinking I'd only eat a couple of bites. A few minutes later, the sandwich was history, and I was wiping peanut butter off my chin.

I hoped to see the hot guy in the sports car again, but all was quiet at the Prendergast house. A UPS truck stopped at the curb, and the driver dashed up the porch steps, dropped a brown bag on the doormat, rang the bell, and raced back to the truck. A moment later, the door cracked open, and a hand poked out to snatch the bag.

Finally, the flashy red sports car cruised by and rolled into the driveway. The top was down, and the guy's hair glistened in the sun. My heart pounded as I ducked down.

He climbed out, leaned into the car, and honked the horn a few times. The front door swung open, and out stepped an older, dumpy woman with frizzy platinum hair and a crazy amount of eye makeup—Peggy. I was parked one house down on the opposite side of the block, so I had a clear view.

I stayed low and held up my phone to video the scene. The windows were down, so I hoped I'd catch a good sound bite. Peggy didn't show any signs of being in pain as she scurried to the car. The sexy young driver passionately embraced her, his hand slithering down her back to squeeze her ample tush.

After a steamy Hollywood kiss, he pulled back and, in an accent somewhere between Spanish lover and Italian movie heartthrob, said, "I need more money, mi amore."

Peggy, looking stressed, replied, "Antonio, I'm trying—but you need to be patient. It's going to take time." He dropped his hands, and she turned my way, patting the sports car's hood. "I don't know how much longer I can afford the payments."

Antonio grabbed her shoulders and gave her a hard shake. "We have a deal, remember?" His sexy accent gone, he roughly shoved her away, stepped over the car door, and slid into the driver's seat. The engine roared to life, and he tore out of the neighborhood.

Peggy glanced around, looking gloomy and defeated. Her shoulders slumped, she plodded back into the house.

I was so excited! She obviously wasn't injured, and I couldn't wait to show Maxie my video.

But I couldn't help feeling a little sorry for her. Her sexy boytoy was a total jerk.

———

I burst through the office door, waving my phone. "I've got proof! Right here! Prendergast is a big phony!"

"Hold on!" Maxie's voice echoed from the bathroom. A moment later, the toilet flushed. Then flushed again. The door creaked open.

"No more solid food for me today," she groaned.

"Oh, I'm sorry. What set you off?"

"Soda crackers and ginger ale."

"Flu food made you sick?" I asked.

"I need to take a break from eating." She pinched her flabby middle. "A little fasting wouldn't kill me. So, what's this about you having proof on the Prendergast woman?"

I sat on the couch and patted the cushion. "Come sit. You're gonna love this."

She joined me, grabbed a red lumbar pillow, scrunched it against her tummy, slipped on her cheaters, and sighed. "I'm ready." Then grimaced. "Wait." Clasping her hands, she did a few slow yoga breaths while staring at her knees. "Okay."

I tapped the camera icon on my phone, then the video, and held it in front of her face. "Check this out."

Maxie squinted at the screen for a few seconds. "Am I supposed to be impressed by your forehead? Because that's about all I'm seeing here. That, and what's outside the back window."

"Huh?" I leaned in for a look. Stupid me, I'd held the phone camera in the wrong direction. "Dammit! Maxie, I swear to you, she's fine. She's got an incredibly hot, young boyfriend, and, oh my God, her eye makeup is atrocious. And I heard him tell her he needs more money." I clicked play again and turned up the volume.

Antonio's voice rang out: "We have a deal, remember?"

Maxie smiled. "Well, I heard that. I wonder what their deal is?"

"I don't know, but he was mad and shoved her." I dropped the phone onto my lap. "Some investigator I turned out to be."

She patted my arm. "The good news is you know she's not injured. So, you'll give it another whirl tomorrow."

"Geez, I really blew it."

Maxie chuckled. "Have I got some stories to tell you one of these days. Talk about blowing it. You're new to this, and I've thrown a lot at you all at once. So don't beat yourself up."

CHAPTER TEN

TUESDAY • SEPTEMBER 1
Posted by Katy McKenna

Around five-fifteen this morning, I made a potty run. When I crawled back under the covers, it hit me—I'd completely forgotten about my new job when I made that doggy playdate with Eric. No way could I make it home, grab Daisy, and get to the park by five. I work until five. I think. Still a little fuzzy on what my hours are.

I didn't want to cancel, but it was too early to text him to reschedule. Plus, he'd see the time I sent it and think I was desperate.

Then my thoughts drifted to yesterday's stakeout video fiasco. I fretted for a few minutes, feeling like the biggest idiot on the planet (not the first time), and finally accepted that sleep was over.

I was backing out into the street when Maxie called.

"Hi, boss. I'm almost there," I fibbed.

She laughed. "Running late, huh?"

"Busted."

"Don't bother coming in."

"I'm fired?"

"Fired? Heck no! You're the best thing that's happened to me in a long time, girl."

I almost burst into happy tears.

"You still there?" she asked.

"Yeah. It's just...you know. What you said."

"I meant every word. Now, do a U-turn, head home, and pack yourself a sandwich if you haven't already. No need to show up at the office today. I'm running late too. I need you to go all-in on taking down Ms. Prendergast."

"Got it, boss! I promise I won't mess it up this time!"

———

I cruised into Peggy's neighborhood just in time to catch a glimpse of a dusty white Prius backing out of her garage. Behind the tinted windows, I spotted Peggy in the driver's seat. I slowed down and followed at a polite, non-stalkerish distance.

We wound up at Walmart. Peggy's one of those people who has to have the closest parking spot to the door, no matter how long it takes to get it. While she waited for a woman who was loading what looked like a thousand dollars' worth of groceries into her minivan—while yelling at her unruly brood—I parked Veronica a few spots farther away and strolled toward the entrance to wait.

Finally, the frazzled mom got into her van and backed out. For the time Peggy spent waiting on that spot, she could've finished her shopping. As she headed toward the entrance, I stepped aside, pretending to be engrossed in my phone while secretly recording her. And yes—this time, I had the camera pointed in the right direction. Peggy grabbed a shopping cart, and I followed suit. I set my purse in the cart's child seat, with my phone sticking out of the side pocket, camera pointed at my quarry, and the tailing began. I paused behind a kiosk to check what I'd recorded so far to make sure I had a good angle. Perfect.

We passed through the ladies' underwear section, where she stopped to admire some rather risqué bras. She tossed a big, lacy, padded scarlet number into her cart. Then she moved on to the bootie enhancers, selecting one that could've given Kim Kardashian a run for her money. She held it up to her already generous backside, checked herself out in the mirror, nodded with smug satisfaction, and dropped it into the cart, along with a red thong.

As I followed her through the aisles, I couldn't help picturing her prancing around for her loverboy in that red bra and matching thong.

Next stop: groceries. She shopped like she was prepping for a family of eight—or the apocalypse. I added random things to my cart to blend in: a box of crackers, canned peaches, spaghetti sauce. Then came my brilliant move. You're going to love this.

We were in the cereal aisle. I'm 5'9", and Peggy's a good two or three inches taller, so neither of us has trouble reaching the top shelf. Unless, of course, you're nursing a neck injury. Which she supposedly was. But she wasn't wearing a neck brace or wincing as she tossed three boxes of Honey Nut Cheerios into her cart.

"Excuse me?" I said, approaching from behind, holding my phone aimed at her.

She turned, a friendly smile in place, her black-rimmed, turquoise-shadowed, spider-lashed eyes wide with interest. "Yes?"

"Hi. My boyfriend wants me to get some..." I glanced at my screen, as if I were reading a list. "Grampa Schneiderson's Whole

Grain Gluten-Free Muesli." I looked up at the top shelf. "I took a nasty fall the other day and pulled something in my neck." I winced. "And my back, too. I can't reach that high."

Peggy smiled, flashing perfectly capped pearly whites. "I'd be happy to."

As she effortlessly grabbed the cereal, I added, "Normally I'm the one reaching for top-shelf stuff for the vertically challenged, being five-nine and all."

"No problem," she said, dropping the red-and-white box in my cart. "Always happy to help. Perhaps you should be in bed."

"You're probably right." I was dying to say, *Gotcha!* But I didn't. I pushed it a little more. "I should see a doctor too," I said, throwing in a grimace for effect. "But no insurance. I thought about suing the store where I fell—but it's not like anyone pushed me."

I let my gaze drift over her cart. "Wow. Looks like you've got a big family."

"Nope. Just a hungry man. He's into bodybuilding and marathons."

I nodded sympathetically. "These days, food's gotten so expensive. I've had to cut way back. No more steaks at my house."

"That's what I've told Antonio. Several times. But he doesn't seem to hear me."

I smiled. "Thanks again. Have a great day."

———

I barged into the office, waving my phone triumphantly. "I got her! Yessiree, I got her good this time!"

Walter, sprawled on the couch, gave me a look like I'd lost my mind. "Got who good?"

I collapsed into a chair just as Maxie emerged from her office. "Got what?" she asked.

"Peggy. I got her so good. Hold on—Maxie, I'm texting you the video, just to be safe."

Then we all sat down together. Maxie and I on either side of Walter—for the big reveal. "I've already watched it, so I know I didn't goof this time."

I cranked up the volume, mostly for Walter's benefit.

Video: "Excuse me? Hi. My boyfriend wants me to get some, uh..."

"Whoa, you weren't kidding about the makeup," Maxie laughed. "Yikes."

When the video ended, we high-fived all around.

"Girl, you are amazing," said Maxie.

"Gotta admit, Katy," said Walter, "you did good."

Maxie shook her head, chuckling. "When you said maybe you should sue, oh my God! Brilliant!"

"It just came to me," I said, still riding the adrenaline. I inhaled deeply, then exhaled loudly. "So...now what?"

"Now I contact Suzy, she contacts the insurance company, and we put this damn lawsuit to rest."

"Will Peggy be arrested?" I asked.

Walter harrumphed. "Could happen. Insurance fraud can get you five to ten. But it's unlikely."

He leaned forward, elbows on his knees. "Most businesses have cameras now. Nine times out of ten, they can prove a false claim."

"What about bathrooms?" I asked.

He shook his head. "Nope. Too risky. Think of the lawsuits that would trigger. But insurance fraud's no joke. Your pal Peggy might be facing a hefty fine and some quality time in the county clink."

"She seemed so nice," I said. "I wonder why she did it?"

"Lots of nice people do rotten things," Walter replied.

Maxie raised an eyebrow. "My bet? Antonio is a very expensive gigolo."

———

That evening, I texted Eric and rescheduled the playdate for around six-ish. I say "ish" in case I'm running late. I like Eric, but I'm still not sure if it's a romantic like. Time will tell.

CHAPTER ELEVEN

Posted by Katy McKenna

I was applying a second coat of mascara when Ruby called.

"Whatcha doing, sweetie?"

"Mascara."

"Don't forget blush. You've been looking a little peaked lately. Are you getting enough protein?"

"Ruby, dear grandma. You've asked me that at least a thousand times—and yes, I am getting enough protein."

"You don't eat meat, so I worry."

"Neither do horses, cows, or elephants."

"You always say that." Silence on her end for a few moments. "Anyhoo—when are we going to get together and work on my *Ready-Set-Ruby[KD1]* influencer stuff?"

"How about Saturday or Sunday?"

"Why not sooner?"

"I have a job, remember? The one you arranged for me, thank you very much."

"Oh, pooh. You were more fun when you were unemployed."

"I'm liking this job. It might even become a permanent Monday-through-Friday gig."

I swiped my cosmetics off the counter and into the top drawer of the sink cabinet. Then I pulled out the blush and brushed on a little extra to make my grandma happy.

"Oh! I just remembered!" she said. "You've got that date tonight with the teacher. Are you nervous?"

"Not really. It's a doggy playdate at Lago Park. Hopefully, our dogs will get along."

"And if they don't?"

I let her ominous question hang in the air and said goodbye.

———

I was the first one in the office that morning, busy checking emails, when Maxie arrived.

"Hey girl," she said. "How's our newest and brightest private investigator this fine morning?"

"Feeling great. Still riding high from yesterday."

"And you should be. But I gotta warn you—you'll have your fair share of failures, too. I've certainly had mine." She glanced out the window. "I wonder if Walter plans to grace us with his presence today."

She came over and flipped open the desk calendar. "Let's see what's on the agenda."

A loud engine growled outside, revving dramatically a few times before falling silent.

"Speak of the devil," she chuckled. "He may be old and grumpy, but he still drives that muscle car. Or hot rod, as he calls it."

"How come it's so loud?"

"It's the muffler. High-performance—translation: noisy. Back in the day, the teenage girls probably loved it. I've seen pictures of him as a teen. He could've passed for Frankie Avalon. I was in grade school when Frankie was popular—and he was so cute."

Maxie headed to her office, and I pulled out my phone to Google "Frankie Avalon." Yup. Very cute. Pompadour hairdo and all.

Walter trundled through the door a few minutes later, huffing and puffing. He flopped onto the couch and hollered, "Did you get it?"

"Get what?" Maxie asked.

"My friend at the DIA. Did he send anything yet?"

"I just checked the emails," I said. "Nothing from him yet. But it's only been a couple of days."

"It's Washington," Maxie said. "Have you watched the news lately? They've got their hands full. We can't exactly expect them to drop everything and run to our rescue."

"Well, if you ask me," he grumbled, "if they used a little common sense, they'd have fewer fires to put out."

Maxie shook her head. "You're preaching to the choir, Walter." Then she glanced at me. "Why the mopey look?"

"Me? Oh. Sorry." I sighed. "I was thinking about Peggy Prendergast and her boyfriend, Antonio. I wonder how he's going to take the news that the lawsuit isn't happening."

"Most likely, he'll dump her and move on to the next sugar mama," Maxie said. "With his looks, he'll have no problem hooking up fast."

———

Maxie knew I had a date and kicked me out a little after four. My meetup with Eric was at six-ish, which gave me less than two hours to get ready and get to the park.

Yes, I know. It was just a doggy date, but I had major butterflies and wanted to look my best without looking like I tried. I refreshed my makeup (meaning I added another layer) and changed into casual-cute play clothes.

Meanwhile, Daisy gave me the side-eye, probably wondering why her mama was acting like a teenager going to the prom.

"Hey, kiddo. Ready to meet a super cute guy? His name's Dundee."

That's when it hit me. Dundee was, in fact, a he. Things could get...interesting. Daisy's spayed, but still...

"This could be a very short date." And then I realized I'd called it a date. Cue another wave of butterflies.

———

We arrived a few minutes before six. As usual, Daisy dragged me to the gate. The dog park has two sections: one for pups and one for mid-size and up. Our side was the party zone—dogs cavorting everywhere, tails wagging, noses sniffing.

We pushed our way through the welcome-wagging committee, but much to Daisy's dismay, I didn't let her loose.

"Hold on, girl. I want you to meet Eric and Dundee first. We're a little early."

"Katy! Over here!"

I scanned the park and spotted Eric lounging on a bench at the far end. Dundee sat calmly beside him, looking like a model dog citizen.

"Come on, Daisy," I said, tugging her through the canine chaos. "Trust me, this'll be worth the wait. Then you can party all you want."

Dundee noticed my gorgeous girl and stood, tail wagging furiously. Eric got to his feet too, leash in hand, thankfully not wagging anything.

I smiled with more confidence than I felt. "I hope they like each other."

He walked toward us. "Me too."

Dundee, the gentleman, allowed Daisy to sniff as much as she wanted. Then she paused and gave him the same privilege.

"Daisy's fixed," I said with a shrug. "No surprise puppy pregnancies for us."

Eric nodded. "Same here. No worries."

We watched them circle and sniff for a bit, and then he said, "I think it's safe to unleash them now."

As soon as we did, they tore off like rockets to join the other frolicking dogs.

We sat down, and with a sigh, I said, "Kids. They—"

"Grow up so fast," he finished.

The pups played for about an hour. We didn't go for dinner afterward—not because of the dogs, though. It was his mother. He had to get home to make sure she ate.

We made a tentative plan for a dogless dinner on Friday.

———

It was a balmy, perfect summer evening. Daisy and I sat on the porch swing after dinner, reading the paper. The big story: another person had been found dead in a tent at the homeless encampment in Maiden Lane Park. This time, the victim was a woman, possibly in her mid-thirties. No sign of foul play.

"Two dead in a matter of days. It's got to be drugs," I muttered.

Homelessness is a nationwide problem, but here on the Central Coast, where the weather is mild year-round, the situation is especially overwhelming. For a long time, it was mostly the big cities. But now? Even towns like ours are struggling.

I know many homeless people are decent individuals who have fallen on hard times. It can happen to anyone. So many these days are just one broken leg away from not being able to pay rent. No work, no paycheck. If you don't have friends or family to catch you, you end up on the street.

But a lot of the unhoused are mentally ill, abandoned by their families. And many more are addicts. Addiction feeds crime. If you need drugs, you need money. And money doesn't grow on trees in Maiden Lane Park.

Every night, there's another story on the local six o'clock news. The encampment has ballooned to hundreds of people. The park's public restrooms are likely locked now. Close to the park, there's a small Asian food market, a gas station, a Panera Bread, and Greazie's—a popular fast-food chain.

Maiden Lane is a long street that stretches through the downtown and ends in the warehouse district. It's lined with shady trees, boutiques, and upscale restaurants. But in the blink of an eye, it's a shadow of itself. Sidewalks are crowded with panhandlers—some aggressive, some unconscious, some zipped up in pup tents. Navigating the street has become a miserable obstacle course, and it's killing local businesses.

When I asked Pop why the police don't clear the sidewalks, he explained that they legally can't—unless someone is blocking a business entrance. Sidewalks are public property.

Three sides of the park are bordered by grand old homes from the late 1800s and early 1900s—gorgeous and wildly out of my price range. Just beyond that lies my neighborhood: modest, cozy homes built between the 1920s and 1950s. Old, yes, but nothing stately.

A smaller article beneath the headline said deputies have been urging campers to leave for months, citing an urgent need to replace the park's outdated irrigation system with a more water-efficient one. The original closure deadline was September 1—yesterday—but it has now been pushed to the 15th. City officials say they've offered shelter options, but so far, no one's taken them up on it.

One quote stuck with me:

"Recently, workers collected over 200 pounds of human waste

and more than 1,200 syringes in a two-week period in the encampment area."

Daisy suddenly sat up, a soft growl rumbling from her throat, the hair on her back standing at attention. Her eyes locked on a shabby man shuffling down the street, pushing a shopping cart piled high with all he owned. A skinny, mangy German Shepherd on a rope followed close behind.

The dog glanced at Daisy with such sad, pleading eyes that it nearly broke my heart.

Without thinking, I yelled, "Wait!"

The man paused, eyeing me warily.

"Wait a sec! Please!" I told Daisy to stay and ran inside.

From under the kitchen sink, I grabbed a plastic produce bag and filled it with kibble. A glance out the window confirmed he was still there. I snagged a dog biscuit from the cookie jar and rushed back outside.

Waving the bag, I yelled, "Here! I have food for your pup!" I was suddenly nervous. Would he ask for money? Was this a mistake?

But then he smiled, revealing dark, broken teeth. "Thank you. You are so kind."

"Can I give your dog a cookie?" I asked, wishing I'd brought one for him too.

"George would love that."

I stroked the dog's head while he munched the cookie. "Nice to meet you, George."

"Likewise," the man replied.

And for a minute, the three of us stood there, connected in an unexpected moment of friendship.

CHAPTER TWELVE

Today was "Take Your Doggy to Work Day!" On the way to the office, I decided to make a quick detour past Maiden Lane Park to see if people were vacating. In less than two weeks, it'll be September 15—D-Day for the encampment, and everyone's supposed to be gone by then.

Instead of the exodus I'd hoped for, it looked like the population had tripled overnight. With the recent mysterious deaths, you'd think people would be running for the hills, not setting up camp.

I parked across the street and surveyed the growing shantytown. Thankfully, I didn't see any children. But there were plenty of dogs, every size, shape, and scruff level, from Chihuahuas and Yorkies to mutts and one majestic, dappled Great Dane. He stood on the edge of the park directly across from me, proudly holding a Greazie's hamburger bag in his drooly mouth.

I glanced at my girl in the backseat. "Daisy, how can anyone afford to feed a Great Dane fast food?"

Daisy quivered as she stared out the window at the friendly-looking giant. The Dane dropped the paper bag, pinned it with one paw, and tore it open, fries flying across the grass. He chomped down the burger in one slurp, letting pickle slices and lettuce slide out the sides of his mouth. Then he went back and cleaned up the pickles and fries, one by one.

A tall, slim guy with long, beachy blond curls sprinted over, yelling, "You damn dog! That dude gave that food to me, not you!"

———

After I parked at the office, I turned to Daisy in the backseat and gave her my serious-parent face.

"Do you remember what we talked about? This is where I work. You need to be on your best behavior if you want to come with me sometimes. Not every day, of course, but maybe once or twice a week."

Her big, brown, soulful eyes locked on mine, and I swear she nodded.

Before heading inside, we did a full sniff-and-tinkle tour around the parking lot perimeter, ending at the screen door of Dara's Donuts.

"Sorry, Daisy. We can't go in there."

A cheerful voice called out, "Of course you can!"

"I've got my dog with me," I said.

"She looks like a good dog. Bring her in for a dog biscuit."

I opened the screen door and was greeted by a warm, welcoming smile. The woman behind the counter was a cute, middle-aged Asian lady with short, stylish hair and a floral bib apron.

"Come here, sweetheart," she said, waving a treat at Daisy.

Daisy happily accepted. I thanked her as I scanned the glass display case full of fresh, glistening pastries.

"You must be the new girl Maxie hired," the woman said. "I'm Dara. And you're Katy, right?"

"Yup, that's me. Pleased to meet you. Do you happen to know what Maxie's favorite donut is?"

"I sure do." Dara pointed to some unusual-looking donuts sprinkled with sesame seeds. "Cambodian Noum Kong donuts."

"I've never heard of those. They look amazing."

She used a white bakery tissue to lift one from the case and handed it to me. "My treat. But don't tell Maxie—not until her stomach settles down."

"You know about that?"

"Of course. We've been business neighbors and friends for years."

I took a bite. "Oh. This is incredible."

———

Daisy waited patiently at the agency's glass door while I unlocked it. Inside, she followed me straight to the alarm panel. Then came her official office tour, conducted while I polished off the last of my donut.

Once she'd sniffed everything and seemed satisfied, I started a pot of decaf for Maxie and settled in at my desk. Daisy flopped down beside me with a groan, already settling in for her morning catnap.

I scanned the day's appointments. Maxie tries not to schedule anyone before 9 a.m. or after 4 p.m. First up: 9:30. Elderly gentleman suspects his wife of cheating.

About ten minutes later, Maxie arrived. I held Daisy's collar so she wouldn't charge the door, as if she owned the place. Maxie knew she'd be here and came prepared.

"And who do we have here? A new hire?" Maxie slapped her thighs, and I released the pup.

"I brought you a goodie. Shh—don't tell Mommy."

Daisy gratefully accepted the large biscuit, then returned to her spot beside me and crunched away, tail wagging.

"She's having a great morning. Two treats already." I told Maxie about meeting Dara.

"Dara and her family are great people," she said. "They're living the real American dream."

"How so?"

"They came to the US after the Khmer Rouge war in the late 1970s. Millions were killed. The Khmer Rouge was trying to create a classless agrarian society. Americans didn't know the full extent of what was happening over there. Sure, it was on the news —but I didn't really know until I met Dara's family."

"Sorry to interrupt and admit my ignorance, but—where was this?"

"Cambodia. Dara was just a toddler when they arrived, so she doesn't remember any of it, thank God. But her mother used to tell me stories that would make your hair curl."

"That was before I was born," I said.

"A lot happened before you were born—or before I was, for that matter. But we have to know history. It has a nasty habit of repeating itself when we're not paying attention." She reached down and patted Daisy's head. "Don't we, girl?"

"I guess I need to read up on that war."

"Watch *The Killing Fields*. It's probably on Prime or Netflix. Supposed to be pretty accurate. Came out in the 1980s. I remember my husband and I were absolutely blown away."

As I quickly texted myself a reminder, Maxie added, "Before we dive into the day, I need to check my emails. Hopefully, we've received the age-progression photo."

"Fingers crossed."

She poured herself a cup of decaf, muttered something about how pointless coffee is without caffeine, and disappeared into her office.

A couple of minutes later, I heard her growl, "Dammit."

I called out, "Nothing?"

"Nothing," she said. "We need to give poor Phyllis some hope."

CHAPTER THIRTEEN

FRIDAY • SEPTEMBER 4
Posted by Katy McKenna

Around five this morning, the *thwack-thwack* of the dog door flapping woke me. A few minutes later, Daisy returned to the bedroom, flopped practically on top of me, and immediately conked out. I rolled over, dumped her onto her side of the bed, curled into my "go back to sleep" position, and tried to turn off my brain.

No luck. My thoughts drifted to my doggy date with Eric.

The more I see him, the more I like him. But—and this is a big, selfish *but*—he's got some serious family baggage that I'm not sure I want to unpack. He even admitted he probably shouldn't be dating right now. But c'mon, he's a millennial. If he wants a family someday, shouldn't he be in the game?

Then again, and yes—this is another big *but*—I need to tread lightly. Keep it cool and casual. The last thing I need is to get tangled up with someone who can't go to the next step. It's admirable that he's taking care of his mom, but...does that leave room for anyone else? I thought Josh was the one and look how that turned out.

I fretted for several minutes, no doubt blowing everything out of proportion, then got up.

Coffee in hand, I turned on cable news. First: twenty minutes of politics. Then, a slew of disturbing clips—people getting shoved onto subway tracks, some jerk in NYC going around punching random elderly women in the face and getting released to do it again. Can someone explain that logic to me?

Disgusted with the world, I took a hot shower. After drying off and getting dressed, I still had a couple of hours to kill before work. So I poached an egg, plopped it on a piece of toast, poured a second cup of coffee, and curled up on the couch to watch the recorded early morning edition of our local news.

Sofie Gundersen, the perky young morning anchor with Sharpie-stenciled eyebrows, enormous, red-rimmed glasses, bulging lips, and showing way too much cleavage, dialed down her beaming smile for the next story.

"There's been another mysterious death at the Maiden Lane homeless encampment. At 11:30 last night, a resident of the camp reported a man between the ages of forty and fifty who appeared to be dead."

I set my coffee on the side table and muttered at the screen, "*Appeared* to be dead? What does that even mean? You either are or you aren't."

"There were no signs of foul play," Sofie added. "And forensics has not yet released a report. Our reporter, Megan Martinez, is live on the scene."

Cut to Megan, the early morning mist frizzing her hair, surrounded by the camp's residents. Behind her, a scrawny, deeply tanned, bald, bearded guy grinned and waved at the camera.

She extended the mic. "Sir? I'm told you discovered the deceased?"

"Yup." He yanked the microphone right out of her hand. "It

was me, all right. Name's Theodore Herbert Hastings III. That's me—not the dead dude. You can call me Teddy."

Megan tried to reclaim the mic, but Teddy held on like it was his prize. So, she raised her voice and asked, "Why were you in the man's tent at that time of night?"

He scratched his beard like he was pondering the great mysteries of the universe. "That's a good question. The fuzz asked me that, too."

Suddenly, another hand reached in and snatched the mic from Teddy. The camera spun to reveal a whiskery man with long blond curls—a face I recognized.

"I'll tell you what I know. His damn dog ate my Greazie's burger. Fries, too."

Megan blinked. "And what does that have to do with the man's mysterious death?"

"Yesterday, I'm sitting in front of Greazie's, collecting funds for, uh, a good cause, when some dude walks out and hands me a couple bags of burgers. Says a customer inside gave the burgers to him to give to the hungry-looking beggar out front. Evidently, that was me. The dude said to me, 'Enjoy this with a friend,' and even tossed me a fiver. I head back to my tent, and I run into the now dearly departed. Says he's starving, so I give him one of the bags. We're talking triple cheeseburgers with the works. Just as I sit down to enjoy mine, his friggin' dog sneaks up and steals it. Bag and all. Serves him right that he's dead."

Poor Megan had completely lost her composure. "And... sir, your name?"

"Hank."

"Hank who?"

"That's all you need to know."

Teddy chimed in, "Hank's a highly decorated soldier." He straightened up and gave a sharp salute. "Marines. Afghanistan did a number on him."

Hank turned on him with a glare. "So, what's your excuse? World War I?"

Megan chortled nervously, out of her element. "So, Hank...you think the victim deserved to die because his dog ate your burger?"

"Nah. I'm talking about the dog. The dead dude's dog died too."

"Oh my God!" I yelped.

Daisy came bounding into the living room, ready to save me from whatever crisis I was having.

"I'm okay, honey," I said, patting her head.

She jumped on the couch and snuggled close.

"That guy on TV—that's the man we saw yelling at the Great Dane eating the burger. That poor doggy died."

———

I didn't think I should bring Daisy to the office two days in a row. Turns out, I was wrong.

Maxie and I pulled into the lot at the same time, and the first thing she said was, "Where's my Daisy?"

"And good morning to you, too," I replied. "Daisy had a previous engagement today. With the couch."

"Please inform her she's on the schedule for next week."

"Will do."

While I set the boss's decaf to brew and turned the kettle on for my instant coffee, she said, "Phyllis is coming in at ten this morning. Walter emailed the age-progression photos to me last night, so I'll make a copy for her. Oh, that reminds me. You need an official company email address. Do you want it to be Katy@DiligentDetectiveAgency or Katy McKenna or what?"

"Katy's fine."

Once our coffees were ready, I asked if we could take a minute to talk. We sat on the couch, and she gave me a look of curious anticipation.

I took a deep breath. "Okay, you just said I need an email address, so...I need to know. Is this a temp job, or is it—"

"Permanent? It is if you want it to be."

"I do."

"Then I guess we need to talk about salary, benefits, and vacation time," she said, shaking her head with a little smile.

"There's just one thing," I said, taking a sip of my coffee.

"Already making demands, huh?"

"I am. And this one is non-negotiable—we need another coffeemaker."

———

I handed Phyllis a copy of the age-progressed photos. There were a few photos on the page, showing different views of how he might look now. The face had aged over the decades but still held familiarity.

Phyllis leaned in close, her voice barely above a whisper. "This is how he would look today?"

"More or less," said Maxie. "It's incredible how accurate these AI age-progression photos can be."

"Can I keep this? I want to show it to my son."

"Of course," Maxie said.

"What's the next step?" Phyllis asked.

"We'll visit the local homeless shelters," Maxie explained. "See if these photos ring any bells. We'll call you the moment we hear anything. How's your son doing?"

Phyllis smiled faintly. "A little better today."

After she left, Maxie had me print out fifty copies of the photos.

"I want you to visit every shelter on the Central Coast," she said. "Start with Santa Lucia. Then branch out to food banks and other locations that might be able to help. Leave the photos with them. Meanwhile, I'll contact the media and see if they'll run a story." She reached into her desk drawer and handed me a credit card. "For expenses. Gas, food—whatever you need."

"Really? I could just keep track," I offered.

"What century are you living in, girl? That's too much work for both of us."

I reluctantly took the card. "Are you sure? I mean, what if I fill my tank and then go to the store for something personal? You shouldn't be paying for my toothpaste run."

She laughed. "Fair point. Use the card for work-related meals and keep track of your mileage. Submit your bill on the first of the month. But you'll have to do the math—not me."

I searched online for shelters in Santa Lucia County and found several. With a population of around 250,000, I couldn't help wondering what percentage might be homeless.

Lately, I've noticed the media using the term "unhoused." In the past, they were called bums, hobos, vagrants, or transients. I know a few people I'd call bums—but not because of their housing situation. It's their rotten behavior.

My first stop was the county health services center. I'd driven past the modern structure of metal and wood countless times without realizing it was also a shelter.

I parked, butterflies fluttering in my stomach, but reminded myself that Ben volunteers at a women's shelter and has shared countless stories about the kind and decent people he's met.

Inside, the space was open and bright. This was nothing like the grim dungeon I'd expected. One side was occupied by offices, and across a courtyard was an emergency shelter that accommodated up to twenty-five people. I showed the photos to several staff members and volunteers, but no one recognized Graham Brownstadt.

"I know it's a long shot, but if he's alive and in the area, we need to find him as soon as possible." I explained about Alex and left one of the copies of the photos for the community bulletin board.

Next stop: a Catholic church I often pass and admire for its beautiful old stonework. I had no idea the building behind it was a homeless shelter. A couple of volunteers were changing bedding, but the shelter was empty—it only opens at 6 p.m., and everyone has to leave for the day after breakfast.

Again, no recognition of the man in the photos, but they promised to show them to the evening crowd.

Those two visits took up the entire morning, and by noon, my stomach was growling. I stopped at Panera Bread, which is a few doors down from Greazie's. Guess which one was busier?

Hank, the guy from the morning news with the long curls, was camped outside Panera Bread's entrance, seeking donations for his "good cause."

A man walking past said, "So what's your good cause, buddy? Meth? Fentanyl? I hear crack's making a comeback."

Hank replied, hand on heart, "No, sir. I have found the Lord, and I'm seeking donations for my church."

"Yeah, right," the guy snorted, pushing through the door.

"Have a good day, sir!" Hank called out with exaggerated cheer. Then I heard him whisper, "Asshole," as I went inside.

My next visit was a small shelter at the north end of town. No good news there either.

After that, I headed to the Maiden Lane encampment. I hesitated at the idea of walking through the camp, showing photos to residents, but it was broad daylight, and not having a home doesn't make someone a criminal.

I found a parking spot about a block and a half away. After feeding the meter, I started toward the park, nerves fluttering. I was maybe half a block from the encampment when police cars, an ambulance, and a fire truck came screaming around the corner.

They stopped at the park's curb.

I turned back toward my car, a knot forming in my stomach.

Please don't let it be another dead person.

———

Eric and I planned to meet at six for dinner at the SlapDash Brewing Company in Clam Beach, which is about halfway between our houses. It's one of several restaurants and shops located on a long, wide pier. The food is casual and tasty, the beer is cold, and the view is spectacular.

At this stage, I prefer meeting up instead of being picked up, mainly to avoid the awkward good night moment. You know the one: the lingering kiss that might lead to an invitation inside, which could and probably would lead to my bed.

Don't get me wrong, I'm not opposed to inviting Eric into my bed if I see a future with him. I'm thirty-two, not getting any younger, and I don't want to mess this up. If it's meant to be, it will be.

Besides, I totally fumbled things with Kyle just a couple of weeks ago. I can't believe I'm already dating someone else. Neither can Samantha.

She called me during lunch and said, "I know I'm going to sound like your mother, but please take it slow with Eric. Are you even ready for this? You just broke up with that Kyle guy."

"First of all, I don't think a couple of dates with Kyle——"

"It was three dates."

"Okay, three dates. Still, I wouldn't call that a breakup. I just said I didn't want to go out with him anymore. And technically, you can thank Ruby for me going out with Eric. This is her fault."

"All right. But Spencer and I are gonna want to meet this guy, young lady."

"Yes, Mommy."

"Speaking of moms, doesn't this Eric person have to get home to take care of his mother? Like he did the other night?"

"He asked the daytime caretaker to stay late."

"How late is late?" she asked, full snark mode activated.

"Not that late."

CHAPTER FOURTEEN

SATURDAY • SEPTEMBER 5
Posted by Katy McKenna

"Dish, girl, dish! I want all the juicy details!" Ruby leaned in, waving a slice of toast like a wand, her eyes sparkling with pure gram-ticipation.

We were supposed to be having one of our "work" breakfasts at her dining table—planning next steps for *Ready-Set-Ruby*—but clearly, the conversation was about to veer into date recap territory.

"There's not much to tell," I said. "I tried a flight of sample beers. The Bad Girl IPA was the standout. Oh, and the black bean burger I had was amazing, and he—"

"Stop! You're killing me! I don't want to hear about the food. I want to hear about Eric. Like how you feel about him. Will he be the father of my great-grandchildren? You know..." She shrugged. "The juicy stuff."

"I can't say yes, and I won't say no. Time will tell. It's a little early to start dreaming about great-grandkids—we haven't even kissed yet."

Ruby let out a dramatic groan. "You are too much! I'm seventy-five, and—" she shifted into her elderly woe-is-me voice, complete with a quiver— "who knows how much time I have left? Did I tell you about my friend Cathy?"

I didn't want to ask. But I knew I had no choice. "What about Cathy? Did she die?"

"No. But she could have. She tripped over her dog in the kitchen."

"Did she break her back? Her hip? Is she paralyzed?"

Ruby sighed. "She cracked her elbow. Her right elbow. So now she can't fix her hair or put on makeup, and she said it really hurts."

Okay. I shouldn't have laughed. I know cracked elbows hurt— I've had one. But still. How could I not laugh?

"All I'm saying," Ruby huffed, "is life can turn on a dime. One minute everything's hunky-dory, and the next—you've bought the farm."

"Or you can't put on your makeup," I said, struggling to keep a straight face as I stood and hugged her from behind. "I love you, Granny. Now let's talk *Ready-Set-Ruby* strategy."

Ruby uses one of the two bedrooms in her cozy cottage as her dressing room/closet. It's got a wide, upholstered chair that opens into a twin bed, a makeup table with flattering lighting, and fun prints on the peach-colored walls.

"We need to set up a spot where you can talk about all things fabulous—makeup, clothes, the works," I said. "And I'm thinking your dressing room is perfect."

"My closet? Are you kidding?"

"It's not just any closet. It's Ready-Set-Ruby's boudoir."

She mulled that over. "Nope. Not a boudoir. But...probably a good place to vlog."

We stood at the doorway, quietly surveying the room.

Ruby broke the silence. "I guess I'll need to rearrange things, so I've got a blank wall behind me."

"Not blank," I said. "The backdrop can be a couple of prints, maybe your scarf rack—stuff that adds interest without being distracting."

She raised an eyebrow. "You sound like you know what you're doing."

"I don't have a clue," I admitted, shrugging. "But I've watched a lot of YouTube. You're supposed to tell me what to do, and I'll help you do it. Eventually, you'll be so good at this, you won't even need me."

She gave me a wry smile. "That, my dear, will never happen."

We spent a couple of hours rearranging the room. Ruby paused every ten minutes to tell a story from her youth—my favorites are the ones about all the rock concerts she went to with Grandpa. They saw Jimi Hendrix, Janis Joplin, The Who—and other big-name bands I can't remember now—many I'd never even heard of, which drives her nuts.

———

When I got home, Daisy met me at the door, clearly annoyed I hadn't taken her to Grandma's.

"Wanna go for a walkie?"

Forgiveness was immediate. She dashed off to grab her harness.

On the sidewalk, we turned left and strolled past Simon's house. He'd gotten the well installed. I'd pictured one of those old-fashioned, fairytale wishing wells—with a crank and a bucket —but it was just a white pipe sticking out of the ground near some bushes. Hardly noticeable.

What was noticeable was the large green water tank, half-buried in the ground on the side of the house. It looked like a spaceship had landed.

The front door opened, and Simon stepped out. "What do you think?"

"The tank? Uh...it's, uh...well—"

"Don't worry," he said with a grin. "You won't even see it soon. I'm planting berry bushes next week to camouflage it."

"Is it full of well water?"

"Nope. I'm going to capture all the rainwater from the roof— 5,000 gallons worth. I wish the city would do something about all the water that runs down the drains when it rains."

I stared at him. Does he not know it never rains in California?

Then he changed the subject. "I'm in the mood for pizza. Know any good places?"

"As a matter of fact, I do."

"Feel like sharing one?"

He must've seen the flicker of panic cross my face. "Not a date," he added quickly. "Just neighbors having pizza. That's what friends do, right?"

The thing is...Simon is very attractive. And I am very attracted to him. And I know you're thinking, but what about Eric? Hey, I'm only human. I can't help what my hormones are feeling. Is it against the law to be attracted to more than one man? But Simon and I agreed that dating neighbors is a bad idea. Very bad.

"You know what?" I said. "I could go for some pizza."

"Then it's a date." He caught himself. "I mean...plan."

Daisy was getting antsy, so we continued our loop around the block. When we got back to our corner, I crossed to the other side of the street to avoid walking past Josh's place. Silly, I know. But what if he was there, saw me through the window, came outside to say hello—and then it would be weird and awkward and messy and...enough.

I walked halfway down the opposite side, then crossed back and returned home.

Halfway up the walk, Daisy sniffed out the newspaper hiding under a bush and retrieved it. Good girl.

Back inside, I gave her a treat and made myself a cup of coffee.

As it brewed, I unfolded the newspaper on the kitchen counter. The front-page headline screamed:

ANOTHER HOMELESS MAN
FOUND DEAD

My mind flashed back to yesterday's scene—police cars, a fire truck, and an ambulance swarming the park. That makes four deaths at the Maiden Lane encampment.

The article included an autopsy report for the first victim: a lethal cocktail of fentanyl and xylazine.

The piece closed with a public safety alert from the DEA:

The US Drug Enforcement Administration is warning of a sharp increase in the trafficking of fentanyl mixed with xylazine. Xylazine—also known as "tranq"—is a powerful sedative approved only for veterinary use. This combination is making fentanyl, already the deadliest drug threat the US has ever faced, even more lethal. Because xylazine is not an opioid, naloxone (Narcan) does not reverse its effects. The DEA reports that six out of ten fentanyl-laced fake prescription pills now contain a potentially lethal dose.

I sat down at the kitchen table, the weight of it sinking in. I'm so naïve about these things. Sure, I smoked a little weed back in college, but my drug of choice is wine. I wouldn't even know where to find this stuff.

Do the people in the encampment even realize how dangerous that combo is? And where are they getting the money to feed these habits?

———

Simon chauffeured me to my favorite restaurant, Klondike Pizza, in Cala Grande, in his new, as in recently acquired, old—and very cool—2014 Ford Solar Energy Concept car.

Before we got in, he patted the roof lovingly. "Only a few were ever made. I was lucky to snag this baby. It can run entirely on solar power, but you can also plug it in or fill it with gas. Has a 620-mile range."

"This is brilliant," I said. "Just think—on a long road trip, it charges itself through the solar roof. Why didn't they ever produce these for the public?"

"It was more of a learning experiment. Never meant for mass production."

We ordered a veggie pizza—half, no cheese. Simon's vegan, so no cheese for him. It was his first time at Klondike's and his first visit to the charming village of Cala Grande.

After we stuffed ourselves, we took a stroll through the village, saying hi to all the free-roaming roosters. We had a good time, and the conversation never ran dry.

Now, I know what you're thinking. And yes, Samantha, Mom, and Ruby, I know you're reading this and I am talking to you.

No, Simon and I are not heading toward "relationship" territory. The guy's great, but as I've already said several times, I won't be getting involved with someone who lives in the neighborhood.

Friendship? Absolutely.

Anything more?

Not unless he moves across town.

CHAPTER FIFTEEN

MONDAY · SEPTEMBER 7
Posted by Katy McKenna

Yesterday

Sunday was a catch-up day: laundry, vacuuming, dusting, watering my parched houseplants, and grocery shopping. Now that I'm working full-time, I have to be a lot more disciplined with my routine. Or at least I *should* be.

———

Dinner at the folks' was veggie lasagna with béchamel sauce—and a generous helping of Mom's third-degree interrogation.

We'd barely sat down when she asked, "You're not doing anything dangerous with this new job, are you? I watch those private detective shows on TV and—"

"And they're fictional," said Pop, shaking his silver buzzcut head. "All those shows—police, FBI, detectives, whatever—are made up by writers who've never done a day on the job. It's entertainment, not real life. So quit worrying, honey."

She shot him a look. "Says the man who had to retire from the force early because...he...got...shot."

"Mom's got you there, Pop," I said, loading salad onto my plate. "But don't worry—I'm a receptionist, not James Bond."

"I admit it," Pop said. "Domestic calls can be dangerous—more so now than ever. But that was the only time I ever pulled my gun in the line of duty." He patted her hand, and she looked like she wanted to smack him. "If police shows reflected real life, they'd be canceled after two episodes."

"I watch the news, too, you know," she countered. "Officers getting attacked by rioters, ambushed while they're sitting in their cars. Life's dangerous now. Speaking of the news... Katy, did you hear they found another dead homeless person this morning in Maiden Lane Park? How many does that make?"

I paused mid-bite. "Another one?"

"Yeah," Pop said, nodding. "I think we're up to four or five."

"Pretty sure it's five," I said, suddenly not hungry. "Sounds a lot like murder."

Mom brushed a stray lock of brown hair off her forehead. "I can't believe the police haven't cleared that place out yet."

"It's public property," Pop said with a sigh. "It's not as easy as it sounds. As long as they're not blocking businesses or doorways, they're not technically breaking the law."

"Like you told me the other day about people camping on sidewalks?" I said.

"That's right, Katy. The laws haven't kept up with what's going on these days."

"Laws or not," Mom huffed, "this is out of hand. Taxpayers pay for that park. They should be able to use it."

"No one's stopping them," Pop replied.

I set my fork down. "Really, Pop? Would you take your kids there now? You can't even see the playground—it's buried under tarps and tents strung up on the swings and slides."

"Of course not. I was merely stating a fact." He took a long sip of his IPA. "We used to have some good times there when Katy was little—" He looked at my mom. "Didn't we, Marybeth?"

"We did. And with Katy's baby sister, Emily, after she came along. Picnics, band concerts, craft fairs..." She shook her head slowly. "I don't get it. What's happening to the world? Everything's changing—and not for the better."

———

Last night, I forced myself to stay up and watch the eleven o'clock local news. Curiosity got the better of me. I had to know what had happened at Maiden Lane Park.

And who should pop up on the screen but Megan Martinez, the same reporter from the other night. She looked like she'd rather be anywhere else.

"Early this morning, another homeless man was found dead in the Maiden Lane Park encampment. Police are investigating it as a possible homicide. This marks the fifth death in the camp over the past several days. No names have been released, as authorities are still working to identify the victim and notify next of kin."

———

This morning, I didn't go to the office. Maxie told me to keep visiting shelters. Honestly, I couldn't help wondering if this whole search was pointless. The man walked away decades ago. Even if he's still alive, he could be anywhere—across the country, across the globe—or six feet under.

At one shelter, a volunteer mentioned a podcast called *Have You Seen This Person?* She said they might take up my case and help track down Graham Brownstadt. It felt like a long shot, but when I got back to my car, I pulled up their website. There were photos of hundreds of missing people.

I fired off an email to their contact address—but I'm not

holding my breath. Whenever I email a website contact, I never hear back. Like, never ever.

Then I filled my gas tank and realized I'd forgotten to jot down my mileage. Gas is ridiculously expensive now, so I downloaded an app to track it. Found another one that finds the cheapest stations nearby.

Next, I stopped at a little café next to the gas station, got some fries, and continued my shelter quest until I ran out of flyers a couple of hours later. No, I didn't visit fifty places—but several asked for extra copies, so the stack vanished fast.

On my way back to the office, I treated myself to an oatmeal cookie and a latte from Starbucks. I walked through the door mid-cookie bite and was greeted with:

"Where's Daisy?"

No hello. No "How are you, Katy?" Just "Where's Daisy?"

"Sorry, Maxie. I didn't want to drag her around in the car for hours. She would've thought we were going to the park and driven me up the wall. She's home, no doubt snoozing in a sun puddle with Tabitha, her kitty sister."

———

I made a detour past Peggy Prendergast's house on my way home. I was curious whether it had sold yet. Being so close to the Maiden Lane Park homeless encampment has got to be hurting her chances. The other day, I looked up the listing. She's asking $2.3 million.

Since the last time I cruised the street, three more homes had sprouted For Sale signs. Peggy's was the largest and probably the priciest.

The red Porsche 911 Carrera sat topless in the driveway, which meant loverboy was home. I parked two doors down on the opposite side of the street, and while watching the house, I mulled over Peggy's fraudulent lawsuit fiasco, still wondering why she wasn't in jail.

The side door facing the narrow driveway swung open, and Mr. Hunk exploded out of it, screaming like a banshee. He vaulted down the steps to the car and reached inside—hauling out a derelict-looking man I hadn't noticed before. Must've been slumped low. Sleeping. Or passed out.

Antonio dragged the bearded, scrawny guy over the door and dumped him onto the concrete, then delivered a few swift kicks to his ribs.

I could hear the man groaning, trying to roll away from Antonio's shiny tan leather shoes.

"You drunk bastard! Get the hell outta here!"

Peggy stepped out, wearing pink leggings and a tank top. Not a pretty sight. "Stop kicking him!"

"Goddamn homeless loser's trespassing. I bet he tried to steal my car!"

Antonio grabbed the man under the armpits and dragged him to the curb. He paused and glanced straight in my direction. Heart hammering, I slid down low in my seat, fingers gripping the steering wheel. *Should I call the cops?* I wondered.

"Don't leave him there!" Peggy shouted.

Antonio glanced around again, then started hauling the man elsewhere. His pants were soaked, and when his face turned toward me, I saw blood dribbling from his nose and mouth. He looked...familiar. I couldn't place him, but I knew I'd seen him before.

Hands trembling, I tried snapping some photos without drawing attention. I didn't want to get beaten up, too.

Antonio shoved the whimpering man into the neighbor's bushes, then stalked back to his Porsche and leaned in. "Dammit. He pissed on the leather seat!"

He straightened, fists clenched, glaring toward the bushes. "I'm gonna kill him!"

"NO!" Peggy shrieked. "We do not need the cops coming after us. Just leave him be!"

He stood there fuming, then turned on his heel and stormed back into the house, slamming the door behind him.

I was frozen. Should I try to help the man? What if Antonio saw me and made me his next punching bag?

I called 911. Told them what I saw. They asked for my name. I figured they already had my number, so I gave it to them. I also told them I was leaving the scene—I didn't want to be spotted. If the police needed to speak with me, I'm easy to find.

———

It's two in the morning now, and sleep won't come. Every time I drift off, I see Antonio kicking that poor old man.

The police haven't contacted me, so I'm assuming the man survived. He might've been gone by the time they arrived. Or if they arrived. *If* being the keyword. Like most towns, ours is short on officers.

CHAPTER SIXTEEN

TUESDAY • SEPTEMBER 8
Posted by Katy McKenna

I can't get the image out of my head of Antonio pummeling that man yesterday. I understand being furious about someone sleeping in your car. But that kind of rage? That vicious beating was unwarranted.

There was nothing about it on the morning news. No police blotter story in the newspaper. So, what happened? Did the man walk away? And I still can't shake the feeling I've seen him before.

After my second cup of wake-up juice, I called Maxie and filled her in on what I'd witnessed.

"I'll swing by the police department on my way in," I told her. "Ask if there's any report on the incident. Not that I'm expecting anyone to know what I'm talking about."

"Good idea," she said. "I know we're done with Peggy Prendergast's bogus lawsuit, but maybe we're not done with her boyfriend." Then she added, "And instead of coming into the office afterward, how about checking a few more shelters today?"

The police station was in the middle of a major remodel, and the racket was ear-splitting. I approached the front desk and hollered, "Hello?"

The officer pulled out his orange, noise-canceling earplugs, dangling from a blue string around his neck, and gave me a friendly grin. After I introduced myself and explained why I was there, he began typing on his keyboard.

"Yes, I see you reported a crime yesterday afternoon," said Officer Cramer, squinting at the screen through cheaters balanced on the tip of his bulbous nose. "When the patrol officers arrived at the address you gave—the one where you said the victim was left in the bushes—he was gone. They knocked on the door of the home and—"

"What?" I leaned over the counter. "It's hard to hear you over all the noise."

Cramer offered a weary shrug and raised his voice. "Sorry. We're remodeling."

"Yeah, I noticed." I glanced at a burly guy on scaffolding at the far end of the room, plastering a wall. "What are you doing?"

"Adding more holding cells. Now, if only we could hire more officers."

Our police chief complains about that constantly. As older police officers retire, no one is replacing them. Bad for public safety. Great if you're a criminal.

Just then, a man in baggy, gray overalls adjusted a ladder against the rear wall. His broad back was to me as he slammed it into the scaffolding hard enough to nearly knock Mr. Plaster off his perch. A flurry of colorful cursing followed.

I turned back to Cramer, raising my voice. "So, what were you saying?"

"I said the officers knocked on the door where the victim was dumped, but there was no answer."

"What about the house where the beating happened?"

"They visited that one too," he said. "No answer there, too."

Gee, I wonder why? I thought. "So that's it?"

Cramer took off his glasses and sighed. "I'm afraid so. Unless the alleged victim files a complaint, there's not much else we can do."

"It's not alleged. I was surveilling the house where the beating occurred. I saw the whole thing."

He raised a bushy gray eyebrow. " 'Surveilling'?"

"Yes. I work for the Diligent Detective Agency." Saying it made me feel very cool. Like...real PI cool. I left out the part about being the receptionist. Less cool.

"Do you have any photos of the incident?"

My moment of cool melted. "I'm new at this, and none of the photos turned out well enough to ID Antonio. I was worried he'd spot me."

Cramer shook his head in visible frustration. "Did you say 'Antonio'?"

The ladder guy paused. Even with the face mask and chalky dust covering his hair, I caught his glance when the cop yelled the name, "Antonio." He looked our way—just for a beat—then went back to work.

"Yeah," I said. "That's the guy's name. The one who beat up the homeless-looking man. He's the boyfriend of the woman I was surveilling."

"Got a last name?"

I shook my head, feeling like a rookie. "No."

"My best advice?" he said, leaning in slightly. "Stay away from this guy. He sounds like a ticking time bomb."

I stepped out of the noisy chaos, grateful to hear the crows squawking in the giant oak tree out front. Sliding into my car, a thought struck me. The ladder guy. He'd glanced our way when Cramer yelled, "Did you say 'Antonio'?" Only his eyes had been visible—but they were dark, intense, and unsettlingly familiar. And though the overalls masked his build, he looked tall and strong like Peggy's Antonio.

I snorted. "No chance," I said aloud. "That pretty boy would never be caught doing real work."

CHAPTER SEVENTEEN

WEDNESDAY • SEPTEMBER 9
Posted by Katy McKenna

Eric called this morning. "I'm between classes and only have a few minutes before the next wild bunch rolls in. How about I bring dinner and a bottle of wine to your place around six? We could watch a movie. Something stupid funny, like *Airplane*."

"*Airplane?*"

He laughed. "Yeah, I saw it years ago at a friend's house with his grandpa. It's hilarious. Leslie Nielsen's in it. Someone brought it up in a chat I was in this morning, and it reminded me how much we all laughed. I thought it'd be fun to watch it with you."

Who's Leslie Nielsen? I wondered. "Sounds good to me. But what about your mom?"

"An old friend—someone Mom still remembers—is taking her to a potluck at the senior center. I hope it's not too much for her, but...maybe I'm overthinking it."

———

Later in the afternoon, I cruised past Maiden Lane Park on my way to check in at the office and report that, once again, I'd had no luck on my hunt for Graham Brownstadt. No surprise. I could've just called, but I feel better talking to Maxie face-to-face.

From what I could see, the park hadn't emptied out at all. If anything, it looked more crowded than ever. So much for the town's deadline.

I spotted a sharply dressed man chatting with a scruffy vagrant at a picnic table. It struck me as odd, so I pulled over to play detective for a moment.

The two of them were munching on cookies, sipping hot drinks, and looking like old friends catching up. Still, the contrast between them was striking—one was rail-thin, grimy, ragtag and wearing a gray beanie, while the other looked like he'd just stepped out of *GQ* in his perfectly fitted dark jeans, crisp white shirt, and Panama hat.

Then came the guilt. Maybe I was being a snob for even notic-ing. Who's to say they weren't old high school buddies—one down on his luck, the other just being a good Samaritan?

"Turn around, Mr. Fancy Hat, so I can see your face," I whis-pered, squinting through the windshield. I was almost certain I knew who he was—but it didn't make sense.

I was about to drive on when a noisy car roared past. Both men turned to look, giving me the perfect view.

The hat and sunglasses obscured half his face, but the chiseled jawline and 5 o'clock shadow made me feel 99% sure Mr. *GQ* was Antonio. The same guy I'd seen roughing up a homeless man just days ago. And now here he was, sharing cookies, coffee, and friendly chitchat with one.

Maybe Mr. Macho's got a soft side too, I thought, still trying to make sense of it.

Antonio glanced in my direction. I slouched low in the seat, hoping he couldn't make out my face through the windshield. But he might've recognized the car. There aren't a lot of orange Volvos on the road these days.

After seeing him shove Peggy and beat that poor guy bloody, the last thing I wanted was for him to recognize me.

I've lived thirty-two years without ever laying eyes on this man. Now, suddenly, I can't seem to stop running into him.

———

The doorbell rang, and my guard girl went berserk.

"Daisy, sit," I commanded in a not-so-stern tone.

She obeyed, tail thumping a happy rhythm on the floor as I opened the front door. There stood Eric, all smiles, looking adorable and holding a cloth bag that smelled divine. He placed it on the entry table, pulled me into a warm hug, then leaned back to take a good look at me.

"You have no idea how much I've missed you."

My heart did a happy dance, fully expecting a kiss, but instead, he bent to greet Daisy, and then Tabitha, who was weaving around his legs, leaving a generous trail of gray fur on his black pants.

"You must be Tabitha," he said, scratching behind her ears. She leaned into his hand, purring like a lawnmower.

In the kitchen, I placed two wine glasses on the tile counter. He filled them halfway, handed me one, and raised his own in a toast. "To life, the passing show, and the eyes of the prettiest girl I know."

We clinked glasses and sipped. Then he set his glass down and moved in for a kiss. Gentle. Sweet. He took my glass, set it beside his, and kissed me again—this time deeply, passionately, and thoroughly.

Let me pause here and take a deep breath so I can relive it all over again before continuing. Sigh.

I was surprised by my response—eager, joyful, excited, and yes...horny. Especially considering how I still feel about Josh.

Is it possible to be attracted to two men at once? Wait—make that three because I do find Simon incredibly alluring. But that's not going anywhere.

But Eric? I find myself very much in-like with him. And so far, he's checking a lot of boxes:

Kind heart: He's caring for his mother. A good son, but not a "mama's boy."

Loves dogs and cats: He's passed the Daisy-and-Tabitha test.

Loves kids: He's a teacher. A noble profession.

Funny: Mandatory.

Smart: Honestly, have you ever met someone funny who isn't smart?

Good looking: Not a priority, but a nice perk. Learned my lesson with my ex— Chad-the-Cad. A good soul outlasts a pretty face.

Well groomed: Clean, dresses nicely. I'm not into slobs.

Eric had brought a spread of vegetarian delights from the Whole Foods deli, and when I noticed the lack of meat, I asked, "Don't you eat meat?"

He looked sheepish. "I do. However—"

"No worries. I don't have any vegetarians or vegans in my circle, but hey—to each their own."

He smiled. "I've been researching diets for people with Alzheimer's. Turns out plant-based is best. So Mom and I have cut out meat. However, getting her to eat anything besides sweets is a daily battle. She used to be such a healthy eater. Now? Some days she doesn't even recognize me. On those days, I'm the *hombre malo* who makes her eat *mala comida*."

I raised my eyebrows. "Sorry—my high school Spanish is rusty."

"Mean man who makes her eat bad food," he translated, half-grinning, half-deflated.

I touched Eric's arm. "I'm so sorry. That has to be incredibly hard. What's her name? And does she speak English?"

"Adelina. She was born and raised in Modesto. Her parents were from Veracruz and spoke Spanish at home, but she raised me in English. Lately, though, she's slipping more and more into her childhood."

He refilled our wine glasses. "And, as I've probably said too many times already, that's why I was hesitant to start dating again."

Right on cue, Daisy nudged his leg—like an invisible Hallmark director was staging our lives. Eric scratched her head.

"And yet...here I am. With two lovely ladies." He glanced down at Tabitha. "Make that three lovely ladies."

"We're glad you're here," I said. "I'm not in a big rush. Let's take it slow and see where this goes."

Cue another kiss. And we did.

If I'm being honest, I was no longer all that interested in dinner—if you know what I mean—but good sense prevailed (barely). We filled our plates and settled on the couch.

The movie? Hysterical. Laugh-out-loud, stupid funny.

The meal? Tasty.

The company? Sensational.

The good night kiss? Over the moon.

But it's still too soon for a sleepover. My feelings for Josh are too strong, too messy, and far from sorted. Maybe I need therapy.

CHAPTER EIGHTEEN

THURSDAY • SEPTEMBER 10
Posted by Katy McKenna

Around dinnertime, Samantha FaceTimed me—shrieking like she'd time-traveled back to eighth grade.

"Oh. My. God! I just read your blog, and I am losing it!"

Chelsea popped into view behind the sofa where Sam was sitting. "I'm so impressed, Aunt Katy!"

"You read my blog?" I asked, immediately thinking, That's not good. I've shared some very personal stuff—stuff not meant for sixteen-year-old eyes.

"Nope. Mom told me." She sighed dramatically, fluttering her lashes. "Sooo romantic."

Sam cut in, "I couldn't help myself, Katy. She heard me screaming. How could I not tell her?"

Chelsea laughed. "Yeah, I thought she was in labor!"

"We've still got a few months to go," I said, grinning.

Casey clambered over the back of the couch and crash-landed next to his mom. "Hi, Aunt Katy. Why's everyone screaming?"

Sam gave her daughter a pleading look.

Chelsea extended a hand. "Come on, little bro. Let's give the besties some space." As she led him out of the room, she yelled, "Love you, Aunt Katy!"

"Wow," I said. "She's in a good mood."

"Yeah, I know. Our moody girl hasn't shown her grumpy face in days. Probably because she got her phone privileges back."

"Remember when we got cell phones in high school?" I asked.

"How could I forget? We were the last in our group. We thought we were so cool with our matching pink Motorolas. And don't forget MySpace! I wonder if those fake dog accounts we made are still out there?"

"They're probably floating in cyberspace somewhere. Then Facebook took over everything."

"Chelsea says Facebook's for old people."

"Like us. Early-thirties and already extinct. And now look at you—handing out the same punishment our parents invented. I still remember Pop saying, 'Young lady, if you want that phone back, those grades better improve. A "D" in history doesn't cut it.' "

"That was a punishment for me, too, you know. I had to call you on your landline."

"Oh, horrors!" I laughed. "The wall phone in the kitchen with the ten-foot curly cord. To get privacy, I had to stretch it into the pantry and close the door."

"Those were the good old days. So, back to Eric. Is it too soon to have you both over for dinner?"

"Way, way too soon. It's not like we're a couple."

"Uh-huh. Sounds like you might be heading that direction. Keep this old, married, pregnant lady in the loop."

CHAPTER NINETEEN

FRIDAY · SEPTEMBER 11
Posted by Katy McKenna

Another death occurred last night at the Maiden Lane Park encampment. I saw it on the late-night news. The reporter referred to the deceased as "allegedly deceased." Behind her, the "allegedly deceased" was on a gurney in a black body bag.

I don't know about you, but a zipped-up corpse on a stretcher is usually a pretty solid deceased indicator.

———

I was on my way to work when Mom called.

"Honey, I just read your blog and have some news for you. We didn't invent the 'no phone privileges' punishment. That was your grandmother's doing. Or maybe her parents. Or possibly Alexander Graham Bell himself. All I know is that if I didn't behave, I didn't get to use the phone. The ultimate punishment for a teenage girl."

When Daisy and I walked into the Diligent Detective Agency, Maxie was waiting at the door with a steaming mug of coffee me and a dog cookie for my girl.

"Just the way you like it," she said. "A pound of sugar and a quart of cream."

I took a sip and sighed. "Perfection."

"Great. I've got a little surprise for you." She turned and gestured toward the coffee station. "Voilà!"

"Oh, wow. Just—wow."

"It's the Cadillac of coffee pod makers. Holds two quarts of water and keeps it hot, so there's no waiting. I ditched the old machine." She opened a drawer to reveal an impressive choice of pods.

I hugged her. "Thank you, Coffee Queen."

After she made herself a cup of decaf, we settled onto the couch with Daisy snuggled between us.

"You know what today is?" I asked.

She nodded, her mood instantly shifting. "Nine-eleven. 2001. The day nearly 3,000 Americans were killed by al-Qaeda. I'll never forget it. I had a lousy cold and was sleeping in. Tim came into the bedroom, and I told him I'd get up in a while. And he said, 'You don't want to.' I knew right then something awful had happened."

"I was in elementary school. They canceled classes for the week. I stayed home with Mom, and she cleared her schedule at the beauty shop. Pop was a cop, so he went to work, of course."

"We didn't know what was coming next. It felt like the end of the world. We figured the West Coast would be hit, too."

We both petted Daisy, who rolled over, begging for belly rubs.

"Thank God for dogs," Maxie said softly. "They give such innocent, unconditional love." After a quiet moment, she straightened up. "All right. Time to catch up on cases."

"Did you hear there was another death at Maiden Lane Park?"

She nodded. "I did. How many now?"

"Six, I think," I said, counting on my fingers. "This is starting to feel like a serial killer."

Maxie shook her head. "Not really. If they were being shot or stabbed, sure. But this is drugs. Sad, self-destructive choices."

"Do you think they could have been poisoned?"

"It's possible," she said. "But why? The news said the first victim had fentanyl and xylazine in his system—a deadly combo of drugs."

"Maybe someone's selling tainted drugs," I said. "You hear about that all the time. People think they're buying cocaine or whatever, and it turns out to be laced with something lethal. When I was a kid, we were warned not to take stickers from strangers in case they were soaked in LSD. Remember the D.A.R.E. program? I went through it in sixth grade."

"I remember. And Nancy Reagan's Just Say No program. If kids want to do drugs, a catchy slogan isn't going to stop them."

"You're right. I still remember Olivia Ozback and Tiffany Welder sharing a joint behind the dumpsters on D.A.R.E. graduation day."

"And you were back there because...?"

"I was on my way to lunchtime crossing guard duty," I said proudly. "I was on the safety patrol."

"Did you narc on them?"

"No," I said, a little deflated. "But I wanted to. They were such stuck-up snobs."

"Probably best you didn't. They would've made your life miserable."

"You're right." I sipped my coffee. "You know, I'm glad I'm not trying to sell my house right now, since I'm just a few blocks from the park."

"Didn't you say Peggy Prendergast is trying to sell hers?"

"I did. She's asking 2.3 million. Big old Victorian, gorgeous house, but it's half a block from the chaos. Not long ago, being near the park was a selling point. Not anymore."

Maxie let out a wicked little laugh. "Serves her right."

"There are several other houses on the block up for sale. I don't feel sorry for Peggy, but I do feel bad for the others." Changing the subject, I asked, "Any new cases?"

"Nope. It's going to be a quiet day."

I must've looked worried.

"Don't panic," she said. "This happens all the time. Feast or famine. We'll be fine. Ready to check out a few more shelters[KD5] for Graham Brownstadt?"

"Yup." I already had a fresh stack of flyers waiting in my car.

"How about heading north today," she suggested. "Then maybe Santa Barbara on Monday. I know this is a long shot, but it's good training for you, and we're building connections that might come in handy later. How's your car running? I don't want you stranded."

"Veronica? She's great. I take good care of her."

Maxie raised an eyebrow.

"My Volvo. I named her Veronica when I was a kid—after the girl in *Betty and Veronica* comic books. Mom had a huge stack of them from when she was a kid, and I loved reading them. She was our family car, and my parents gave her to me when I was a teenager. I don't plan to part with her anytime soon—if ever. Although I wouldn't mind a few modern upgrades."

Maxie grinned. "Like a tape player?"

I nodded. "And built-in cup holders!"

———

Searching for Graham Brownstadt is like looking for a needle in a haystack, except the needle doesn't want to be found, and it might not even exist.

We had his photos printed in the *Santa Lucia Times* local news section. Nothing. They've been posted multiple times on every online platform I can think of. I've Googled his name repeatedly, hoping that if he's dead, it might show up on an obituary site.

I even set up a Google Alert for "Graham Thomas Brownstadt." So far, I've received a handful of alerts, but none of them are the right man. You'd be surprised how many people have that exact name.

The drive from Santa Lucia to the first town up north only takes about twenty minutes, but it felt like crossing through a climate portal—cool ocean breeze to brick oven set to "broil." It was a blistering 96 degrees, and my car doesn't have AC. Now that's an upgrade I'd love to have! I was glad I'd left Daisy snoozing under my desk.

I stopped at every shelter. Handed out flyers and explained that it might be a life-or-death situation. Everyone was kind, but I could see the doubt in their eyes. The same doubt I carry with me. Most likely, Graham Brownstadt is already long gone.

Still, I read somewhere that people who disappear don't always go far. Maybe he stayed close. Maybe he watched from the sidelines as his son grew up—playing soccer, Little League...

Maybe he was there through the years, just out of sight.

CHAPTER TWENTY

SATURDAY • SEPTEMBER 12
Posted by Katy McKenna

Eric's cousin Brian is in town for a short visit. He's got a wife, two kids, and a house painting business in Bakersfield. Now and then, he makes the trip over from the valley to give Eric a break from caregiving. So, we made a dinner date. I suggested meeting at Suzy Q's, which is about a half mile from my house—an easy walk that takes me past the homeless camp.

As I strolled by the park, Hank, the guy with the gorgeous, long blond curls, was talking to TV news reporter Megan Martinez. The fact that she was filming probably meant there'd been another death. That and the three cop cars still on the scene. I checked my watch. I was running early, so I walked over to join the crowd and listen.

"I'm tellin' ya, these dudes were poisoned," Hank said. "Don't try to tell me they all just happened to die from accidental fentanyl overdoses just because the first guy supposedly did. "Or" —he made air quotes—"'allegedly,' like you reporters love to say. That's bullshit."

Martinez, dressed unprofessionally in an orange tank top and jeans, looked somber as she said, "People are dying by the thousands all over the country from that drug."

Hank continued. "And I'm tellin' ya that this latest victim, Jack, didn't do drugs. Alcohol, yeah. The guy was a drunk, but he didn't touch drugs. His kid died from a heroin overdose years ago, and Jack never got over it. That's why he stayed away from drugs." He shrugged, then added softly, "It's also why he's—" he paused, grief flashing in his eyes. "Was a drunk."

Megan, trying to remain professional, turned away from Hank to wrap up her segment. "At this time, it's unknown what killed the latest victim in the Maiden Lane deaths."

I racked my brain, trying to tally up the victims. Five? Six? Maybe seven? Could this be the twisted handiwork of a serial killer? Or is it just an unintentional, lethal mix of drugs, poor health, and alcohol? Every time I turn on the news, there's another grim tale about fentanyl. And the Mexican drug cartels are so ruthless that they make the Mafia seem almost virtuous by comparison.

I caught Hank staring at me—one of those slow, heavy-lidded, up-and-down lazy looks that makes a woman feel like she's being undressed. Not always a bad thing, if it's the right person doing it. When our eyes met, Hank grinned.

If you can see past his squirrelly behavior, he's a good-looking guy. Tall, tan, slim, and muscular. Maybe mid-thirties to early forties. Straight, white teeth. He wore a snug, black, sleeveless T-shirt and camo pants. A military-looking tattoo decorated his forearm. I recalled his campmate, Teddy, saying on the news that Hank had served in the Marines. I smiled politely, but when he stepped in my direction, I made a dramatic show of checking the time and hustled off.

———

Eric was waiting on the bench outside Suzy Q's entrance.

"Am I late?" I asked.

"No, I'm early," he said. "Soaking up the sun's vitamin D and trying to make sense of my day yesterday."

"Oh? Not good, I take it?"

He stood. "Not so much. Let's get a table and a bottle of wine, and I'll tell you a little story about what it's like to teach these days."

Yesterday, a freshman girl in one of Eric's classes apparently decided it was the perfect time to refresh her makeup—and livestream it for her followers.

Get this: Kylie pulled out a cosmetics bag, set up a light-up mirror, and propped her phone up to record herself applying mascara—all while sitting at her desk. When Eric told her to put it away, she ignored him and kept going like he didn't exist.

After asking her nicely three times, he collected her makeup gear and placed it on his desk, telling her she could get it back after class. Kylie immediately whipped out her phone and texted her mommy to complain that her "mean" teacher was harassing her. Within minutes, the principal swooped in and took over the class.

Now Eric is on suspension while they investigate. Can you believe it?

My heart breaks for him. He loves teaching, but this is just beyond ridiculous. Public school teachers rarely get the support they need, especially from administrators terrified of lawsuits. I suggested he consider private schools, and he said he's thinking about it. It's no mystery why there's a teacher shortage.

In this day and age, I know I'm not cut out to teach anyone over the age of, say, ten. I can picture myself marching over to Kylie's desk, sweeping her little beauty salon setup onto the floor, then yanking that phone out of her hand, saying "bye-bye" to her followers, and then stomping on it. Yup, I'd last about a day.

Wow. I just wrote, "in this day and age." Am I officially a cranky, old curmudgeon?

CHAPTER TWENTY-ONE

MONDAY • SEPTEMBER 14
Posted by Katy McKenna

This morning, Daisy and I headed south to Poza Tica, the first large town in north Santa Barbara County. The population is approximately 122,000, according to the most recent census. Four shelters were listed online, but, no surprise, no luck finding Graham Brownstadt.

You might be wondering why I didn't just email my questions along with a photo. It would save me a lot of time and gas, right? But here's the thing: I've found I'm way more likely to get an answer if I show up in person. I can't tell you how many times I've emailed the contact_address on a website and never received a response.

Case in point: I recently reached out to a local soup kitchen to offer a donation—thirty-six pounds of rice and another twenty of lentils that I ordered during a doomsday prepper phase last year. That was weeks ago. Crickets. I still think the world's on its way out, at least for us humans, but I've decided if the apocalypse comes, I'd rather go out stuffed with dark chocolate than lentils.

Obviously, I know I can't visit every shelter in the US, or even in California, so I'm contacting them via email—but for now, I'll visit the ones within reasonable driving distance—at least until Maxie tells me otherwise.

After leaving Poza Tica, Daisy and I made our way through the neighboring towns, then hit a long stretch of 101 before we reached another city big enough to have shelters. By 3:00, we were hot, tired, and ready to call it a day.

On the way home, I swung by a local shopping center for some takeout. As I rolled toward the parking lot exit, I spotted Hank standing on the corner with a cardboard sign, knocking on car windows. I had just enough time to veer off toward the other exit and avoid being seen.

What's his story? Why is a guy like that living on the street? He looks healthy and strong, so why is he panhandling? Is he using? Drinking? I've never seen him drunk. I know he served in Afghanistan—Teddy said he was a Marine, so maybe he's wrestling with some heavy PTSD. I wonder if he's settled into that life or if he still dreams of something more.

I know I have PTSD. Most of my worst experiences happened right here on the Central Coast because I couldn't seem to mind my own business. Like the time I was tied up in the attic and left to die. The rats up there did not help! For the most part, I think I'm handling it. But sometimes, in the middle of the night, I wake up in a cold sweat from a nightmare tied to one of those memories. And I wonder...maybe it's time I talked to someone.

When I got home, I pulled into the garage, grabbed my things, and stepped out of the car. I was reaching for the button to close the garage door when something outside caught my eye— a red sports car, cruising by slowly. The top was down.

At the wheel: Antonio. Staring right at me.

My heart shot into my throat, and I ducked behind a stack of boxes. Was it just a coincidence? After all, Peggy's house isn't far from mine. Maybe he drives past all the time.

Or... does he know I'm the one who called the cops after I saw him viciously beating that homeless man?

CHAPTER TWENTY-TWO

TUESDAY · SEPTEMBER 15
Posted by Katy McKenna

Now that I'm working full-time, I've started a new routine for Daisy. A couple of times a month, maybe more, she'll go to doggy daycare at Rolling Hills Pet Resort. Today was her first day. The ranch is just outside town, surrounded by shady oaks.

I signed Daisy in at the office, and then we waited outside for a staff member to come and collect her. Soon, I spotted a familiar, smiling face heading our way.

"Chloe Sarantos! Or is it Chloe Fargate now?" I asked, remembering that she and her fiancé, Justin Fargate, had tied the knot in Lake Tahoe.

She gave me a hug. "It's Fargate. I saw your name on the list and wanted to do your dog's intake personally." She tousled the fur on my dog's neck and got a happy grin in return. "And you must be the famous Daisy!"

A little backstory: I joined a Jane Austen book club a while back, and Chloe and Justin were members. Her short brunette hair and huge upturned eyes remind me of a young Audrey

Hepburn. If you follow my blog, you're aware of what happened at the book club. No more book clubs for me!

"I thought you worked in HR at the hospital," I said.

"I got tired of the politics," she replied.

"So now you work here?"

"Justin and I own the place! We inherited it from my great-aunt Louise. It's always been my happy place. The taxes and insurance are brutal, though, especially fire insurance, so Justin's income sure helps. He's still a full-time nurse anesthetist, but he helps out here, too." She pointed to a cozy log cabin nearby. "That's our home."

"I love it! And you had a baby, right?"

"Yes, Ava. She's a lively toddler, keeping us on our toes."

"Ava Fargate. Sounds like a movie star." I turned my head, taking in the surroundings. "This place is beautiful."

Chloe smiled at Daisy. "Looks like she's ready to make some new pals."

———

"Where's our receptionist?" asked Maxie as I entered the agency.

"Right here." I glanced at my watch. "And I'm early."

"No, Katy. You're the office manager. Daisy McKenna is the receptionist."

"Wait, what? I'm the manager?" I laughed. And I wasn't sure about Daisy's typing skills.

"You betcha," said Maxie. "And with your promotion, you get a raise."

"A raise? Seriously? Already?"

"I couldn't keep paying you the temp rate now that you're officially part of the team. So yeah, girl—you're getting a raise." She turned toward her office door. "And even though you're the manager, you're still on coffee duty."

"Ma'am, yes ma'am." I saluted, heading for the coffee station. "I'm on it, boss."

Shaking my head with joy and wondering how I got so lucky to land here, I dropped a decaf coffee pod into place and set it to brewing.

A moment later, Walter juggled his walker through the door. "I smell coffee. Don't mind if I do." He collapsed onto the couch with his usual groan.

"You're next. This one's for the boss." I paused, then added, "You know what, Walter?"

He gave me a wary look. "I don't think I'm going to like this, but what?"

I patted the coffee maker. "I'm going to teach you how to use this fancy machine, so you'll never have to ask for coffee again."

"Lucky me," he grumbled.

Now, I know what you're probably thinking—that making coffee is beneath my new promotion and pay grade. But here's the thing: I love my job, and all that comes with it.

After everyone's caffeine needs were satisfied, I sat at my desk to check the calendar and wonder what fresh new duties came with my shiny new title.

Walter interrupted my thoughts. "I've been thinking about your Graham Brownsteen search."

"Brownstadt," I corrected.

"Yeah, that guy."

I waited for him to continue. He didn't, so I asked, "What have you been thinking?"

"Do you know if our missing Mr. Brownstadt ever served in the military?"

"I have no idea."

"Well, I was thinking—if he did, maybe he's in a veterans' home."

I stared at him, and suddenly, Phyllis's wedding photo and her words clicked into place in my brain. "He was!" I shouted. "He served in Vietnam. Why didn't that cross my mind before?"

Maxie walked into the room. "What's all the shouting about, and what didn't cross your mind?"

"Graham was in the military," I said, "and Walter suggested he might be in a veterans' home."

Maxie threw up her hands. "Oh, for crying out loud! Of course. I should've thought of that. I must be losing my edge." She grabbed a cookie from our snack basket. "Let's focus on that angle instead of visiting more shelters today."

I dove headfirst into my new mission with a fresh burst of energy. First, I hunted down all the veterans' homes in California. According to the CalVet website, these homes offer affordable long-term care to aged and disabled veterans, as well as their eligible spouses and domestic partners. There are 1,380 VA healthcare facilities across the country, offering a range of services from independent living to round-the-clock skilled nursing care. California has more VA hospitals than any other state. Maybe it's because we have the largest population.

I started alphabetically, beginning with Barstow in San Bernardino County, deep in the Mojave Desert. At last count, the population was over 25,000. I've never spent time in Barstow, but I've topped off the tank there en route to Las Vegas for one of those "girls gone wild" weekends with Mom, Ruby, and Samantha. Care to guess who was the wildest of the bunch?

I composed my letter, attached the photos, and emailed it. Hopefully, someone will respond. However, I plan to follow up on all my inquiries by phone. And, like the shelters, visit those within driving distance.

Next up was Chula Vista. Several emails later, I ended up with Yountville, California. Founded in 1884, it's the largest veterans' home in the United States, serving about 1,000 veterans. It's nestled in Napa County's wine country.

Then I shifted my search to Nevada. Found a veterans' home

in northern Nevada, another in southern Nevada, two in Oregon, and three in Arizona. After sending off my final email to Arizona, I leaned back with a big sigh, muttering, "Only forty-six states to go. I need a break."

Walter looked up from his Wordle game. "While you're taking your break, how about grabbing us some donuts?"

"I'll take one, too!" hollered Maxie from her office. "I mean just one, not two. Take the money out of the snack fund."

I hollered back, "What about your stomach?"

"Oh, pooh! You're no fun."

I strolled down to Dara's Donuts, letting my nose lead the way. Dara wasn't there, but a friendly teenaged boy helped me. I got Maxie her favorite—the Cambodian Noum Kong. Walter failed to tell me what kind he liked, so he got a glazed donut, which happens to be my favorite.

———

I couldn't wait to hear how Daisy's first day at doggy daycare had gone. When I arrived, Chloe was in the office. She called for a staff member to bring Daisy out, then turned to fill me in.

"Daisy had a great day! She was a little shy at first, but Greta—our senior rottweiler who's here five days a week—took her under her paw and showed her the ropes." Chloe smiled and glanced out the window. "Here she comes now."

"I've booked her for next Tuesday, so I'll see you then. Say hi to Justin for me."

"Will do. Don't be surprised if Daisy crashes as soon as you get home. She had a big day."

———

Now I'm on the couch, wrapping up my daily blogging with

Heartland streaming in the background—though it's nearly impossible to hear over Daisy's snoring.

Tabitha, fed up with the racket, went to bed an hour ago. I finally gave up on the show and switched over to the local news.

A marine layer is rolling in tonight, and tomorrow's high will barely hit the low 60s.

In other news, the Premium Trust Savings and Loan Bank in Santa Lucia was robbed of $762 by an 83-year-old man wearing an ankle monitor and a clown mask. He was apprehended while trying to flee...on a skateboard.

I patted my snoring girl. "Geez, Daisy. You can't make this stuff up."

Just then, the anchor said, "And now we go live to Megan Martinez at the Maiden Lane homeless camp."

As I feared, there's been another mysterious death at the camp. At this rate, there won't be many people left in the park much longer.

Today was supposed to be the deadline for everyone to vacate —but clearly, that's not happening.

CHAPTER TWENTY-THREE

WEDNESDAY • SEPTEMBER 16
Posted by Katy McKenna

I left the house early this morning to do a little recon at Maiden Lane Park before work. I parked about a block away, and with my trusty sidekick/bodyguard on a leash, we took a casual stroll toward the encampment. I wasn't too concerned about safety in broad daylight.

I wore jeans, a loose tank top, a light sweater, and navy Converses instead of my usual sandals. I looked like your average everywoman out walking her dog.

At the corner, I paused, scanning the area. Should I circle the perimeter or cut through the middle?

I opted for both. First, I looped around the perimeter. The park takes up an entire city block, so it was a bit of a trek. I smiled at folks along the way and kept my distance from those who looked strung out or lost in their own world.

When I circled back to my starting point, I cut diagonally through the park, heading kitty-corner to the far side, carefully dodging garbage, syringes, and feces. I was glad I hadn't worn sandals. I kept my expression friendly and, hopefully, nonjudgmental.

Whenever I pass someone panhandling or camped in a doorway, I usually avoid eye contact, partly out of guilt for not giving money. I used to give, until police chief Angela told me that handouts usually feed habits more than hunger. Still, if it's a family with kids? That's different. How could I not help?

However, Sam recently told me she gave ten bucks to a couple near Costco with a sign reading, "Please help our hungry kids." The kids were sitting on the ground playing with toys. But when Sam came out of the store, she saw the family drive off in a brand-new Hyundai Santa Fe SUV. Not the first time I've heard a story like that.

As I passed behind a makeshift tent—blue tarp propped up with branches and rope—I heard a voice that stopped me cold.

"I'm telling ya, Teddy, it's murder. That's why the cops ain't doing nuthin'. That's a crime in itself. I guess we're not worth the effort."

That voice was unmistakable—gravelly, with a weird blend of Midwest and Southern twang that you couldn't place but never forgot. It had to be Hank.

Teddy replied, "It's like we're invisible—society's eyesore. Maybe the cops are even relieved. It's like a twisted solution to the problem. What's that line from *A Christmas Carol?* You know, the one Scrooge says about poor people? You're the one always reading the classics at the library, so you should know."

" 'If they would rather die,' " Hank quoted, " 'they had better do it, and decrease the surplus population.' "

"Yeah, that's it. I remember it from watching that old movie as a kid. I guess we're the surplus population. But I'm not ready to die yet."

Hank grunted. "We need a committee. Or a neighborhood watch to guard the camp. Someone's out there killing us, and I won't rest until I find out who."

"I almost feel sorry for the guy, knowing what you're capable of," said Teddy.

"That was war. And who says it's a dude? Plenty of lethal women out there. You never met my mother. I joined the Marines to get away from that heartless bitch. Doesn't take muscle to poison someone, you know."

"You really think it's poison?"

"What else can it be?" Hank said. "They said the first death was from a lethal mix of fentanyl and something else."

Teddy answered, "Xylazine."

"Yeah, that's it. That mixture's poison. Fentanyl is killin' people left and right. Xylazine makes it way worse."

Teddy coughed—wet and congested.

"You gettin' sick?" Hank asked.

"Allergies," Teddy replied. "I need some allergy meds, but I'm broke. That stuff's expensive."

I turned, trying to coax Daisy along, but in her excitement, she bumped into me, and I went crashing, butt-first, into the back of the tent.

"What the hell?" Hank barked as he stomped around the collapsed tarp. "What the hell are you doin'?"

I flailed, tangled in rope and plastic. Hank offered a hand, which I ignored.

He stared, then his expression shifted. "Wait a minute. I saw you the other day when that reporter was here. Yeah, you were checkin' me out."

"No, I wasn't. You were, Hank."

He gave me that same cocky, testosterone-fueled grin I remembered. "So you do remember me." He extended his hand again. I took it, reluctantly.

"Are you okay?"

"Yes," I hissed as he helped haul me to my feet.

"You know my name, so I should know yours, right?"

"It's Katy. Sorry about the tent. I was just walking with my dog and—" I spun around, panicked. "DAISY?"

"Relax. You dropped her leash when you fell. She's sayin' hello to my buddy."

His friend was crouched nearby, petting her, her tail wagging with delight.

Hank crossed his arms, giving me a quick once-over. "So, you were just walking by? Through this dump? Like I'm gonna believe that."

I brushed pine needles and dirt off my pants, tucking my hair behind my ears, and coming away with a brittle redwood twig. "Well... It's the truth."

He wasn't buying it.

"Okay, fine. I'm not being totally honest."

"No shit, Sherlock."

"The thing is...I work for a detective agency."

He laughed. "Like, I believe you're a detective."

I'm not, I thought, but said, "I'm not on assignment or anything—at least not about this place. But I am concerned about the recent deaths."

"So you're doing a Nancy Drew and nosing around." His tone edged into flirt territory again.

"Maybe more like Jessica Fletcher," I replied.

"She's too old. How about Stephanie Plum? Cute and sassy."

"I thought you only read the classics."

Hank grinned. "I've been known to indulge in lighter fare. How long were you listenin' to us?"

"Long enough to know you think the deaths are murders—and you want to catch whoever's doing it. And I agree with you."

"You care about us? A bunch of lowlifes bringing down the neighborhood property values? I'd think you'd be glad someone's killing us off."

"I'd be lying if I said I liked this." I gestured to the surrounding camp and kicked a syringe out of Daisy's reach. "Not long ago, this was a beautiful park for families, kids. Now look at it. It's a dangerous, disgusting dump. Everyone was ordered to leave, but instead, the population keeps growing."

"And dying."

I met his gaze. "You know what? This park may be public property, but it is not meant to be a residence. I would think you'd all want to get out of here before you wind up dead, too."

"I'll move on," he said. "But not until I catch the killer."

———

When Daisy and I arrived at the office, Maxie was at her desk, talking on the phone. As soon as she hung up, she waved me into her office.

"Katy, I'd like you to meet Alex Brownstadt."

A man about my age stood and offered his hand. "Hi. It's good to meet you. My mother speaks highly of you all."

Although thin and pale, Alex was good-looking. He had an engaging smile, a friendly face, and a nice head of dark, wavy hair. He looked very much like his father, though I didn't say so.

"It's nice to meet you," I said. "How are you feeling?"

"Pretty well, all things considered."

Maxie said, "I told him we're researching the VA homes and shelters."

"I don't expect any miracles," he said, his tone resigned. "I barely have any memory of my father. Just flashes." He paused. "But good flashes. Reading books. Rolling a ball to me. Sitting on his shoulders at a parade." Alex shook his head as if trying to shake off the fog of memory. "I honestly think he's dead. Probably for years."

"We haven't found any confirmation of that," Maxie said gently.

"But even if he were still alive, that doesn't mean he's a match," Alex said.

I didn't know what to say, so I just nodded and stayed quiet.

Alex continued, "I'm on the waiting list and doing everything I can to stay as healthy as possible, so I don't get bumped off."

"Alex told me he was in the army," Maxie added.

He looked over at me. "Straight out of high school. I didn't have a direction and hoped I'd find one there. My father was in the army and—" he shrugged—"I don't know. Maybe I thought it might bring us together somehow. Obviously, it didn't. But I don't regret enlisting. My dad, the real one, David, the one who raised me, was in the army too. That's where he discovered his love of auto mechanics. He wound up owning a repair shop until he passed."

"And did you?" I asked. "Find a direction?"

"I did," he said with a nod.

Maxie asked, "Where were you stationed?"

"First in the Bahamas."

"The Bahamas?" I blurted.

He grinned. "Yeah, I know. Tough duty. It was like a paid vacation. Then I got stationed in El Salvador. Vacation time was over. A lot of people don't know that the military, all branches, do good work in impoverished countries. We repaired schools and water systems and worked with kids in our free time. That's what led me to want to teach."

"That's right. Your mother told us you're a teacher." I nearly added that my boyfriend is a teacher too—then thought, *My boyfriend? A little soon to be throwing that word around.*

"When I got out," he said, "I had a direction and was ready for college. And the army paid for it."

"And then you got married," I said.

"Yes. To my college sweetheart. She's got great parents, so between them and Mom, our kid will have doting grandparents. I just hope I'll be around to be a good dad and part of the family."

My heart cracked. Why did something like this have to happen to such a nice guy?

After meeting Alex, I'm more determined than ever to help him and his family.

———

I couldn't stop thinking about Teddy's miserable allergies. So, on my lunch break, I ran to the nearby CVS and picked up some allergy medicine for him.

Hank looked surprised when I approached his tent.

"You here to knock down my humble abode again?" he teased with a laugh.

He looked even more surprised when I handed him the small pharmacy bag. "These are for Teddy."

CHAPTER TWENTY-FOUR

THURSDAY • SEPTEMBER 17

Posted by Katy McKenna

I woke up feeling like I could conquer the world. To keep the good vibes rolling, I skipped my usual morning ritual of drinking coffee while watching the news and questioning humanity's survival odds. Instead, much to Daisy's uncontainable joy, I opted for a brisk walk around the block before heading to the office.

We turned left and spotted our neighbors, Randy and Earl, camped out on Simon's porch steps. The guys—excluding Simon, who's more of an herbal tea kind of guy—were drinking coffee and smoking weed, all looking glum.

"Hey guys! What's the haps?" I asked. Yes, I was in that kind of mood.

Simon furrowed his brow like I was speaking a foreign language.

"Hey, Katy," Earl said, offering me the joint.

I waved it off. "Nah, I have to work. One hit and I'd want chocolate and a nap."

"The haps is," Randy said, sighing, "Simon's well went dry."

"What? Why?"

"Apparently," Simon said, shaking his head, "that earthquake the other night dropped the water table, and it all drained away."

"Yeah. Probably in China now," Randy muttered.

I looked at Simon. "Are you still hooked up to city water?"

"I am," he said, eyeing the little white well pipes poking out of the ground. "But I spent a fortune on that well, and the water was amazing."

"Amazing," Earl echoed solemnly.

"Like bottle-it-and-sell-it amazing," Randy added, flicking the end of his joint into a flowerpot.

"So, what now?" I asked, watching Daisy snuggle up to the brooding boys.

Simon perked up. "I'm installing that atmospheric water harvester next week. The one I told you about. It's shipping from England and should land in San Francisco on Monday."

———

After entering the office, I unclipped Daisy's leash, and she made a beeline for Maxie's office like she had urgent PI business to report.

"Daisy! Have you been smoking a doobie?" Maxie called out. "Because, girl, you reek!"

I laughed as I followed her in. "I probably reek, too. We stopped to say hi to the neighbors—and their porch pot party."

"Whoa!" yelled Walter from the entryway. "Where's the party, and why wasn't I invited?"

We joined him, and Maxie said with a smirk, "Yeah, like you've ever indulged, Mr. Straight Arrow."

Walter chuckled while peeling off his ratty navy cardigan and settling on the couch. "You're right. But hey, it's legal now, and I hear it helps with aches and pains. Might give it a whirl."

Daisy hopped up beside him, and he leaned over to sniff dramatically. "Daisy! That's you?"

"Yup," I said. "She's a total party animal."

Walter shoved his walker aside and propped his loafered feet on the coffee table. "I know! Let's go to one of those fancy dispensaries. How about it, Katy?"

Maxie said, "Uncle Walter. If you want to go, I'll take you. I'm nearly out of edibles, anyway." She must have noticed my surprised look and patted my arm. "I take them at night—helps with the ol' tummy and catching some Zs."

"Sleep? What's that?" Walter snorted. "Haven't seen a full night's sleep since Clinton was in office."

Maxie grinned. "Katy, let's make it a company field trip. Sounds like Walter needs CBD gummies."

"I don't want to chew marijuana!" he bellowed.

"They're tasty. Strawberry-flavored, cherry, orange," said Maxie. "Then we can grab lunch at Suzy Q's."

I raised my hand. "Count me in. What day are we doing this?"

Maxie glanced at my desk calendar and tugged up the sleeves of her lemon-yellow sweater. "How about today?"

I shook my head. "I haven't heard anything from the veterans' homes I contacted, so I was thinking about driving to the one in Fresno today, if that's okay. I might stand a better chance of getting an answer if I'm in their face."

She glanced at her watch. "Oh, okay. Work before play. It'll probably take you two and a_half hours to get there. If you leave now, Katy, you'll be there by late lunchtime."

Walter piped up, "What's a good shopping day for you next week? Just not Monday—I've got a dominoes showdown that day."

I thought a moment, gazing at Daisy. "Tuesday. That's doggy daycare day."

She wagged her tail like we were going for a walk.

"No, sweetheart. Not going for a w-a-l-k. We're going bye-bye!"

Even better, she must have thought. She pranced to the door, eager to hit the road.

It was a balmy seventy degrees outside, so I let Daisy have her backseat window half-open so she could enjoy the wind in her face and, hopefully, air out her fur as we drove northeast on CA-41 to the central valley.

———

The CalVet veterans' home of California–Fresno is a 300-bed, long-term care facility tucked away on thirty peaceful acres. I didn't know what to expect, but I was pleasantly surprised. If you have to live in an assisted living situation, and let's face it, most of us eventually will, it seemed like one of the better options: tranquil grounds, friendly staff, and fellow residents with shared history and war stories.

Everyone was kind and helpful, and Daisy was an instant hit. People lit up when she trotted over, tail wagging like she was on a goodwill tour. But, unfortunately, no Graham Brownstadt in residence. I can't say I was shocked. Still, I left in relatively good spirits, despite the dead end.

Two and a half hours later, we rolled back into town, and I was ravenous. I swung by Greazie's for a veggie burger and fries to go. My plan? Veggie burger, a generous glass of wine, and an old movie. I've been chipping away at AFI's 100 Best Movies of All Time, which—newsflash—are usually about as cheery as a funeral. Tonight's pick: *Pulp Fiction*. I'd never seen it. It came out when I was a kid and probably wasn't on my parents' approved viewing list.

I parked, cracked the windows for Daisy, and promised I'd be right back. As I grabbed the glass door handle, a tall guy wearing dark glasses, reeking of expensive cologne, and carrying enough takeout to feed a battalion, pushed past me. No "excuse me," no smile. I was about to shout, "You're welcome!" when I got a good look.

It was Antonio.

My stomach dropped. I turned my head fast, grateful for my sunglasses. He didn't glance my way, but even if he had, would he have recognized me? Probably not. Just because I know who he is doesn't mean the reverse is true. Still...a few days ago, I caught him slowly cruising past my house, eyes locking on me like he did recognize me. Or maybe I was just being paranoid.

But considering I'm the one who exposed his girlfriend Peggy's fake injury, which torpedoed her multimillion-dollar lawsuit—money I'm guessing Antonio was counting on—I sure don't want him to know who I am. I've seen flashes of his temper, and I'm not eager to see it directed at me.

Suddenly, I wasn't hungry anymore.

I trailed him outside, staying behind parked cars. He slid into his flashy Porsche, rolled down the window, and revved the engine. Daisy spotted me and woofed a greeting.

Antonio leaned out and snarled at her, "Shut the fuck up!"

I hid behind a silver minivan just as he peeled out of the lot, tires screeching.

Heart hammering, I ran to my car, fumbling the keys with shaky hands. Daisy was barking her head off, equally rattled. I didn't stop to soothe her. I threw the car into gear and tore out of the lot, following him.

Why did I do that? Honestly, I don't have a logical answer. It was a chaotic cocktail of anger, adrenaline, and plain old curiosity. I've seen both sides of this guy. Once, sharing a muffin with a homeless man, and once, beating one bloody. But yelling at my dog? That was my line in the sand.

I thought maybe he was headed to the park, to the same place I'd seen him before. But when he passed Maiden Lane, I figured I was wrong. What are the odds a guy like that hangs out at the park twice?

Just as I was about to give up and turn right, he pulled over—about half a block past the park entrance. I cruised by, turned at the next street, and parked.

I turned to Daisy, who looked more annoyed than shaken now. "I'll just be a couple of minutes, promise. Then we're going home. And yes—goodies."

Her ears perked up at that magic word. Mine too, honestly.

I jogged to the corner and peered around it just in time to see Antonio heading into the park. He waved at a couple of guys near a picnic table beside a tent, and they waved back like old pals.

I ducked behind a redwood tree and watched as a gaunt, elderly woman joined the small group of jovial people. Antonio set the food in the center of the table, as if it were a holiday feast. Everyone grabbed burgers and fries, laughing and talking like old friends.

I blinked. What the heck?

The impulse to run over and yell, "Don't eat that—it's poisoned!" was strong. But then Antonio grabbed the last burger, unwrapped it, and took a huge bite.

I stared, baffled.

"Antonio," I whispered, "what's your deal?"

———

I texted Eric to see if he wanted to come over for dinner tomorrow night, Saturday, or Sunday—his choice. I even promised to cook. The whole shebang, as Ruby would say.

But alas, Eric turned me down. On the bright side, not seeing him too often keeps things light, interesting, and most important, uncomplicated.

There was some good news, though. Eric's going back to work Monday! The school board finally wrapped up the "Kylie-makeup" investigation, and get this, they suspended her. That's right. Justice prevailed! Fingers crossed her mom doesn't immediately slap the district with a lawsuit and a press conference.

According to Chelsea, Sam's daughter, who knows Kylie, the girl is a self-absorbed teenage drama queen. She's apparently making bank as a beauty influencer, with sponsorships from major cosmetic brands and over a million followers hanging on her every eyeliner tip. I don't get it. The girl is fifteen.

Chelsea sent me the link, and...I lasted about twelve seconds. It was a nonstop vanity-selfie-a-thon, full of kissy-face videos that made me want to stomp on my phone.

Maybe I should ask Kylie for advice on boosting Ruby's glam-granfluencer vlog. Ruby has seventy-three followers right now—only 999,927 to go, and she'll hit that million-mark milestone.

CHAPTER TWENTY-FIVE

FRIDAY · SEPTEMBER 18
Posted by Katy McKenna

Before Daisy and I headed to the Ventura veterans' home this morning, I checked the news. If there had been another death at the Maiden Lane encampment last night, I'd have to tell Angela about Antonio feeding the vagrants. Fortunately, no fatalities were reported.

———

The veterans' home in Ventura is much smaller than the Fresno facility, with just sixty beds. It's located near the United States naval base.

Daisy walked sedately beside me as we approached the main office, soaking up the compliments like a movie-star canine and spreading doggy love to the residents along the way.

In the main lobby, with my girl sitting quietly at my side, I recounted my story at the reception desk and showed photos of Mr. Brownstadt—both the younger version and the AI-aged one.

I've told this story so many times now that I practically have it memorized.

The woman at the desk took the photos and studied them, shaking her head slowly. I braced myself for the usual: "No, we don't have anyone like that here." But before she could speak, a tall, lanky man leaned over her shoulder to look at the pictures.

"When was that taken?" he asked.

"Which one?" I replied.

He pointed to the age-enhanced image and took it from the woman. "This one."

I explained it was a digitally enhanced photo, showing what Mr. Brownstadt might look like today. Then I launched into the rest of my story. "I know it's a long shot," I said, "but if he's still alive, he might be able to save his son's life." I glanced at his name tag. "Mr. Schmidt."

"Call me Austin." The rusty-haired man walked over to a file cabinet, returned with a thick folder, and set it on the counter. "We haven't moved everything to the cloud yet—too much work, not enough staff. And honestly, it's a lot easier to open a file cabinet, so we're not in a big rush." He flipped open the folder and turned it toward me.

"Oh, my God!" I tapped the folder name. "Graham Thomas Brownstadt. That's him. How did I not find this? I checked all the online military vet sites."

"Those are not complete. Over 2.7 million Americans fought in Vietnam."

My heart was pounding. "May I meet him?"

Austin closed the file. "I need to ask him first. This is going to be a huge shock—hearing about his son out of the blue. Can you come back tomorrow? Maybe around 9 a.m.? That's if he's okay with it."

"I live up in Santa Lucia, so could we make it a little later? Maybe ten or eleven?"

Austin nodded with a smile. "Tell you what. I'll go talk to him now. Who knows? He might be up for meeting you today." He gestured toward some chairs in the lobby. "Have a seat over there."

"Mind if I wait outside? I won't go far, but my dog could use some fresh air and a good sniff around."

After Daisy had her fill of exploring, I settled on a wooden bench dedicated to Alvin York, a World War I hero. I snapped a photo of his name, intending to look him up later. Twenty minutes dragged by before Austin returned. I stood up, my initial hopes dashed by the grim look on his face.

As he approached, file in hand, he shook his head. "I'm so sorry, Katy. Mr. Brownstadt became extremely agitated when I told him about your request. He kept saying he died long ago."

"He thinks his son died long ago?"

"No. He believes he is the one who died." Austin sighed. "And in a way, I guess he did." He motioned for me to move over so he could sit.

"Why do you say that?"

"Several years ago, Mr. Brownstadt was found in a hotel room with a self-inflicted gunshot wound to the head." He opened the file, glancing at the top page. "Christmas, 2011."

I hung my head, feeling devastated on so many levels and not knowing what to say.

Austin continued. "He survived the gunshot; however, it left him a paraplegic. I guess one good thing came of it—it got him off the streets and into a VA home. He has severe PTSD, which led to drinking and drugs, and you know the rest. A sad, wasted life."

I told Austin about the night his wife tripped over his drunk, passed-out body and lost the baby. "He probably blames himself for his unborn baby's death, too."

Austin pushed his gold wire rims back up his nose, slowly shaking his head. "That heartbreaking story isn't in his file."

"I wonder why his wife, I mean ex-wife, or his son wasn't informed about his condition?"

"That I don't know. It was long before my time here. Even if he is a match, he's in no condition to donate a kidney. Alcohol and drugs destroyed his health. No doubt his kidneys, too."

I leaned over to hug Daisy. "Do you think he would want to see his son?"

"I don't know, but I can't broach the subject right now. We had to give Mr. Brownstadt a sedative to calm him down."

I sat up straight. "Well, you don't always get a happy ending in real life."

"You're right about that. Life sure isn't like a Hallmark movie, is it?" He ruffled Daisy's ears. "I'll check in on him tomorrow morning. Who knows? Maybe he'll be open to it then."

I gave Phyllis's and Alex's telephone numbers to Austin and left.

As soon as I was buckled into my car, I called Maxie with my news. Her first reaction was dead silence.

"Hello? Earth to Maxie! Can you hear me?" I shouted. "Are you there?"

"I'm here," she said. "Just stunned. Katy, you actually did it. You pulled off the impossible!" She sounded like she might burst into tears. "I'm... I'm absolutely gobsmacked. I'll call Phyllis and set up a meeting. Can you come in tomorrow? I know it's Saturday, but this can't wait."

———

During the drive home, my thoughts kept circling back to Phyllis's strange marital situation. What was the legal status of her marriage to her deceased husband, David Kaplan, now that Graham—her first husband—had been found alive? They were never officially divorced, and although Graham had been declared legally dead before she married David, does that declaration still hold now that he's back? Is she technically still married to Graham? It's not my place to ask, but it's something to ponder.

The drive dragged on, thanks to a traffic jam that brought me to a standstill in Santa Barbara. Luckily, my gas tank was full, and I had snacks and entertainment. I've been hooked on a true crime podcast lately, and the latest episode got me thinking about Antonio and Peggy. Talk about an odd couple.

I flashed back to when I heard Peggy telling him she didn't know how much longer she could afford the payments. I assumed she meant his fancy car. Then he grabbed her arm and reminded her—none too gently—that they had a deal.

I turned off the podcast, seeing the scene play out in my mind. Antonio had jumped into his car and sped out of the neighborhood, leaving Peggy looking utterly miserable.

"What is their deal?" I asked snoozing Daisy. "And what's up with this damn traffic?"

———

This evening, I looked up Alvin York. According to Wikipedia, his full name was Alvin Cullum York, born in 1887 and passed away in 1964. They called him Sergeant York, and he was a country boy from rural Tennessee who became one of the most decorated American soldiers of World War I.

CHAPTER TWENTY-SIX

SATURDAY • SEPTEMBER 19
Posted by Katy McKenna

I arrived at the office half an hour before we were scheduled to meet with the Brownstadts so that I could grab some donuts from Dara's. I was excited in a mixed-up way:
• Happy to have found Graham.
• Sad that he could not be a donor.
• Happy that Alex and Phyllis would now know what had happened to Graham.
• Sad about the miserable life Graham has lived.
• And hopeful that Alex and his father might forge a friendship.

Maxie arrived just as my coffee was gurgling into my cup. "Ahhh, heavenly," she said with a smile, peeking into the pink donut box and selecting a chocolate-covered cake donut. We settled into the seating area, and after a big bite, she mumbled with a full mouth, "Breakfast of champions!" Halfway through her donut, she turned to me. "So, fill me in on Graham Brownstadt."

When I finished, she said, "That sure is a letdown." She sat straighter in her chair and clasped her hands. "But hey, let's look on the bright side."

"What bright side would that be?"

"You found him. You tracked down Alex's long-lost father. Even if he can't be the donor, maybe they can reconnect. Become a family again."

I sighed, feeling the weight of the world on my shoulders. "Yeah. Before it's too late for both of them."

"Let's not write off Alex just yet. There's still hope that a donor will be found."

"If he can survive the wait." I leveled my eyes on hers. "Maybe I could be the donor." The words just popped out of me. I paused, thinking about it. "Yeah, maybe I could."

Maxie's brows furrowed. "Now, Katy, we don't know if you're a match. And we're talking about giving someone you barely know a kidney. That's serious business."

"I can't decide anything until I know if we're a match," I replied, refilling my coffee as I mulled over the idea. "But what if I *am* a match, and then I chicken out? That would devastate Alex and his family."

Maxie shook her head. "They wouldn't know."

I sat down, picked up my donut from its napkin on the coffee table, took a bite, and realized I'd lost my appetite. "How do you know that?"

"My husband, Tim, had liver cancer. I was tested, but unfortunately, I wasn't a match. Of course, he knew I was getting tested, but that's when I learned how the system works. You go through psychological evaluations and medical tests. It's all confidential, and the recipient only knows if you want them to."

"I'm so sorry you weren't a match. That must have been hard."

"Yes, it was. But there was a bright side. There was a little local boy with whom I did match."

"So, you donated to him?"

She smiled, looking wistful. "I did. It made Tim happy to know that the seven-year-old cutie had a chance to live a full life."

A few minutes later, our clients arrived. After I made coffee for Phyllis and Alex's wife, Hillary, and poured a glass of water for Alex, we got down to business.

I laid everything out—what went down at the VA home, Graham's condition, the self-inflicted gunshot wound, and his fragile mental state.

Phyllis was the first to break the silence. "First off, I'm amazed you even found him."

"Honestly, so am I," I admitted. "It was pure dumb luck."

She shook her head. "No, it wasn't just luck. You worked hard."

Alex shook his head slowly. "It's hard to wrap my mind around the fact that he's been so close all these years. I don't know how to process this."

Hillary, a slim, pretty brunette, took her husband's hand. "We truly believed he was dead. It's a miracle."

"What really would have been a miracle," said Phyllis, "is if he were healthy and—"

"A viable donor," finished Alex, looking down at his hand in his wife's.

Hillary squeezed his hand. "We're going to find a donor. I know it. We've had one miracle, so who says we can't have another?"

I handed Alex a note. "Here's your father's contact information. Ask for Austin Schmidt. He'll do everything possible to get you and your father together."

CHAPTER TWENTY-SEVEN

SUNDAY • SEPTEMBER 20
Posted by Katy McKenna

While sipping my morning coffee, I realized it was Sunday. Sunday Funday!

I've spent so many years working for myself that Sundays haven't felt special in ages. However, I now have a job with weekends off. So, what does one do on Sunday Funday?

Catch up on errands: laundry, grocery shopping, and yard work. Fun! Not. Should've done it on Saturday.

I stripped the bed, stuffed the sheets into the washer, and started sorting through my laundry basket.

As I separated whites from colors, it hit me—my wardrobe is seriously lacking anything suitable for my new job title. Maxie's style leans casual-boho, but I feel like I should elevate my look a bit when I'm out representing the firm.

I love shopping at hardware stores, but clothes? Not so much. Still, it had to be done. A little help wouldn't hurt, so I called my fashionista grandmother, who pounced on the invitation.

"You mean you want to shop in a real store?" she said. "Not online?"

"No, I don't want to, but I have to. Will you help me?"

"Count me in, kiddo! Hey, we can do a *Ready-Set-Ruby* segment! I'm on my way."

Fifteen minutes later, I heard the honk outside. I opened the door and waved at Ruby, who was parked at the curb in her cute little 1964 red Triumph Spitfire, top down, looking retro chic with a long, pink chiffon scarf wrapped around her head and neck.

From the porch, I called, "Hey! How about I drive? No need to use up your gas." The truth is, I'm not fond of her driving, and she knows it.

"Hop in, sweetie pie! Time's a-wastin'!"

Reluctantly, I opened the passenger door and slid in.

"Sweetie, don't worry about my gas. I've got plenty. And I mean that literally. I'm suffering from IFS."

"Oh my God! What's that? Is it serious?"

She giggled. "Involuntary farting syndrome. And I got it bad."

And then she proved it.

———

"Hey there, all you fabulous fashionista Boomers! It's your girl, Ready-Set-Ruby, back at it again—and today, I'm on a mission to style my granddaughter! Honey, show the world that pretty face of yours!"

I switched the phone camera to selfie mode and forced a cheerful grin that was more jovial than I felt. Then I flipped it back toward her.

"Today's fashion adventure takes us to my all-time favorite local boutique, Golden Gals! In fact, my entire outfit was purchased here." Ruby did a little spin, then motioned me to follow her through the entrance. "I bet we're gonna find some cute outfits for my grand gal here."

She made a beeline for a nearby rack and immediately held up a sequined jean jacket. "Trendy, youthful, and perfect for you, Katy! Go ahead, try it on!"

Let's pause for a moment here. Yes, Ruby always looks fabulous. She's seventy-five and dresses like a stylish fifty-something. It works for her. But it won't work for me, because I'm in my early thirties, and glittery sequins are a hard no. Probably always will be.

Before I could protest, she thrust the jacket into my arms and snatched the phone. "I'll handle the camera while you slip into this snazzy little number."

Just then, a sixty-ish, grey-haired saleslady approached at what I can only describe as boutique warp speed. "Hello, ladies! I'm Christine."

Ruby swung the camera toward her. "Hello, Christine! I'm Ready-Set-Ruby, and this is—"

"Oh my gosh! You're Ready-Set-Ruby? I love your vlog! I never miss a post. That segment you did on snail facials? Brilliant!"

Ruby turned the camera on Christine, who squealed, "Oh my gosh, am I going to be on your vlog?"

"Snail facials?" I said, no doubt sounding as horrified as I felt. "I must've missed that one."

"Betty's been helping me since you started working full-time. And let me tell you—slime is all the rage. Plus, it doesn't cost a dime to slime!" Ruby and Christine burst into giggles like two middle-schoolers on a sugar high.

"Wait—was that your friend Betty with the snails on her face?" Christine asked. "I adored her turban. Very exotic."

"Yup, that was Betty," said Ruby. "She's exotic, all right."

I was still struggling to believe any of this had actually happened. "So...do you kill the snails, mash them up, and smear them on your face? Because if that's the case, I'm out. No way."

Ruby brushed a strand of hair from my face and said, "No, sweetie. It's cruelty-free. You just lie back, place a couple of live snails on your freshly washed face, let them work their slimy magic, and then release them back into the wild. Snail mucin is packed with antioxidants, hyaluronic acid, and proteins for healthy skin."

She slipped on her cheaters and leaned in for a closer look at my face. "You might want to give it a go, Katy. They say an ounce of prevention is worth a pound of cure."

"Or a pound of snails," joked Christine, taking the jacket from my arms. "I'll start a dressing room for you."

I glanced around at the other shoppers, thinking, *This is so not my vibe. Maybe in thirty years.*

The sequined jacket was a no-go; it felt like stiff chainmail. I did end up buying a couple of cute, flowy tops and a pair of olive-green ankle pants. Honestly, I might even shop there again.

But the snail facial? Still a hard no.

CHAPTER TWENTY-EIGHT

MONDAY • SEPTEMBER 21
Posted by Katy McKenna

After some late-night research, I'm having second thoughts about donating a kidney to Alex. This isn't like rolling up your sleeve to donate blood—you're handing over a vital organ. The remaining kidney has to pull double duty, working harder than it was ever meant to, through something called hyperfiltration, which can lead to complications like diabetes, high blood pressure, and obesity.

Then I picture Alex, his pregnant wife, Hillary, and his mother, Phyllis. How can I not at least find out if I'm a match?

———

"Good morning, Maxie!" I said as she came into the office. Daisy scooted out from her cave under my desk and trotted over to greet our boss.

Maxie dropped her purse and a newspaper onto the couch,

then stooped to soak up some doggy love. "Oh, Daisy. This grumpy old lady is so happy to see you and your mom."

Raising an eyebrow, I asked, "Why are you a grump?"

Maxie popped a decaf pod into the coffeemaker. "It's good, but it sure ain't caffeine. Damn colitis."

I resisted the urge to say, *Did someone get up on the wrong side of the bed?* She probably would've clobbered me.

She grabbed the *Santa Lucia Free Press* from the couch. "According to this morning's paper, it won't be long before this weekly rag is our last printed one. *The Santa Lucia Times* is going fully digital in a few months. I get it—but that doesn't mean I gotta like it."

"I don't like it either. Although there is an upside. Ruby won't be able to read the obits with her morning coffee and then call me every time someone she knew, or barely knew, has died. So, fewer funerals for me."

Maxie shook her head. "Hate to burst your bubble, girl, but the online version has obits too. I think you can even sign up for daily email alerts."

She snagged a cookie from the jar at the coffee bar, then flopped onto the couch and opened the paper. "I always start with the letters to the editor. That's how I know what to be mad about."

Daisy climbed onto the sofa and snuggled close, placing a paw on the paper to get her attention.

Maxie set her coffee on the side table and scratched Daisy's ears. "Yes, dear, I see you. But Auntie Max wants to read the paper."

A few minutes later, she said, "You have got to be kidding me."

I was at my desk deleting the usual flood of junk emails. "What now?"

"Listen to this letter," she said. " 'Dear Editor: It's about damn time our city follows through on clearing out the homeless camp in Maiden Lane Park.' "

I nodded. "Can't argue with that. The place is a mess—garbage, rats, needles—"

Maxie kept reading. " 'Those of us who are homeowners nearby are being hit with theft, vandalism, and plummeting home values. My house is on the market, but who wants to buy near a homeless encampment? It's not safe for us, let alone our children. Every day, drugged-out vagrants stagger down my street, passing out in our yards. According to my Realtor, the value of my home has dropped by over $300,000 in the last few months. Soon, I won't be able to give it away.' "

"Geez. That is awful," I said. "I'm glad I'm not trying to sell right now. That encampment's only a few blocks away from me."

"Yup. There's more." Maxie read on: " 'If the city won't take action, we citizens will. It's time to protest, to make those vagrants' lives miserable, to force them out—whatever it takes to take back our town! Join me on my Facebook group—Take Back Santa Lucia.' " She set her gaze on me. "And get this. The letter is signed, Peggy Prendergast—Concerned Citizen."

"Oh my God!" I grabbed my phone. "Here it is. She's already got 262 followers. She's planning a protest for Sunday. At the park. Two p.m."

"Are you going to follow her?"

"Heck no. It's Peggy Prendergast."

"Are you going to protest?"

I paused. "I don't know." I thought for a second longer. "Yeah. I think I am. As long as it's a peaceful protest. And you?"

Maxie tilted her head, eyes narrowing. "I'll go. But we're sticking to the edge. Crowds aren't my thing—especially if things turn ugly."

I laughed. "Deal. If it gets crazy, we make a run for the nearest coffee shop."

She raised her coffee cup. "And you're buying."

Eric called on his lunch break and let me tell you—he sounded like he'd just won the lottery. He's thrilled to be back with his students and even more ecstatic that "Kylie the Social Influencer" is on temporary hiatus—expelled for lying. Bonus: The school board is now considering a ban on cell phones on school campuses.

Apparently, schools across the country are hopping on the no-phone bandwagon. Who knew that prying tiny screens out of kids' hands could actually work? Grades are climbing, bullying is nosediving, and there's no more fear of being immortalized on YouTube while doing an impromptu chicken dance.

Plus, these schools are returning to the socializing experience they once were in my day. Kids are talking to each other instead of texting. Who would've thunk?

Friday is a half-day, so we're plotting a get-together. No details yet, but we'll have to wrap it up before his mom's caregiver punches out. Still, I can't wait. It's going to be so good to see him.

I miss the guy.

———

I had lunch at my desk while sorting through old files and uploading decades of paper documents to the cloud. It's a massive job, and Maxie refuses to let go of even the dustiest folders.

She always says, "You never know when something might come back to bite you in the butt."

As I popped the last Ruffles chip into my mouth, Maxie called from her office. "Katy! Guess what I forgot!"

I racked my brain for something clever but landed on, "What?"

"Uncle Walter's birthday! It's this Thursday. We need to do something special for him."

I tossed my trash and walked to her office. "How old is he turning?"

"Eighty-three." She stood, looking excited. "Grab your purse. We're going shopping."

CHAPTER TWENTY-NINE

WEDNESDAY • SEPTEMBER 23
Posted by Katy McKenna

Last night, I slipped into my favorite Oreo cookie-print flannel pajamas and red, fuzzy slippers, poured a glass of red wine, and settled in on the couch with Daisy to catch up on my blog while watching *Grumpy Old Men*. The 1993 classic stars Jack Lemmon and Walter Matthau, who reminds me of Maxie's Uncle Walter.

Around 9 p.m., just as the two grumps started bickering over their sexy new neighbor, played by Ann-Margret, Daisy sprang up, barking—loud and frantic.

"It's okay, baby. It's just a movie. They're not really fighting."

She tore off to the entryway, barking and clawing at the door like something, or someone, was out there.

"Daisy, cut that out. You're scratching the wood."

She didn't stop. In fact, her frenzy only intensified.

"Dammit, you're making me nervous."

Feeling a little anxious, as I always do when Daisy does this at night, I paused the movie and got up to check the door. Daytime, I'm fine. But not so much at night. The door was bolted. The porch light was on. I edged over to the side window and inched the opaque curtain aside just enough to peek out. The porch, sidewalk, and street were empty.

Across the street, Violet—Randy and Earl's senior pit bull—had joined the commotion, barking furiously from their front window. I could see her silhouette clearly. But no sign of the boys.

"Daisy, it's probably just a raccoon," I muttered. "Whatever it is, you're not going out there to chase it. So, get over it. Wanna cookie?"

Just like that, she stopped barking and bolted into the kitchen toward the cookie jar on the counter like nothing had happened.

As she crunched away on her treat, I said, "Hey, Cookie Monster. I guess it wasn't that terrifying after all, huh?"

I think I've watched too many horror movies because I turned off the living room lamps, then tiptoed back to the window and stood there watching the empty front yard for several minutes.

No longer in the mood to blog, we settled back on the sofa. I unpaused the movie, forwarded through several commercials—and then an eerie, un-raccoon-like sound pierced the night air. It was like someone was in agony.

I tossed the remote on the couch, sprinted to the kitchen with Daisy on my heels, snatched a couple of dog biscuits from the treat jar, and tossed them on the floor for Daisy to chase down. Slamming the kitchen pocket door shut, I dashed back to the front door, cracking it open just enough to listen.

Rustling, leaf-crunching sounds came from the thick, tangled manzanita and photinia shrubs along the property line between my house and Simon's. My mind raced. Was it an injured animal? A rat? A squirrel? A raccoon?

Then came the unmistakable sound of a human moan. A chill zipped down my spine.

"Oh, crap," I muttered. "So do not want to go out there."

I grabbed the little, super-bright flashlight from the antique cabinet drawer in the entryway. Just as I was about to step outside, I thought of calling Simon for backup. I snagged my phone from the couch and dialed his number. My call went straight to voicemail.

Taking a deep breath, I chided myself for being a scaredy cat, yanked the door open, and stepped onto the porch.

"Hellooo? Anyone out there?" I called, straining to hear a response. "Hellooo? Do you need help?"

It was a full moon. Crickets chirped. An owl hooted softly from the pepper tree in my backyard. Peaceful, soothing night sounds were suddenly extinguished by an anguished moan, followed by a faint, desperate, and very spooky, "Help me."

Reluctantly descending the wooden porch steps, I flicked on the flashlight and shouted, "Where are you?"

Dry leaves rustled under the bushes. "Help me," came the weak reply.

My heart was racing as I approached the bushes, directing the beam at the ground. A chilling, gurgling sound reached my ears.

I called out, my voice trembling. "Where are you? I want to help you!"

The gurgling turned into the gut-wrenching sound of vomiting. Panic gripped me.

"I'm calling for help! Just hold on!"

Suddenly, something latched onto my ankle with a vice-like grip and yanked me off balance. I crashed face-first into the bushes. Branches and leaves dug into my skin as I struggled to break free. Then I felt a sharp pain in my leg.

Twisting free, I fell backward onto the lawn, gasping in shock. A filthy, gnarled human hand gripping a bloody pocketknife emerged from the shrubbery. His arm reached out, and I could faintly see his pale face in the moonlight filtering through the leafy bush.

I shimmied backward on my butt, putting several feet between us. I yanked up my pajamas, horrified at the sight of blood oozing from a deep slash on my calf. Oddly, the pain was already fading.

"You stabbed me?" I gasped as the reality hit me like a sledge-hammer. "Why? I was trying to help you!"

"Sorry," the man rasped. "I thought you were going to..." His voice trailed off.

I squinted, trying to see his face more clearly, when a wave of dizziness crashed over me.

"I need help!" I screamed. My vision blurred, everything turning bright white. I knew from experience I was about to pass out. "HELP!"

I bent forward, pressing my head between my knees, fighting to stay conscious as warm blood dribbled into my slipper.

I heard Simon's front door slam, and a moment later, he was at my side, towering over me with a handgun. He snatched the flash-light from my hand and aimed it at the motionless figure in the bushes.

"I have a gun pointed at you," he said. "Move, and I'll shoot. I'm calling the police."

"I think he's unconscious," I mumbled between my knees.

Simon dialed 911, gave his report, then tore off his T-shirt and crouched beside me, tying it tightly around my leg to stop the bleeding.

"Hang in there, Katy. You're going to be fine."

Daisy's frantic barks echoed from the kitchen. That brave dog had saved my life before, and I knew if she got out, she'd tear the throat out of the guy who hurt me.

Simon sat beside me on the grass, cradling me with one arm, still aiming the gun at the man in the bushes. Minutes later, sirens wailed in the distance, growing louder until the street was flooded with flashing lights—police cars, an ambulance, and a fire engine.

An EMT gave my wound a once-over. "You'll need stitches, but you're lucky—he missed the artery." She handed me a bottle of water, and as the cool liquid slid down my throat, I felt some strength return. While bandaging my leg, she turned to Simon.

"I don't think this calls for an ambulance ride. Can you get her to the ER?"

"Of course."

"I'll alert them that you're on your way."

The man in the bushes wasn't so lucky. After police pulled him out, they confirmed he was dead. I couldn't see his full face—and didn't want to—but he seemed vaguely familiar. A filthy, scrawny man with a shaggy beard and a bloody gash on the back of his bald head.

"Looks like another overdose," an officer muttered.

But what about the head injury? I wondered.

Before taking me to the ER, Simon ran home to grab a shirt. For those curious about the details: the man is very nicely built—very. Even in my panicked, dazed state, I noticed his six-pack.

———

Luckily, I was the only patient in the ER, so there was no wait. One of the perks of not living in a big city. By then, the initial adrenaline rush had worn off, and the pain hit me hard. After a numbing shot, twenty-two stitches, a tetanus jab in my upper left arm (ouch!), a crutch, and a little plastic vial of painkillers, they sent me home.

Simon helped me up the steps and onto the porch swing before heading inside to calm Daisy down. I could hear him talking to her in that gentle voice of his, and it warmed my heart.

"Now, Daisy, your mom has a big cut on her leg, but the bad man is gone. You need to take care of her, okay?"

She woofed in agreement.

"No jumping on Momma, got it?"

She woofed again.

Simon led me to my bed (unmade, of course), where Daisy and

my cat, Tabitha, fussed over me—sniffing at the bandaged wound and offering their unique brand of furry comfort. He set me up with ginger ale, mint chocolate chip ice cream, and a bag of Ruffles. The holy trinity of recovery.

After making sure I was comfortable, he offered to stay the night. I assured him I'd be fine, and after setting his number on speed dial on my phone, he promised to check on me first thing in the morning.

Once he left, I lay there thinking about Simon in a way that was far from innocent.

Too bad he's my next-door neighbor.

———

Thank goodness for painkillers!

I limped to the kitchen this morning, made my coffee, then headed straight to the couch to call Maxie. She freaked out when I told her what happened last night. She insisted I take the rest of the week off, but there's no way I'm missing Walter's birthday surprise tomorrow. He's going to be over the moon about it.

Next, I called Simon and told him I was fine. I wasn't—but I was such a mess that I preferred he didn't see me in my current state. I was also feeling a bit shy after my late-night, pain med-fueled, inappropriate thoughts about him. Thankfully, he had no clue. He offered to go to the grocery store for me, but I assured him my fridge was well-stocked.

Then I switched on the news to see if there was any mention of last night. I kept dozing off, so I set it to record for later.

After that, I called my folks, Ruby, and Sam. You can probably imagine how those calls went: lots of "Are you sure you're okay?" "Eat some soup!" and "Get plenty of rest!"

Finally, I waited until Eric's lunch break to call him. This wasn't a text or voicemail kind of conversation. I needed to hear his voice.

He sounded upset. Frustrated that he hadn't been the one to come to my rescue.

"How could you? You don't live next door, let alone in Santa Lucia," I said, trying to lighten the mood.

He let out a long sigh. "Yeah, I know. I just feel like I'm not a very good boyfriend."

Whoa. *Boyfriend?* That was the first time I'd heard him say that out loud.

Eric continued, flustered. "Sorry about that. I know we haven't been dating long. I've just, uh, been thinking—"

"It's okay," I cut in. "I'm not seeing anyone else, and I really enjoy our time together, so—"

He jumped in. "So...will you be my girlfriend?" Then he laughed. "Wow. I sound like a dork."

"I like dorks," I said.

Eric laughed again, sounding relieved.

———

Around noon, my folks tapped on the front door and let themselves in.

"We've come bearing lunch," said Mom. "Butternut ravioli and a salad from Suzy Q's, and—"

"Cookies," said Pop. "From that cookie store chain you said you liked."

We ate in the living room so I could keep my leg propped on a pillow on the couch.

"Honey?" said Mom, fork paused mid-air. "I read your blog post about the protest rally at the park on Saturday. Given your injury, I assume you're not going."

"What rally?" asked Pop.

I answered, "It's to protest the encampment at Maiden Lane Park. And it's on Sunday, not Saturday. They were supposed to be cleared out by now, but the city's doing nothing, and the situation is getting worse." I gestured at my leg. "As you can see."

Mom set her plate on the coffee table and reached out to feel my forehead, going full-on maternal.

"I don't have a fever, Mom."

"I'm worried about infection."

"They gave me a tetanus shot and antibiotics."

"Nevertheless," said my father, "I don't think it's a good idea to get mixed up in a big crowd. You could get jostled—and things could turn ugly."

"I probably won't go. But it's..." I paused, counting on my fingers. "Four days from now. I'm sure I'll be fine by then."

Mom let out one of her classic sighs of disapproval. "If you do go, then I'm going with you."

"Me too," said Pop.

"Uh, no," I said. "You're in that fundraiser golf tournament on Sunday, remember?"

He looked disgruntled. "How did I get myself roped into that? I haven't golfed in years."

"You did it to raise funds for homeless vets," said Mom. "It's a good cause."

"And pretty coincidental," I added, "considering what's happening in our town."

———

The morning news I recorded didn't mention anything about last night, but the five o'clock broadcast did. It was just a brief segment—no video, thankfully. The anchor, Don Davenport, reported that an unidentified unhoused man had died, apparently from a drug overdose. Don added that before the man's death, he had attacked a middle-aged woman.

"I wonder who that was," I muttered.

"—in her yard on Sycamore Lane with a knife, leaving her—"

"Wait a damn minute!" I shrieked. "You're calling me middle-aged?"

"—with a life-threatening injury. She's expected to survive."

"Yeah, I survived," I muttered, giving my two snuggle buddies, Daisy and Tabitha, a pat. "But next time we hear strange noises outside, we're not going to investigate, okay?"

Daisy rolled over for a belly rub, sealing the agreement.

"And I am so not middle-aged."

———

The dead man is haunting me. I feel like I know him. And why didn't Don Davenport mention the bloody gash I saw on the back of his head?

The man's last words were, "I'm sorry. I thought you were going to..."

Going to...what?

CHAPTER THIRTY

THURSDAY · SEPTEMBER 24
Posted by Katy McKenna

My leg wound is healing, but sleep has been a challenge. If I accidentally roll onto my left side—which just so happens to be my favorite sleeping position—the pain from the gash and the tetanus shot in my arm wakes me up immediately.

Luckily, my furry companions came to the rescue. In the middle of the night, Tabitha curled up against one side of me, while Daisy flopped down on the other—effectively sandwiching me in place and making sure I couldn't roll over in either direction.

Tonight, I'm going to try some liquid Sleepytime. No, not wine. The stuff from the drugstore.

———

Ruby called while I was putting on makeup.

"I read your blog, and you can count me in on the protest rally on Sunday. It'll be a girls' day!"

"Yeah, that's my idea of a fun girls' day—protesting a homeless encampment."

"Ya know what, sweetie? I could use this for my *Ready-Set-Ruby* vlog."

I set my concealer on the counter, turned, and leaned against the sink. "Your vlog is about makeup, clothes, and whatever—for senior women."

"And, like you said—lifestyle. Being a concerned citizen and actively involved in your community is part of a fulfilling lifestyle. Senior women need to stay connected and have a voice."

———

The next call was from Sam.

"You still going to the protest on Sunday?"

"Yes," I said. "Or I'm pretty sure. Depends on my leg. But pretty sure."

"I'd like to go with you," she said. "Casey wants his park back. One of his buddies always has his birthday party there, and it's coming up soon."

"Looks like he may have to have it somewhere else this year."

"No," she said firmly. "This is ridiculous. That park is for the citizens. The kids. The families. If the city won't take it back, then we, the people, will take it back!"

"Sounds like you're running for mayor," I said.

"Well, our current mayor doesn't seem to be doing anything. So maybe I will—after I have the baby. And she's in school. High school. No, make that college. And I retire from nursing. Then watch out!"

———

Daisy and I rolled into the office lot at 8:50. Just as I parked,

Maxie ran out of the office, rushing over to grab Daisy and give me a hand.

"You should've taken the week off," she scolded as I clumsily balanced on my loaner crutch.

"I'm thinking you may be right. But I didn't want to miss seeing Walter's face when he sees his gift."

"It arrived yesterday afternoon. I'm so excited." Maxie unlocked the office door and held it open for me. "I have a cake in the car. I'll go grab it."

Daisy scooted ahead of me and immediately planted herself on Walter's birthday gift: a dark red chenille electric recliner.

"Daisy! Off! You'll get your dog hair all over it."

I hobbled to the teal couch, spread a blanket on one end, and patted it. "Here. This is your spot."

She loped over, jumped on the couch, and dropped onto the blanket with a dramatic harrumph, and let out a sigh like she'd just been betrayed by the universe.

"Here it is," Maxie announced, setting a plastic cake keeper on my desk. As she lifted the lid, she beamed. "And now...the big reveal. Walter's childhood favorite—Creamsicle cake. Baked it myself last night."

The powdered sugar and orange zest–topped cake looked delicious. "Okay. Confession. This isn't the original recipe. That one called for powdered Dream Whip, and no stores around here carry it. But I'm excited about this one. I found it on a Facebook cake mix group. It's a white cake mix with orange soda."

"Plus, eggs, milk, oil, and whatever, right?"

"Nope. Just those two ingredients. Stir and bake. Everyone was raving about it."

"Wow," I said, trying to sound enthusiastic. "Just...wow. Can't wait to dig into that."

CHAPTER THIRTY-ONE

FRIDAY • SEPTEMBER 25
Posted by Katy McKenna

In the early hours of the morning, I woke from a bad dream about the dead man in my bushes. Eyes wide open, staring at the dark, shadowy ceiling, I could almost see him. How, and why, did he die in my front yard? And why did he seem familiar?

Suddenly, it hit me, and I sat up. I was pretty sure he was the same man I'd seen on the news with that guy, Hank—the one with the gorgeous hair.

I smacked the comforter. "What the hell was his name? I know he said it." I squeezed my eyes shut. "Think, Katy."

Daisy, who had been slumbering on the floor, climbed up onto the bed to check on me.

"Honey, I'm fine." I switched on the bedside lamp and gave her a quick snuggle. "Okay, enough. I need to think."

I glanced at the clock on my phone. Crud. 3:34.

The image from the news story played in my mind. It was about the second—or maybe third?—dead person found in the park.

Wait a sec!

I threw back the blankets and limp-dashed into the living room, with Daisy and Tabitha on my heels. I stopped at the couch while they beelined to the kitchen, convinced it was treat time. I gave them dog and kitty cookies to appease them, grabbed a people-cookie for myself, then flopped onto the couch, opened my laptop, and searched for KSLU News.

I wasn't sure what day I'd seen the segment, but it didn't take long to find it.

There he was—the scrawny, bald, bearded, squirrely old guy, waving at the camera behind the reporter.

"Sir?" said Megan, the reporter. "I'm told you're the person who discovered the deceased?"

"Yup. It was me, all right. Name's Theodore Herbert Hastings III. That's me—not the dead dude I found in the tent."

I hit pause, took a photo of the screen, and checked the time again. 4:43. Probably too early to call Angela. But not too early to email her.

I opened Gmail and realized I didn't have her address.

Too wired to go back to sleep, I made a cup of coffee and watched the news segment a few more times.

Why was Theodore in my bushes? Why did he die?

————

Maxie had told me not to come into work today because of my injury. My leg was achy, and I was antsy to talk to Angela about Theodore Hastings, but I waited until 8:30 to give her time to get settled in her office.

"Hey, Katy!" Angela answered cheerfully. "How're you doing?"

"I'm doing good. Loving the job and—"

"I meant, how's your leg? I heard you had to get several stitches. What a shocker for you."

"Actually, that's what I'm calling about."

"Oh God. Please don't tell me it's infected."

"No, no. It's healing nicely. And I had a tetanus shot."

I heard her blow out a big sigh of relief.

"Anyway. I know who did it!" I said.

"You do?"

"Yup. His name is—was—I mean, Theodore Herbert Hastings. The third. But I'm pretty sure it was an accident. Like a reflex to protect himself. Although I have no idea why he was in my yard."

"Well, I hate to burst your bubble, but we already identified him after taking his fingerprints. But how did you know?"

"I remembered seeing him on the news. And I even met him once, walking Daisy near the park. Oh! And I bought some allergy medicine for him. He seemed like a nice guy."

"We've ordered an autopsy, of course, but we haven't gotten the results back yet," said Angela. "However, he did have a number of wounds—some fresh, some nearly healed."

"How old was he?"

"Not as old as he looked. Forty-seven."

"Are you kidding me? I thought he was in his seventies at least."

"Rough life."

I was dumbfounded. His skin had been etched with deep wrinkles and sunspots across his forehead, a face that belonged to an elderly man, not someone younger than my parents. What was his story? For that matter, what was the story of anyone in the camp?

"Since you were able to ID him by fingerprints," I said, "does that mean he had a criminal history?"

"No. He was in the military. Therefore, he's in the database. He did have a history, though. He was a hero. Purple Heart."

CHAPTER THIRTY-TWO

SATURDAY · SEPTEMBER 26
Posted by Katy McKenna

I love this time of year on the California Central Coast. The summer tourists have cleared out until the holidays, and the weather is still warm.

Eric and I had originally planned a beach date, but that plan was made before I got stabbed in the leg. There was no way I could trudge through sand with my left leg still wrapped up and throbbing.

So—change of plans.

He picked me up and drove us to a quiet park that overlooks the beach. After parking his blue Toyota RAV4, he helped me out, got me situated with my crutch, and popped open the back of the car.

I hobbled ahead toward the grassy overlook, wearing unsexy but comfortable sweatpants and an orange flowy tank top. Halfway there, it hit me—I should've packed food. And sunblock. And a hat. Honestly, it might be time to start taking that memory supplement they keep advertising on TV.

Luckily, Eric's brain was firing on all cylinders. He jogged past me, laid out a plaid blanket on the grass, and set a wicker picnic basket beside it.

Just as I reached the spot and went to set down my crutch, he wrapped his arms around me and kissed me—a warm, spine-tingling kiss that made me want to yell, *Take me! Take me now!*

"Hey, girlfriend," he whispered in my ear.

"Hey, boyfriend," I replied, giggling like a love-struck seventh grader.

And then involuntarily yelping, "Ow, ow, ow," as he helped ease me down onto the blanket.

Late this afternoon, when Eric brought me home, he stepped inside and slowly closed the door behind him—sending my heart into overdrive. His gaze locked onto mine, his expression serious. Then he cupped my face in his hands and kissed me—softly at first, long and lingering.

The kiss deepened, growing bolder, until my crutch clattered to the floor.

Just as his warm hands slid down my bare arms, and I was hoping they'd find their way under my top—Daisy bolted through the laundry room dog door and slammed into the entryway, prancing around us and barking, "Kiss me! Kiss me, too!"

We both cracked up, and just like that, the moment's intense magic was broken. I had been this close to dragging him to my bed and ravishing him.

Not that I could have, anyway. His mother's caregiver had to leave for the day, which meant he had to head home. And let's face it—probably not the best idea for my slashed leg either.

Big, long sigh here.

I want that man in my bed.

CHAPTER THIRTY-THREE

SUNDAY · SEPTEMBER 27
Posted by Katy McKenna

Protest Day

"Are you sure you're up to this?" Mom blurted as Samantha and I opened my front door at 12:55 to let her in.

"Yeah, I'm sure." I swung my arms. "Look, Ma, no crutch." I glanced past her to spot my speedster, Grammy, skidding to a stop at the curb.

Mom gave me a snarky look. "You'd still need it if your boyfriend hadn't gone home yesterday—if you know what I mean."

Sam elbowed me as my dear mother stepped inside, patted Daisy's head, and hugged my bestie. "Oh my, you're getting big."

Sam patted her round belly. "I'm bigger this time than with Casey. Good thing my tops are stretchy."

Ruby strolled up the path with her flamboyant friend Betty trailing behind, draped in one of her exotic caftans, a matching purple velvet turban, and oversized, black-rimmed glasses. I know it sounds like a fashion disaster, but somehow, she pulls it off. Thank God my grandmother doesn't take style cues from Betty.

On the porch, Betty extended her hand like she expected me to kiss her ring and purred in a low, la-de-da voice, "So good to see you, Katy duhling. How's your boyfriend?"

She doesn't have access to my blog, so I shot Ruby a look.

Ruby shrugged sheepishly. "I may have shared a little."

"Can't wait for the next installment," Betty said. "Though I was really hoping you and my grandson, Royce—you know, the very successful CPA—would've hit it off."

I nodded. "He's a nice guy, but the fact that he's in a serious relationship with his boyfriend, Matthew, is kind of a dealbreaker. For both of us."

Betty gave me a withering glare.

Sam burst out laughing, waving her hands. "Sorry! Didn't mean to laugh. And now I have to pee!"

Ruby jumped in. "Betty volunteered to be my camera crew for my vlog." She eyed my outfit. "Is that what you're wearing?"

"No," I said. "I plan to go naked. You know, for your vlog. Although I'm still not sure this protest is really in your vlog lane."

"My lane is widening. This is real life, and my followers need to see that aging shouldn't stop you from getting involved. We all have a voice and—"

Mom cut in. "Katy, I thought your boss, Maxie, was coming with us."

"She's running a little late," I said. "Anyone want coffee while we wait? I just made a fresh pot."

Once everyone was in the kitchen, I said, "I think we should walk over. It's just a few blocks, and parking could be tough."

Sam pulled a water bottle from her backpack. "I'm all set, but I gotta pee again before we go. One of the many joys of being pregnant."

I set out a plate of store-bought cookies, and we sipped our coffee.

"I miss coffee so much," said Sam, grabbing a cookie. "And wine. And sushi."

"You don't even like sushi," I said.

"Yeah, but now I want some."

"Katy, did you make signs for us to carry?" asked Ruby. "Or were you too busy canoodling with your boyfriend?"

"I should have made that post private! And no. It didn't occur to me to make signs." I glanced around and spotted a pile of grocery bags by the back door. "Maybe we could write something on paper bags."

"Like what?" asked Sam.

"Like, uh, we want our park back. You know what? I don't want to do that. That horrible Peggy Prendergast, who tried to sue Suzy Q's, is leading this protest. I don't want to draw attention to us. I'm just curious to see how this goes."

Ruby glanced at her watch and stood. "It's time to get this show on the road. Let's wait on the porch for Maxie."

"After I pee," said Sam.

"Me too," said Ruby.

"And me," said Betty.

"Me three. Or four," I added.

After we all took turns in the bathroom, I was locking the front door when Maxie jumped out of her VW Beetle and scurried up the walk. "Hold that door. I need to tinkle!"

———

As we walked, I checked Peggy's Facebook page. "Oh, wow. The other day, she had 262 followers. Now she has 1,456. No, make that 1,458. No, 1,462. This may be a bigger crowd than I thought."

"Might as well start vlogging," said Ruby. "Camera girl? Ready?"

"Yes, boss," said Betty. She pulled a phone and an extendable selfie stick from her massive paisley purse. "Ready."

"Okay," said Ruby. "Walk a few paces ahead, then turn around and walk backward as I stroll toward you."

Betty scuttled ahead, turned, and called out, "And... action!"

"Hey, gal pals. Ready-Set-Ruby here. Today, I'm wearing a cute ensemble from *Tarjay*." She winked, did a little spin, adjusted her sequined pink zippered top, and giggled. "Better known as Target. I'm here with my daughter Marybeth, granddaughter and famous local supersleuth Katy, her BFF Samantha, and my buddy and camera gal, Betty."

Betty flipped the phone around, blew a kiss, and dropped her equipment into the gutter.

After a quick retrieval, Ruby continued. "Sorry. Technical difficulties."

She kept vlogging as we walked. "As my local followers may know, there's an encampment for unhoused folks in Maiden Lane Park, here in Santa Lucia. It's grown massively—hundreds of people. Crime has gone up. And..." She raised an eyebrow. "So has our death rate." She paused. "We're attending a rally supporting the dispersal—or relocation—of the camp. And I'm sure my granddaughter, Katy, will be on the alert for clues to the recent untimely deaths."

I gave the phone-cam a weak smile and a wave.

At the edge of the crowded park, Betty was feeling pooped, so she and Ruby settled onto a bench near a picnic table. A stylish blonde—late twenties, maybe—was savoring half a bagel slathered with cream cheese and topped with salmon lox, plus a side of fries. My stomach growled at the sight. The Café Bistro bag beside her meal looked like it still had food in it—probably the other half. And I wanted it.

"Are you all right, Betty?" Mom asked.

Betty waved her off with a smile. "Just a little tired."

"Probably worn out from that tango contest last night," said Ruby. "Ben and I sat it out, but Betty here took third place dancing with that cute new guy, Tommy."

"I noticed you limping," I said.

Betty laughed. "Tommy's cute, but he's got two left feet. My poor toes! Good thing he's a good kisser."

Mom hung back with the grannies while Maxie, Sam, and I wandered closer to the protest crowd. We hung out at the fringe in case we needed a quick getaway. From there, we had a good view of Peggy, standing on the bandstand with a microphone, checking her watch. So I checked mine—1:54.

A voice yelled from behind us, "Use the garbage can, you asshole!"

"Hold on, ladies," I said. "Be right back."

I edged around the outskirts of the milling throng and saw Hank picking up trash with a grappler and jamming it in a big plastic bag. He was shaking his head, looking disgusted, as he plucked up fast food bags, coffee, and soda cups. I remembered that the area around his tent was much tidier than the rest of the camp. Perhaps this was a holdover from his military days. As I started toward him, the KSLU news van rolled onto the grass. Not wanting to be on camera, I veered back to my group, picking up trash along the way.

"Is this thing on?" Peggy yelled, tapping her mic.

"YES!" the crowd shouted.

She glanced at her watch. "It's two o'clock, so let's begin. I'm Peggy Prendergast, project manager for Prendergast Construction. My father founded our company in the 1970s, and we've been building homes for our beautiful Central Coast ever since." She smiled warmly. "We care deeply about Santa Lucia's future."

Antonio emerged from the crowd and stepped up to the stage. Tight black jeans. Half-buttoned white shirt. Gold chain nestled against his tan, sculpted chest. Dark two-day stubble. He looked like he stepped out of a romance novel. And no—I'm not obsessed. Just...perplexed. And okay, a little mesmerized.

Peggy, with her bleached-out, frizzy hair and fuchsia leggings made of fabric so thin they left nothing to the imagination, was beaming as she announced, "Everyone, I'd like you to meet Antonio Lombardi. My significant other. He works in the construction field."

Quite a few gasps rippled through the audience. Peggy moved in for a hug, but Antonio dodged, brushing fingers through his ebony curls. Her smile faltered, and I almost felt bad for her.

"Check him out," muttered Maxie. "Is that who I think it is?"

"Yup. That's Antonio," I whispered.

Sam whistled softly. "Be still, my heart."

"I don't get it," Maxie said. "What's he doing with that woman? He should be modeling or making porn videos." She smirked. "Okay, that was awful. Listen to me debasing him. Just because he's drop-dead good-looking."

"Yeah, show some respect," I teased, elbowing her.

Peggy recovered. "If I can have your attention?"

The crowd of maybe three hundred hushed.

"Thank you for coming. Our town is being overrun with bums, vagrants, addicts, criminals, lunatics. And our leaders are doing nothing. Nothing! So I say we take matters into our own hands and take back our city. Our neighborhoods. Our parks. And take back the damn shopping carts!"

Cheers erupted.

Peggy waited, then signaled for quiet. "Look around. Spent needles. Shi—I mean feces. Garbage—"

"Yeah, garbage!" Hank shouted, waving a dripping Starbucks cup with his grappler. "You nice law-abiding folks want to protest us? How about using the trash cans?"

He shouldered his way to the gazebo and climbed the steps. Antonio moved to block him.

Hank flexed his military-tattooed arms. "You really wanna do this, bro?"

Antonio stepped aside. "Say your piece, bro."

News reporter Megan Martinez rushed to the bandstand alongside her camera operator and climbed onto the stage, extending her microphone toward Hank. He ignored her, turning his attention to the crowd instead. "Yeah, there are drug addicts here. You know why? There's no place for them. No place to get clean. No place to get their lives back on track. A lot of these so-called bums are military vets who fought in the Middle East, some even dating back to Vietnam. Many are struggling with PTSD and not receiving the help they need. Others are so lost that they don't know how to apply for assistance. I'm talking real PTSD—not the stupid, oh-poor-me shit that some whiners complain about these days." His voice shifted to a mocking falsetto. " 'I have PTSD because someone yelled at me at work.' " His tone returned to normal. "That's not PTSD. That's life. Grow up!"

He continued, his voice growing louder. "I'm talking about being sexually abused by your parents every day till you fought back and landed in juvie. Or being a medic in Afghanistan and watching your best friend blown to bits by an IED—his blood and body parts splattered all over you, and you can't save him. Or being held in a POW camp. Starved. Beaten. Every. Damn. Day."

He paused, trembling. "Then you come home, and everyone's gone. Your wife, your kid. Gone. And my one good friend? Ted Hastings. War hero. Purple Heart. Murdered a few days ago. His crime? He was a homeless, screwed-up vet, like me."

Hank's voice shook. "And now I see faces. Dead battle buddies. Blown-apart children. Every fucking day I go to sleep with them, and I wake up with them. That's PTSD. And now I see the faces of murdered drifters."

I was frozen. I'd wondered about Hank's past. Now I knew.

He looked straight at the crowd. "Yeah. Like the lady said, we have a problem. It's no coincidence people have been dying in this encampment. But does anyone care?" He took a ragged breath. "To quote Scrooge: 'If they would rather die, they had better do it and decrease the surplus population.' "

He paused. "We don't want to die. But someone wants us gone. You think the police cares? The mayor?"

Hank let the words hang in the air, then shook his head. And then a piercing scream shattered the quiet.

It came from the far side of the park, where we'd left Mom, Ruby, and Betty. People rushed toward the sound. Maxie, Sam, and I followed, news crew in tow.

The three women were frozen near a crumpled figure. It was the blonde from the picnic table—her back against the locked, graffiti-covered bathroom door.

Mom's hand trembled as she held her phone. "I called 911, but I think it's too late."

I slipped my arm around her. Hank appeared, catching Betty just as she wobbled. He carried her to a bench, then turned to the crowd. "Everyone, move back." He glared at Megan. "That means you, too."

"The public has a right to know," she said.

"Do it from the sidewalk," he snarled.

She motioned to her camera guy, and they backed off.

Hank knelt by the woman, checking her pulse, then put his ear to her chest.

He was about to start CPR when I whispered to Sam, "I think I saw her chest move."

Sam squatted beside him. "I'm a nurse if you need help."

"Medic," Hank said with a nod. Then he smiled slightly. "Yes —she has a pulse." He glanced at me. "Good call."

Her top was streaked with cream cheese. My eyes drifted to the Café Bistro bag still sitting on the picnic table.

Just then, the woman gasped. Sirens wailed in the distance.

Peggy was nearby. Her eyes met mine. Did she recognize me? Did it matter?

Hank's voice was calm. "Hang in there, ma'am. You're going to be okay."

I leaned toward Sam's ear. "Shouldn't you still give her CPR?"

"She's breathing on her own," she said.

I straightened. "I'll check on Betty."

"I've got her," Ruby said.

Ruby sat beside Betty, patted her knee, then stood and waved at the approaching ambulance. I glanced toward Peggy, but she had disappeared.

The EMTs arrived, followed by a squad car and fire engine. The medics checked the woman's vitals and then relayed the information to the hospital ER doctor. After stabilizing her with oxygen and an IV drip, they carefully lifted her onto a gurney, revealing her purse that had been wedged under her.

I stepped forward as a cop picked it up. "Wait! I need to tell you something."

Officer Randall turned to me. "I know you. You're the one who solves crimes."

I blushed. "With a lot of help and even more dumb luck."

"What did you want to tell me?"

"You need to check that bag." I pointed to the bag still on the table, now seemingly guarded by Peggy. "I saw her eating a bagel a little while ago, and she was totally fine. There may still be food in it, and you might find that it was laced with a potentially lethal dose of something. My best guess would be fentanyl and maybe xylazine. There have been several deaths recently, as you know, and—"

"You're right. I should've caught that." Just as Peggy reached for the bag, he yelled, "Don't touch that!" Then he barked at his young partner. "Baxter! Bag that bag!"

After the ambulance drove away, sirens screaming, Hank took off, and Peggy was nowhere to be seen, so the protest was over.

Who was the blonde? Definitely not homeless. Anyone can grab food from Café Bistro—it's a casual, upscale fast-food spot just a block away. Maybe I'm reading too much into this food poisoning theory. She probably just picked up her order and walked over to the park to eat. After all, she was sitting on the edge of the park, away from the heart of the homeless camp. And weren't the other poisonings tied to Greazie's?

Looking at Betty, I asked, "You ladies want to walk back, or should I get my car?"

"I'm fine," said Betty. "We still need to finish our Ruby segment."

We strolled along, following other walkers as they made their way home. Ahead of us, we saw a cluster of people at a standstill in front of Peggy's house. My first thought was when I saw Antonio beat that man who was in his car and dump him at the curb. Just the thought gave me a chill. Was history repeating itself?

"Yeah, I think that's her," said an old man to his wife.

"Her who?" I asked Maxie.

"They're looking at a For Sale sign," she said.

The man waved us over. "Hey! You helped that woman. Tell us. Is this her?"

He stepped aside to reveal the real estate sign: Kerry Williams—Luxury Real Estate. The woman in the photo on the sign looked ready to sprint off and close another deal. She wore a chic pink pantsuit over a revealing patterned blouse, her long blonde waves cascading over one shoulder. Her makeup was flawless, her face slightly filtered, and her long, pink acrylics were perfectly polished. One hand clutched a cell phone to her ear as if she were about to close another deal.

"That's her," Sam said. "She looks like she's on *Real Housewives*."

"My favorite is *Beverly Hills*," the man's wife said.

"Don't get her started," muttered her husband. "She watches all that garbage."

"Nobody asked you," she snapped. "All you watch is sports."

He chuckled. "Touché."

I murmured to Sam, "No wonder Peggy looked worried. I saw

her about to grab that burger bag—maybe she was planning to hand it to the cop."

A flicker in the front window caught my eye. Peggy was peeking through the curtains. Antonio appeared next, nudged her aside, and shut the drapes.

"Luxury real estate?" I said. "Her house is very nice, but I wouldn't call it an estate."

Sam said, "When I think of a luxury estate, I picture a sprawling mansion in the countryside. Maybe a vineyard."

"Pool. Guest house. Stables," added Maxie.

"Betty," said Ruby. "Are you ready for one more segment?"

We waited while Betty moved ahead and got herself situated with her phone-cam. "Ready? Set! Action!"

"What a day," said Ruby to Betty's camera as we walked along.

Sam muttered to me, "We need to walk faster—I really gotta pee."

I slipped an arm behind Ruby to nudge her and whispered in her ear. "Mama-Sam's gotta pee."

Ruby nodded and picked up the pace, forcing Betty to speed up her back walk. She continued her vlog talk. "At the park protest, a heart-wrenching speech by a homeless vet opened my eyes to this huge problem. And a lovely young woman collapsed and was taken away by ambulance. We will update our viewers on that once we have more information." Then she screamed, "Stop!"

Too late. Betty slipped backward off the curb and landed in a twisted heap in the street, screaming in agony.

CHAPTER THIRTY-FOUR

MONDAY • SEPTEMBER 28
Posted by Katy McKenna

Yesterday Afternoon
-Continued-

Betty had taken a terrible tumble, landing in a grotesquely twisted heap in the wet gutter. I reached her first and saw why. Her right foot was turned in an impossible direction, and her ankle bone protruded through the skin about an inch. Surprisingly, there was little blood. The bone was a whitish-beige color with a clean sheen. I can't get the picture out of my head. I've never seen an actual bone sticking through someone's skin. Several fellow pedestrians rushed to join us and then backed away when they saw the injury.

For the second time that day, Mom dialed 911. Sam knelt beside Betty, offering what little comfort she could. Betty's gut-wrenching screams echoed through the neighborhood, drawing people from their homes. One man emerged with a handgun, which sent a quivering chill down my spine. But after assessing the scene, he quietly slipped it into his pocket.

Betty's screams gradually faded, replaced by a shaky but coherent voice. "Where's my phone? Ruby, I think I ruined that last shot."

Ruby looked freaked but replied calmly. "Don't you be worrying about that."

I looked at Sam with questioning eyes.

"It's a normal reaction," she told me. "Adrenaline has kicked in, and she's not feeling the pain at the moment."

The ambulance arrived, and after prepping Betty for transport, they took off with Ruby sitting in the back with her buddy. Just before the EMT closed the door, Ruby hollered, "Don't worry about me, Katy. I'll take an Uber home."

As the sirens faded into the distance, I turned to Sam. "Let's get you home before you pee your pants, you poor pregnant momma."

She gave a sheepish shrug and a half-smile. "Too late. Thank goodness for Preggo-Pads."

Last Night

Ruby called to give an update on Betty's condition. "I'm home now, and Betty's sleeping. They did surgery on her ankle and put it back together. And get this! No metal. They used a new cutting-edge technique that will dissolve as the bones mesh over time. Anyhoo, before you head for work in the morning, pick me up and bring me to your house so I can grab my wheels."

I stayed up past my bedtime to watch the eleven o'clock local news. At 10 p.m. was a *Saturday Night Live* rerun that kept me going, sort of. I kept zonking out but woke in time to see the local news report about the Maiden Lane protest and Kerry Williams, the Realtor. Her part of the story was the lead-in. She is in the ICU in critical condition. Megan, the reporter, had gotten a close-up of the officer bagging the Café Bistro bag. Talk about negative publicity.

There was a short snippet of Hank's speech, then a cut to people waving angry signs. *Get A Job! Go Home!*

Today

I beat Maxie to the office, settled at my desk with Daisy at my feet, and checked the calendar.

Minutes later, Maxie breezed through the glass door and was greeted by Daisy.

After making a cup of decaf, she sat on the couch and invited Daisy to lounge with her.

"What's on the agenda for today?" she asked. "Wait. How's Betty doing?"

I relayed the info Ruby had given me.

"That's interesting about the dissolving parts," she said. "I have a metal screw in my ankle, and it always sets off the airport metal detector."

"They're keeping her another night, so I'll pick up my grandma and see her after work."

"Good girl. Now, what's on the agenda?"

We heard a tap on the door.

"Oh, look. It's Phyllis Kaplan." I got up and opened the door.

"Come on in," said Maxie from the couch. "Good to see you."

"Hi. I know it's early, but I had an appointment nearby, so I thought I'd stop by and update you."

"Would you like a cup of coffee?" I asked.

She trailed me to the coffee machine, picked a pod, then sat across from Maxie and Daisy. A minute later, I delivered her brew.

"Thank you. I needed one of these."

"Don't we all," laughed Maxie.

The entry door rattled as Walter walked in, shoving his walker on tennis balls across the floor. "Howdy, everyone!"

"Walter! You're just in time," said Maxie. "I'd like you to meet Phyllis Kaplan."

Phyllis got up and shook his hand. "Pleased to meet you," he said.

"The pleasure is all mine," she said. "I heard about the work you did to help us find my long-lost husband. I cannot thank you enough."

Walter looked flustered, and for the first time since I've known him, he was at a loss for words.

"Go sit in your birthday recliner, Walter," I said. "I'll get you coffee. Phyllis is about to give us an update."

After we were all seated, she began her story. "Alex and I went to Ventura yesterday to see Graham. His doctor had called on Saturday and said he thought Graham could handle it."

"Whoa!" said Maxie. "How'd it go?"

"I went in first, hoping he would know who I am. He hadn't seen Alex since he was a toddler, so one shock at a time. I was a lot younger the last time he saw me. Anyway, the staff had shown him current photos of us. They felt confident that he was ready."

"And was he?" I asked.

She sighed. "He was. He smiled and—" Her voice quivered, and she paused to sip her coffee. "Sorry. It was very emotional. But in a good way. Graham smiled and took my hand. He was in a wheelchair in a quiet area for visitors. He looked much better than I expected for all he's been through. I guess he's getting good care. He spoke clearly, though quietly. He apologized for everything, although I had told him repeatedly that he didn't need to. That we understood.

"I told him about my husband, David. I married him when Alex was eleven. Several years after Graham disappeared. He was a wonderful father to Alex. But telling this to Graham was hard. I cannot imagine how he must feel. However, he apologized repeatedly, saying he should've been there, but said he was happy I'd found a good man and a good father for Alex. After talking for maybe twenty minutes, he said he was ready to meet Alex."

Phyllis shook her head gently. "Alex was so nervous. He really has no memories of his father. He was a toddler when Graham disappeared."

I remembered Alex saying to us when we first met him, *I barely have any memory of my father. Just flashes. Reading books. Rolling a ball to me. Sitting on his shoulders at a parade.* At least they were good memories.

"How did that go?" asked Maxie.

"When I led him into the room, Graham's eyes were lowered as if he expected a three-year-old to come in. I watched as his gaze rose to Alex's face, lighting up with...with a sad-happy joy. If that makes sense."

"It does," I said.

"They talked for an hour or so, and then Graham looked pretty done in. So we said goodbye with a promise to visit next weekend." She set her cup down and took out her phone. "Here's a photo."

Alex was squatting next to his father's wheelchair, one arm draped around his father's shoulder—both of them smiling.

"I owe this all to you," she said. "The Diligent Detective Agency. We are so thankful."

Maxie, obviously moved, cleared her throat. "So, what's next?"

Phyllis smiled. "Next weekend, Alex will take his wife for a visit."

Maxie asked, "Any news on the kidney hunt?"

She shook her head with a sigh. "No good news there. But thankfully, Alex is feeling good. So, fingers crossed, our prayers will be answered soon."

―――――

When we arrived at the hospital around 3 p.m., we found Betty's room empty, and the bed stripped. We stood, staring at it in disbelief. Ruby stumbled into the room and collapsed into the visitor's chair.

"Katy! She was fine when I talked to her earlier. Just fine. How could this happen?"

I knelt beside her. "She was old, Ruby. And it was a terrible injury. Maybe her heart couldn't take it."

"I'm old, too. Maybe my heart can't take this."

"Don't say that."

"You know it's true. I'm seventy-five. Two years older than Betty. All my good years are behind me. There's nothing ahead except misery."

A young man wearing dark purple scrubs entered carrying folded sheets. "Oh, I'm sorry. I didn't know anyone was in here. Would you mind if I made up the bed?"

Ruby shot him a sharp look. "Can it wait? She's not even cold yet. Where's your heart?"

He looked perplexed. "If I don't do this now, she will definitely get cold."

"You mean somebody has already been assigned to this room?" I said. "That's fast."

"Do you mind moving back so I can get this bed done?" he asked.

He pushed the tray table to the side, and my eyes fell on a cup on the tray. "Ruby?" I pointed at the cup. "Is that what I think it is?"

Her eyes widened in horror. "Oh, God. It's her dental partial. She never goes...I mean, never went anywhere without it." Her voice wavered. "She lost her front teeth taking a trampoline exercise class—jumped too hard, spun out of control, and landed face-first on the floor. Knocked them right out." She let out a shaky sigh. "She always says...or said...she wouldn't be caught dead without her..." Ruby choked on a sob. "Teeth."

The fellow quickly made up the bed and exited the room. A moment later, an orderly entered and placed a jug of water on the tray table.

"Grandma? I think it's time to go," I said as gently as I could. "We can ask what happened at the nurses' station."

"Isn't it obvious? She DIED!"

A piercing scream echoed from the hallway: "You're KILLING me!"

I glanced at Ruby. "That sounds like Betty!"

A front-toothless Betty appeared at the door, hanging onto a walker. "I can't go another damn thep. I'm old, and I've had enough!"

We stared wide-eyed as her physical therapist coaxed her into the room.

"You're alive!" shrieked Ruby, bouncing out of her chair to hug her friend. "It's a miracle."

Betty looked at Ruby like she had just escaped from the nut house. "Are you drunk? Becauth, girl, if you are, I want thum, too!"

Holly, the pretty brunette PT, said, "No alcohol! You're on strong pain meds."

"Then why am I in tho much pain?" She ran her tongue over her lips. "I am done with phythical therapy!"

The PT got Betty into bed and covered her up. "Would you like your teeth?"

"Thank you tho much," she sneered.

I touched Holly's arm. "You probably don't remember me, but I remember you. You were my ex-husband's therapist. Chad McKenna."

She smiled. "I remember you, too. And what you told me about him. Wow. Dare I ask, how's he doing?"

"He's in memory care, and last I heard, I don't think he will be getting out. He was a real jerk, but I wouldn't wish that on anyone."

Holly turned her attention back to her patient. "Now, Betty, I want you to listen and listen well. Do you know why so many elderly people die after breaking a hip?"

"I didn't break a hip," she snapped.

Ruby jumped in. "Because they're old, and a broken hip is an automatic death sentence. Everyone knows that."

"I'll have you know I am not elderly," hissed Betty. "I'm merely older."

Ruby sighed. "We've lost a lot of people at Shady Acres. Carl died a couple of months ago. He broke his knee when he tumbled out of bed while—" She glanced at me. "Never mind."

Holly set her tablet on the tray table. "A hip replacement, knee replacement, shoulder replacement, or a broken ankle— none of those are an automatic death sentence. Not if you religiously do your physical therapy. However, if you don't, your lungs will become weaker, potentially leading to serious complications like pneumonia. Especially in older patients."

"What about elbow replacements?" asked Ruby.

Holly ignored her. "Ms. Adler."

"It's Mrs. Adler," said Betty.

"I stand corrected. While we're at it, what pronoun do you identify with?"

"I am woman. Hear me roar!"

Ruby leaned toward me. "I'll explain that later."

The beleaguered PT continued. "Mrs. Adler. You are eighty-four and—"

"Hold the phone," yelped Ruby as Betty's eyes nearly blew out of her skull. "You've always said you're two years younger than me! But all this time, you've been *nine* years older?"

"*Dahling*," said Betty. "A girl never reveals her age."

"Well, I do! And we're friends. And friends should be honest with each other. That's part of the friendship code."

Betty pursed her lips and wrinkled her nose. "It was just an itty-bitty white lie."

Holly looked like she'd like to scram but instead said, 'We still have a few more exercises to do, Mrs. Adler."

I took Ruby's arm. "Why don't we step outside while your friend finishes her workout?"

"Some 'friend' she turned out to be," Ruby said. "First, she's not dead. And then I find out she's been lying to me for years."

We moved into the hallway and settled into the chairs near the nurses' station. My grandmother was cranky, so I tried to lift her mood.

"Hey! Isn't it great, Betty's not dead?"

Ruby grumped, "If you say so."

"Oh! I know! Why don't we check on Kerry Williams? You know, the Realtor?"

"I remember who she is, Katy. I haven't lost all my marbles. Yet."

I walked up to the station, half expecting to hear that Kerry hadn't made it. "Excuse me, what room is Kerry Williams in?"

The nurse glanced at the monitor. "She's in the ICU in room three. Down the hall on the left as you walk through the ICU doors. Are you related?"

"Yes. I'm her cousin." It's shocking how good I've become at lying. "I'm here with her aunt."

I returned to Ruby and whispered, "She's alive. Room three in ICU."

We stood, and Ruby hesitated. "I don't think we should go in. She doesn't even know us. How about we just walk by and take a little peek?"

"That's all I intended to do."

We pushed through the ICU doors and strolled casually toward room three. As we got closer, a man's voice drifted out, low and pleading. We stopped just short of the entrance, eaves-dropping.

"Please, darling. Please wake up."

Ruby and I exchanged wide-eyed glances. I took a quick step

forward to take a peek inside as I crossed to the other side. Antonio was sprawled across the bed, his head buried against Kerry's perky bosom, sobbing.

Once I was on the other side of the doorway, I motioned for Ruby to follow. Grabbing her arm, I dragged her toward a row of seats against the wall, where we sank in stunned silence.

"Are you thinking what I'm thinking?" Ruby asked.

"Pretty sure I am."

Before we could say another word, the ICU doors whooshed open again. A well-dressed woman with short auburn hair strode in, exuding an air of authority.

I nudged my grandmother. "Is that...?"

"Yes," Ruby said, watching the woman closely. "Our illustrious mayor, Kay Nelson. I knew her back in high school. And it looks like she's still dumping L'Oréal Auburn dye on her head. No way her natural hair would look that good."

I glanced at Ruby, raising an eyebrow. "She's your age... Blondie?"

"Don't give me that look, young lady. Yes, I color my hair, but that woman has had so much work done—lifted, Botoxed, and filled to the brim—that if she so much as smiles, her face might crack. I'd rather age like a fine wine."

"You do Botox."

"Just enough to not look cranky, which I am right now, but you can't tell."

"Glad I didn't vote for her," I said. "She's completely botched the handling of the Maiden Lane encampment, and she's no supporter of the police department. Angela is furious because she slashed a huge chunk of their police funding. The fire department, too. Brilliant move, considering we live in a state notorious for devastating wildfires."

"But why is she here?" Ruby asked.

"Probably visiting someone. That's usually why people come to a hospital unless they're patients themselves."

Ruby huffed, "Don't be a smarty-pants."

"You may need a Botox touch-up, 'cause you definitely look cranky."

"You're not helping."

We watched as Madam Mayor stopped at the nurses' station, spoke briefly with the person behind the desk, and then made her way toward Kerry Williams' room.

Ruby whispered, "This just got interesting."

The mayor froze in the room's doorway, as we scurried to a corner for a better view. She stood like a statue for at least a minute, and I was dying to see her face. Then she silently slipped into the room, moving to a corner unnoticed by the weeping Antonio.

Ruby nudged me. "I wonder what'll happen when he sees her?"

The ICU doors swung open again.

I grabbed Ruby's arm. "Oh my God. Why is she here?" I murmured, nodding toward the new arrival. "Quick, duck, before she sees us!"

We both bent down, suddenly fixated on dusting off our slip-on shoes. I took a glance and whispered, "Okay, she's not looking our way." We got up and moved closer to see inside the room without being seen.

Peggy stood in the doorway; eyes locked on the bed scene. She slipped off her humongous shoulder bag, slowly wrapping the long black leather straps tightly around her hand, and then dashed to the bed and swung the gaudy purse high over her head, screaming, "I knew I'd find you here!" and brought it crashing down onto Antonio's back.

"What the fuck!" Antonio yelped just as the bag came at him again. He threw up an arm to shield himself too late, and his nose got slammed by the bag. He tumbled off the bed, staggering to his feet on the window side. "What the hell is wrong with you?"

Peggy's voice rang out, sharp and furious. "The better question is, what the hell are you doing with her? You promised me you were done screwing around!"

From the corner, Kay said in an ominous tone, "I'd like to know the answer to that, too."

Peggy spun around to face Kay. "What are you doing here?" Her eyes widened. "Wait. Aren't you the mayor?"

Kay crossed her arms. "The real question is—what are you doing here?" Then she nodded toward Antonio. "And what is he doing here?"

"I'm his wife!" Peggy shouted.

Ruby and I exchanged a wide-eyed look, both mouthing the same word: *"Wife?"*

Antonio wiped his sleeve across his dripping, bloody nose. "Why are you here?"

From our hiding place, I whispered to Ruby, "I'm so confused."

"You and me both," she replied.

Kay pointed at Kerry. "I'm her grandmother." She turned her gaze on Antonio.

Antonio squeaked, "You're Kerry's grandmother? The mayor? She never told me."

Peggy grabbed a filled water jug from the sink counter and hurled it at Antonio. He dodged just in time, and the plastic jug smashed against the wall, spraying water everywhere.

"You bitch!" he roared, vaulting over the bed toward her—accidentally shoving the unconscious Kerry dangerously close to the edge.

Ruby and I screamed toward the nurses' station, "We need help in here!" Then rushed in to keep the mayor's granddaughter from tumbling to the floor.

In the chaos, Antonio barreled into me, knocking me down. He scrambled to his feet and lunged at Peggy; arms outstretched as if to strangle her.

A security guard burst into the room, tackled Antonio, and

pinned him to the ground. Pressing a knee into his back, he jerked Antonio's arms behind him and snapped a pair of handcuffs around his wrists just as a nurse rushed in.

Writhing on the tile floor, Antonio yelled, "Let me up."

"Not until you calm down," the guard said, tightening his grip on Antonio's arms.

Ruby stood on the far side of the bed near the window, helping the nurse gently move Kerry to the center of the bed. They tucked the thin white blanket around her narrow shoulders.

Peggy pressed herself against the closet cabinet door, looking terrified, while the mayor stepped closer to the bed.

Shaking her head, she said, "Kerry. What have you done?"

"I could ask you the same question, Grandma," whispered Kerry. Her eyes fluttered open.

Antonio hollered, "You're alive! My darling, you're alive!"

Still holding Antonio down with his knee, the security guard scanned our faces. "Is everyone calm now, or do I need to call the police?"

"I'm calm," I snapped from down on the floor near Antonio. "But I'm not fine."

Ruby circled the bed and helped me to my feet. "Oh, crap. You're bleeding. Your leg."

I followed her eyes to the blood dribbling onto the floor. "The stitches must have popped."

The nurse, dressed in pink scrubs and wearing a medical employee photo ID badge identifying her as Jessica Tanaka, helped me to my feet and guided me to a chair in the hallway, where she examined the leg wound. "Don't move. I'll be right back."

She quickly returned and bandaged it. "You'll need to head down to the ER to have this stitched back up. I'll call someone to take you down."

I heard Antonio let out an exasperated sigh. "Can I stand up now?"

The guard said to Peggy, "Do you want to press charges?"

"No," she whimpered in a broken voice.

"Well, I sure as hell do!" yelled Antonio.

———

While Ruby and I sat in the waiting area in the ER, we expressed our dismay at Peggy's marriage to Antonio.

"I can't believe that Peggy and Antonio are actually married," I said, shaking my head. "I mean, why?"

Ruby chuckled. "Money, honey. Why else?"

"So, why was he sprawled on top of the Realtor?"

Ruby smirked. "Looked like love to me. Or lust. Peggy isn't exactly what you'd call a dish—though, to be fair, that shouldn't matter when it comes to love. She's got to be at least twenty years older than him. Again, age shouldn't be a factor. But let's be real—she's all around awful."

I laughed. "She really is. I mean, suing Suzy Q's over a bathroom fall that never happened? And the mayor? She's Kerry's grandmother? What is up with that?"

"The big question is, what did she mean when she said to Kerry, 'What have you done?' and then Kerry asks her the same question."

"You know what I'm thinkin'—"

"They're both doing the hokey pokey with Antonio?"

Final note of the day

Ruby clued me in on Betty's "I am woman, hear me roar" statement. It is from the hit song "I Am Woman," released in 1972 and sung by Helen Reddy.

CHAPTER THIRTY-FIVE

Posted by Katy McKenna

Ruby drove Betty home from the hospital this morning. I can only imagine the conversation in the car about Betty's little age-fib. And then getting her out of Ruby's sports car? I'm sure that was a miserable challenge.

Personally, I've never understood lying about your age. Shaving off years just makes people think, "Yikes, she's not aging well."

Granny hates it when someone asks how old she is and then says she looks good "for her age." Maybe I'll start telling people I'm twenty years older—just to see if they give me that compliment. But what if they don't?

———

When I was backing out of the garage this morning to head for work, Simon jogged over to my car, looking fine in trim-fitting pants and a snug red pullover.

He set his hands on the open car window frame. "How are you doing? Your leg, I mean. Is it healing all right?"

I opened the car door and pulled up my loose yoga pant leg to show him as I regaled him with my latest adventure and six new stitches.

He shook his head. "You are really something, you know that, Katy?"

"I do. Just what that something is, I have no idea. Still trying to figure that out."

Simon chuckled. "It's a lifelong quest, I believe."

───────

When I got to the office this morning, Maxie was on the couch, nursing a cup of coffee and chuckling at her phone. I grabbed a cup for myself and plopped down beside her.

"You have to see this photo," she said, handing me her phone. "My youngest grandchild, Eden, is potty training. They caught her dumping poop out of her diaper into her little potty."

I laughed. "That's priceless. And hey, at least she knows where it's supposed to go. That's more than I can say for some adults in this town. Did you see the local news this morning?"

Maxie set her phone on her lap with a grim look. "No. Now what?"

"Get this. The mayor and the town council members have voted themselves a 45 percent raise. Can you believe it?"

"Good grief," said Maxie. "The city is closing our library three days a week now, due to budget problems. And they cut funding for the police and fire."

"And last month," I said, "they closed that mental health clinic next to the hospital for walk-ins—you know, like homeless people."

"But they can give themselves a raise? Talk about bad PR.

Maybe if the mayor actually fixed the Maiden Lane Park disaster, she'd be more popular."

Then I filled Maxie in on yesterday's hospital soap opera.

"Wow, wow, wow." She shook her head, blowing out a breath. "Peggy's hubby is screwin' their Realtor on the side."

"And maybe her grandmother, Madam Mayor, too."

"This is like a soap opera. Think this Williams woman will pull through?"

"She woke up. She seemed like she's recovering okay to me."

Maxie's eyes sparked. "Maybe we can take a quick trip to the hospital and—"

"After yesterday's fiasco? They might not even let me through the doors."

Outside, the deep rumble of Walter's hot rod filled the parking lot.

Maxie clapped her hands. "Oh, he is gonna love this story."

Once I finished regaling Walter with yesterday's hospital adventures, Maxie said again, "So...hospital recon mission?"

I hesitated. "I don't know."

Walter shrugged. "This Kerry Williams might need our protection. Peggy may very well decide to pay her another visit, now that she knows her husband has been shaking the sheets with Williams."

Maxie said. "You mean you want to go, Walter?"

"Damn right. I could use a little excitement."

I exhaled. "All right, I'm in. But I'm driving."

"Fine by me." Walter stood, adjusting his black-and-blue plaid shirt and tucking it into his baggy jeans.

I narrowed my eyes. "Wait—you're actually okay with me driving?"

"Just filled up Roddy, and it damn near cost me a hundred bucks."

"What's your mileage in that car?"

"Seven miles a gallon." He grinned at my shocked expression. "Good thing I don't drive much. But when I do? I make it count."

———

As I walked past Kerry's ICU room, I peeked inside, silently praying she hadn't taken a turn for the worse. She was sitting up, watching TV. The tray table was across the bed, and it appeared she was eating. I circled around and rejoined my gang.

"She looks fine. Watching TV."

"Let me take a look-see." Walter shuffled forward, pushing his walker, the tennis ball feet squeaking against the shiny terrazzo floor. A moment later, he confirmed, "Yup. Now what?"

Maxie shrugged. "Now, nothing. Nothing more to see here, folks."

I said, "You're not even going to take a look inside?"

She set her hands on my shoulders, shaking her head. "Mission accomplished."

Suddenly, from inside Kerry's room, Walter's voice boomed. "Hello, missy. How are we doing today?"

Maxie whispered, "What the hell is he doing?"

"I'm Walter. Hospital senior volunteer. Everyone treating you good?"

In a strong voice, Kerry replied, "Yes. May I have some more water? The jug is empty."

"Sink water okay?" We heard him filling the container. "But take it slow. Just little sips. You don't want to overdo it."

"Thank you."

"So, what's a prett—I mean, healthy-looking girl, I mean woman, person, like you doing in a place like this?" Walter asked.

"I was eating a bagel and suddenly felt woozy. That's all I remember. The doctor said I ingested fentanyl."

I jabbed my boss. "I knew it." I peeked around the door frame to see what Walter was doing. Kerry was facing away from me.

"That's awful," Walter said. "I wonder how that happened?

She shook her head as if trying to clear the cobwebs. "It's all kind of fuzzy. Someone gave it to me."

"A stranger?" he asked. "Didn't your parents teach you to never take food? Well, actually, they probably said candy, but anyway, didn't they teach you not to take food from a stranger? You know, stranger danger and all that."

"It wasn't a stranger." She shook her head. "I don't think. I mean, I wouldn't take food from someone I don't know. But I really can't remember. It's weird that I can't. It's like it's there, but it's not there."

Walter nodded. "Sounds like short-term memory loss."

"Am I in trouble?"

"No." He chuckled. "Sorry. Retired cop. Can't help myself. But someone has been killing innocent people, and I'd sure like to figure out who. That would be a real feather in this old man's cap."

"I thought it was just some homeless druggies squatting in the park that got killed."

Walter's tone hardened. "I don't think homeless people deserve to be murdered any more than you or I do."

"I'm sorry. That wasn't nice," she mumbled. "I didn't mean it like that."

He continued. "I gotta wonder, though, how you got so lucky."

"I'm feeling really tired," she said, lying her head on the pillow. "I don't feel like talking anymore."

I whispered to Maxie, "I'm going in."

Maxie set a hand on my arm. "Wait. Did she see you yesterday?"

"No. Pretty sure she didn't." I stepped into the room like I owned the place, hoping I was right about her not seeing my face. "Hello there, Kerry. I'm a volunteer also. I hear you're doing much better today."

"Yeah, I guess."

"I overheard Walter asking you some questions. I know you're tired, but we need to figure out what happened to you. This person who gave you the bagel... I heard you say it wasn't a stranger. Do you recall if it was a man or a woman?"

Kerry scrunched her eyes. "I feel like it was a woman. But it could have been a man."

"Okay. That's a start. What about their age? Hair color? Weight? Things like that?" I sounded like a bona fide detective.

"Um. Maybe heavy set. Wearing a hat. Older. Like maybe your age."

"Psst! Psst!"

I turned toward the hallway, where Maxie stood, waving frantically. She gave me a wide-eyed "yikes" look and motioned for us to come out.

Holding up my phone to Walter, I said, "Duty calls. We're needed on the first floor. Pronto."

We slipped out of the room, quickly putting distance between us and Kerry's room, just as Joann Yee, the police lieutenant, was heading down the hall, staring at her phone. I've dealt with her several times in the past, and she's very nice, but if she saw me, she'd know I was sticking my nose where it didn't belong—as usual.

We sat in the far corner of the main lobby waiting area, away from the elevator, so when Yee came down in the elevator later, she wouldn't notice us.

"Okay, here's what we know," I said, keeping my voice low. "First off. The police are asking questions, so they must suspect foul play. An older person gave Kerry the food. Hold on! She said older, like my age. How old is Kerry?"

"I'd guess mid-twenties," said Maxie.

"And I'm older? At thirty-two?"

"Hey, it happens to the best of us. Get used to it," said Maxie. "And you look good for your age."

"I'm thirty-two." I slumped in my chair, folding my arms and feeling grouchy. "Not one hundred and two."

Ignoring me, Maxie said, "Obviously. Peggy had figured out that Antonio was fooling around with the Realtor. And maybe she thought this would be a perfect way to end it."

"Yeah, murdering someone usually ends things," said Walter.

"And maybe," said Maxie, "she thought that if she made it look like all the other recent deaths in the park—"

"The cops would never make the connection to her," finished Walter. "Although weren't the other poisonings from eating Greazie's burgers?"

I nodded. "I thought so, but maybe I was just assuming."

"Where would she have gotten the fentanyl?" said Maxie.

"Maybe an old prescription," said Walter. "It's prescribed for acute pain. Didn't you tell me she had injured her leg or her ankle?"

"I said she tried to sue Suzy Q's for a bogus fall in the bathroom, but I doubt she was ever prescribed fentanyl." I sat up. "You know what? It can't be Peggy. Kerry knows her—she's her Realtor. Plus, Peggy is married to Antonio, whom Kerry is sleeping with. She would've recognized her. This is all so confusing for my poor little pea brain."

"You're not the only one who's confused. But where does the mayor fit in?" asked Maxie.

"My grandma and I thought maybe both Kerry and the mayor are sleeping with Antonio."

"Eeww," said Maxie. "Although I admit that did cross my mind, too. But that would be too big of a coincidence. No, I think Kay is simply Kerry's concerned grandmother."

"I think I'll call the chief," I said. "She should probably know what happened in Kerry's room yesterday."

I called the police station, put the call on speaker, and asked for Angela.

"Hey, Angela. It's Katy McKenna."

"Hi, Katy. Ready to join the force yet?"

I chuckled. "Not yet, but I was wondering if I could come by. I know it's the afternoon already, but I may have some helpful information regarding Kerry Williams and the drugged bagel."

————

Angela was surprised when I arrived with my crew.

"Maxine, so good to see you." The ladies hugged. Angela looked at Walter. "And I don't believe we've met. I'm Angela Yaeger."

"Walter Hoffman. Please to meet you."

"Walter is a retired police officer," I said.

He laughed. "Long before your time, Chief Yaeger."

"Thank you for your service, sir. And please, call me Angela."

We sat, and Angela folded her hands on her desk. "I'm a bit tight on time. My daughter's flying in for a visit, and I have to pick her up at the airport."

The three of us told her about our hospital espionage mission.

"That is very interesting," she said. "While I can't go into details, you are right about the bagel; actually, it was the cream cheese that was laced with fentanyl. Most of it was uneaten, thank goodness. However, it did not have any xylazine. That leads me to think this was not the work of whoever has been poisoning the park residents. Plus, she's clearly not one of those folks. Interesting that Ms. Williams is the mayor's grand-daughter."

"That's what we thought, too," said Maxie. "I went to high school with the mayor. Not my favorite person. Then or now."

Angela continued. "She's not too popular with her constituents these days, with all these unsolved deaths." She sighed. "The police department is not popular either, but we are stretched so thin now. Under the mayor's leadership and cutbacks, we've lost over 30 percent of our staff. How are we supposed to do our jobs with a skeleton crew? That said, I appreciate you sharing your information."

"I wonder if the person who gave Kerry the bagel has it out for the mayor? Maybe they thought if her granddaughter were a victim, she would do something about clearing out the park."

Angela nodded. "That is definitely something to consider, Katy. Thank you. What I didn't tell you is that Kerry was pregnant. First trimester, according to the medical exam. She lost the baby."

"It must have been Antonio's," Maxie said. "I wonder if he knew."

She came around her desk. "Let's have a look at your leg, Katy."

I hitched up my pants to reveal the bandaged wound.

The chief shook her head with a wry smile. "Only you could get stabbed by a man in your bushes and then get re-wounded in the hospital, of all places."

CHAPTER THIRTY-SIX

WEDNESDAY • SEPTEMBER 30
Posted by Katy McKenna

I dropped Daisy off at Rolling Hills Pet Resort for a day of fun in the sun. The moment we turned onto the property, her tail started thumping the seat. After signing her in, I headed to the office, only to be met with an unexpected surprise in the parking lot.

Hank was waiting by the door. He looked unusually put together. Clean-shaven, hair neatly tied back in a low ponytail, and wearing decent, clean clothes.

Feeling a little hesitant, I approached the door with a sunny smile. "Good morning. Fancy meeting you here."

He returned my smile, though his seemed genuine. "I remembered you mentioned you worked here, and I was wonderin' if I could talk to you. About the situation at the camp."

Before I could respond, salvation arrived in the form of Maxie's grumbling VW Bug.

"Oh, look! There's my boss. I'm sure she'd like to hear whatever you want to talk about, too."

"Is she cool. Like you?"

He thinks I'm cool? "Oh, uh, way cooler."

As Maxie climbed out of her car, I called out, "Maxie! We have a guest. Hank." I turned back to him. "I'm sorry. I don't know your last name."

"Bennet. I don't think I qualify as a guest, but maybe as a client."

He can pay? I thought.

"I see that look on your face. Yes, I have money. Not a lot, but enough. Right now, I just want a consultation. But I'll pay for it."

"Be right there!" Maxie yelled as she wrestled a heavy bag from the front trunk of her VW.

Hank jogged over. "Let me get that for you."

"Thank you, Hank. I got a little carried away at the office supply store," she said, shooting me a quizzical look. "Ah, yes, Hank. Now I recognize you. I was at the park demonstration and heard your speech. I gotta say I was impressed. Ever thought about running for mayor?"

I laughed. "Maxie is not fond of our mayor. Neither am I." I unlocked the door, deactivated the alarm, and held it open for them. Maxie led Hank to our little storeroom, where he stowed the supplies.

"Maxie?" I said. "Hank's here because he wants to talk to us about the homeless camp."

"Let's go to my office." We sat, and she got straight down to business. "So, how can we help you, Hank?"

"First, you should probably tell me the going rate." He slapped a Chase Visa card on the desk. "Don't worry. It's good, and I have a pretty decent limit and a zero balance."

"Before we get into that, why don't you tell us why you're here?" said Maxie.

"We all know the cops dropped the ball on the park murders. I get it. It's not like these are upstanding pillars of the community getting killed, but this is ridiculous. Come on! Innocent people are being eliminated."

Maxie nodded. "Can't argue with that."

"I'm hoping the Realtor getting poisoned will light a fire under their butts," he said.

"It's not a good excuse, but the department lost a lot of funding," I said. "They're severely understaffed."

"You're right. It's not a good excuse." His brows furrowed. "After the second death, Teddy and I started patrollin' at night, watching for anything suspicious. But then, as you know..." He shrugged. "He got killed."

"Do you know why he wound up in my bushes?" I asked.

He shook his head. "No idea. Maybe he was following someone he thought was suspicious, and they attacked him. It was his turn to patrol that night, so that's the only thing that makes sense to me. Whoever did it had to be pretty strong. Teddy didn't look like much, but he could brawl with the best of them." He swiped a tear. "Teddy was a good guy. My best friend. He sure as hell didn't deserve what he got."

"What do you want us to do?" Maxie asked.

"I was thinkin' maybe you could find out why that Realtor was poisoned. I mean, I'm assuming she was poisoned or drugged. It's the same thing, I guess. If she was, what's the connection? She's not homeless. Maybe she has information that could lead the cops to whoever is killing people." He tapped his credit card.

"We're already looking into it, so there's no need to pay for our help," Maxie said. "In fact, we spoke with her yesterday, though she didn't give us much. I also know the police have questioned her, so hopefully..." She shook her head. "But you can still help by staying alert. If you see or hear anything suspicious, let us know immediately, and we'll pass it along to the chief."

"Good idea. The cops are more likely to take you seriously than me."

The sound of the front door opening caught our attention.

"Hold on, I'll check who it is," I said, stepping into the front room. "Hey, Phyllis. Good to see you."

She handed me a white bakery bag. "I was in the neighborhood and thought I'd bring you girls a treat."

I peeked inside. "Ooo, cookies! Thank you. Any updates on a donor for Alex?"

Phyllis sighed heavily. "No luck. It's so frustrating. My son was exposed to harmful chemicals while serving in the Middle East, and the VA refuses to take responsibility. Not that it would magically get us a donor, but it'd be something. At least he has his father back, and we have you to thank for that."

"I just got lucky," I said.

"You worked hard, and it paid off. And maybe we had a little help from upstairs." She glanced at her watch. "I better scoot."

After she left, I returned to Maxie's office.

Hank leaned forward. "I couldn't help overhearing. I know a lot of vets dealing with health issues after serving in the Middle East—physical and mental. Her son's situation sounds rough." He hesitated. "Ever heard of Agent Orange?"

Maxie jumped in. "I have. That stuff was, and still is, a nightmare. The US military used it in Vietnam to clear out vegetation that gave the enemy cover. Turns out it was toxic as hell—linked to cancer, birth defects, and all kinds of health problems. My older cousin was exposed. Died of cancer in his fifties."

"They're still cleaning that poison out of the land," Hank added.

"And imagine what it did to the wildlife," I said. "Still does now."

"I never thought about that." Hank shook his head. "That woman's son needs a donor? Can you tell me what he needs, or is that confidential?"

"Alex needs a kidney," Maxie said, "He and his wife have a little one on the way. His father disappeared when he was three.

Mental health issues having to do with PTSD. Another military vet. Seems to run in the family."

"And you found his missing father?"

I nodded. "We did. In a VA home. Sad story. Alex is determined to be a good dad, you know, give his kid what he didn't get from his father. But if he doesn't get a kidney soon..." I shook my head.

Maxie said, "Katy gets the credit for finding Alex's father."

I swear I could see tears in Hank's eyes as he stood. "Thank you for telling me that. I've taken up enough of your time, so I'll get out of here. I'm recruiting a few solid guys today to help patrol." At the door, he turned back. "You know, I can live by myself, out on the open road, goin' wherever the wind blows me. But most of the people at the camp can't. They need a permanent place, a community. If I ever win the lottery, that's the first thing I'll fix."

"Good luck with that," said Maxie. "Government red tape would probably drown you."

After Hank left, Maxie said, "Who woulda thought? He's a decent guy. I think we all tend to paste the same label on every vagrant we see."

"That's what I'm learning, too." I switched gears. "Any new thoughts on the Peggy/Antonio/Kerry the Realtor triangle?"

"You got me. Thing is, even though I find it all very intriguing, it really isn't any of our business what any of them are doing. No matter how juicy it all may be. However, I'd sure like to know who gave Kerry that food. And why?"

"Luckily, it wasn't a deadly dose," I said. "Angela said she only ate a small portion. Who knows what would have happened had she eaten the whole thing?"

"I wonder if anyone saw the person who gave Kerry the bagel?" Maxie pushed away from her desk. "I'm going to live on the wild side and make myself a cup of the real deal while you check the calendar and tell me what we've got lined up today."

Just then, my phone buzzed with a text from Eric. *Feel like pizza at my place and meeting my mom?*

I hadn't seen him in a few days, and if this relationship was going anywhere, this was the next step.

Sure thing, I replied.

———

After work, I dashed home to feed Daisy and Tabitha, then headed over to Eric's place in Cala Grande. I was a little nervous, knowing his mother has memory issues. That's not something I've dealt with in my own family, so I called Ruby on the way over to get her advice. My car's too old for Bluetooth, so I put the phone on speaker and set it in the cup holder attached to the door.

"Honey, I'm no expert on this, and I pray to the Almighty that I do not wind up in our memory care facility here at Shady Acres. And don't get me going on the expense! However, I suggest keeping it simple. Smile a lot, use short sentences, and don't correct her. Let Eric lead. And don't joke—it might confuse her. Let me know how it goes."

My phone told me I had reached my destination, so I parked in front of a cozy-looking ranch-style house, checked my makeup and breath, popped a Tic-Tac, and crunched it quickly as I headed up the short flagstone walk to the entry. Eric opened the door before I hit the doorbell. He stepped outside, pulled me into his arms, kissed me warmly, and sent goosies marching up my arms.

He pulled back, and I said, all flirty, "We have to stop meeting like this."

"Nah. You mean we gotta start meeting more like this."

Eric led me into their tidy living room, where his mother, Adelina, sat in a leather recliner. "Mama? I'd like you to meet my friend, Katy."

Her warm smile instantly put me at ease. She stood and

wrapped my hand in hers. While continuing to hold it, she said, "Eric has told me so many nice things about you."

I glanced at Eric, and he smiled. I couldn't help but wonder if he'd been pulling my leg about his mother having Alzheimer's.

"Katy," said Eric. "We're having your favorite—Klondike Pizza. I ordered the one you love, the Roadkill. The one with all the meats!"

"Eric," said his mother. "I thought you told me Katy is a vegetarian."

"She is. I'm just joking, Mama."

There is no way this lady has Alzheimer's, I thought.

———

I called Ruby on my way home. "At first, I thought Eric must've been kidding me about the Alzheimer's. Maybe using it as an excuse not to get too involved."

Ruby sighed. "I bet you're going to tell me that after a while, it became obvious, right?"

"Yes. She turned to me at the dinner table, halfway through our meal, and said, 'Who are you?' Just out of the blue. We'd been doing fine, and then she had no clue who I was."

"I'm sorry, sweetie."

"Please take care of yourself, Grammy. You eat too much butter!"

"There is no such thing as too much butter," she said with a laugh. "Or cheese."

"I'm being serious. The other day, I read a university study that said that a high intake of flavonoid-rich berries, like strawberries and blueberries, can delay memory decline in older people by nearly three years."

"I had blueberry cheesecake for dessert," she said. "Does that count?"

CHAPTER THIRTY-SEVEN

FRIDAY · OCTOBER 2
Posted by Katy McKenna

We have a couple of new clients at work. Both are cheating-spouse cases. That means I get to go undercover and do surveillance. I guess I live in a fairytale land, but I do not understand cheating. You're either in or you're out. If you feel like you have to cheat, then you're out. You can avoid a lot of grief and save a lot of money by being honest and getting out before you blow up your whole life. If you don't want to get a divorce, then don't cheat. Get couples therapy.

But what do I know? My husband, Chad, cheated on me, and I was clueless until everything blew up. The strange thing is that I am staying in contact with his former girlfriend/wife/mother-of-his-child/, and ex-wife, Heather. She's a sweetheart. He cheated on her, too, by failing to mention me.

––––––

Ruby is all pumped up to add health advice for seniors on her *Ready-Set-Ruby* vlog. She now has 157 followers. I went over after work to video her making overnight oats. Betty had taken over my film duties, but with her busted ankle, it's back on me.

That meant dealing with my favorite gate guard, George.

"Ma'am," George said, holding a pen and clipboard, acting official. "Please state your name, who you are visiting, and the purpose of your visit."

"George, you know who I am. You know who I'm visiting. And it's none of your damn business what the purpose of my visit is. Capeesh?"

"Regulations require me to ask."

"Regulations, schmegulations. Again, it's none of your damn business that Grammy and I are going to talk about my menstrual cramps and tampons." I winced for effect. "So much blood. Can you recommend a good tampon brand?"

You should have seen his face turn fifty shades of red.

Ever since Ruby moved into Shady Acres a few years ago, I've been dealing with this bozo. Honestly, it's kind of fun—unless I'm in a hurry. This time, I came prepared. I'd printed out a fake rap sheet listing my "past criminal activities," complete with a mock arrest photo: front and side shots of me looking like a grumpy thug.

I'd also made rap sheets for Ruby and Daisy, complete with past addresses and crimes.

The list included towns like Ding Dong, Texas, and Booger Hole, West Virginia—places where we're allegedly wanted for various offenses, like sneaking into a second movie at the Cineplex after ours ended. Daisy is charged with being off-leash and chasing squirrels in Boring, Oregon. Believe it or not, these are real towns. Real crimes.

"George?" I handed him the paper. "I will save you some writing, and you can keep this on file in the future. Because you know

I'll be back." I tried not to giggle as I watched his face as he read the list of crimes. He didn't laugh, so I was at a loss. Then I took it up a notch. Revving the engine, I said, "You gonna open the gate, or do I have to call my...friends?"

"Yes, ma'am!" He leaped into his guard cubicle and pressed the gate button.

———

Ruby had everything set up perfectly for her overnight oatmeal prep. On the kitchen counter, she had a heaping mix of oats, grains, and seeds, along with fresh blueberries and strawberries neatly piled in a bowl. She offered both sugar and maple syrup as sweeteners, along with a zero-calorie option called Allulose, and had milk and oat milk for variety. She had even set up two new round lights that all the vloggers use to ensure the perfect lighting.

To top it all off, her sweet malti-poo, BeeGee, sat on a counter stool, sporting a pink bow on her head. When I walked in, she went berserk with excitement, showering me with doggy kisses before finally settling down to "help."

After a final makeup check and doggy bow adjustment, Ruby was ready.

I held up my movie camera—aka my cell phone—and yelled, "Action!"

"Hey there, gal pals! It's Ready-Set-Ruby! Today, we are starting a new subject on my vlog. Healthy eating! So, let's get to it!"

Ruby made two generous batches—one with milk and sugar, the other with oat milk and maple syrup—both big enough to last for days. Tomorrow morning, I'll be back to film the big reveal and take home the oat milk and maple syrup batch.

When I left the senior community, George swiftly lifted the

gate. As I drove through, I did that classic move—two fingers to my eyes, then pointing them straight at him with a little nod, a silent warning. He looked a little startled, then quickly saluted me.

I think I like this thug life.

CHAPTER THIRTY-EIGHT

SATURDAY • OCTOBER 2
Posted by Katy McKenna

I need a break from watching the news—what a surefire way to ruin a perfectly beautiful, blue-sky day.

And yet, that's exactly how I started my morning. To make matters worse, I tuned into cable news instead of our local station. Big mistake. The lead story? You guessed it—politics. The usual cycle of outrage, with everyone at each other's throats, refusing to work together for the greater good, so not much gets done.

On my second cup of coffee, I switched to our local news, which I had recorded late last night since they don't air a news show on Saturday and Sunday mornings.

Rain is coming our way later in the week.

An EV blew up in a garage while charging.

A group of college students attempted to set a Guinness World Record for the largest number of people on a house roof. Unfortunately, the roof collapsed. Amazingly, there were only minor injuries.

Two more people were found dead yesterday at the Maiden Lane encampment.

The report showed the mayor delivering a brief statement on the steps of city hall regarding the park deaths.

"We are doing everything possible to find the person or persons responsible for the recent fatalities," she said.

A reporter called out, "Mayor Nelson, wasn't the park supposed to be cleared out two weeks ago? What's the status of that? And why did you cut police funding and give yourself a raise?"

A small crowd behind the press began booing and chanting, "IMPEACH! IMPEACH!"

Without responding, the mayor turned and hurried inside, leaving local reporters shouting unanswered questions in her wake.

———

I have plans with Eric tomorrow. His mother's caretaker is giving him the afternoon off, and he is coming over for lunch. And if things go well, we'll have dessert, if you know what I mean. I'm really in the mood for dessert—wink, wink.

But today, it is officially "Spend the Day with Daisy." Even though she goes to work most days with me, it's not like we're doing fun, doggy things, so today is all about her.

I suited up in comfy clothes—yoga pants from my short-lived yoga phase, a loose top, sneakers, and a baseball cap. As soon as I grabbed the cap, Daisy dashed for her halter and leash.

Across the street, the neighborhood boys were raking dead leaves off their dead lawn and gave us a wave. I turned left and spotted Simon out front adjusting his solar panels. I stopped to admire the kale, peas, and broccoli growing throughout his yard.

"I won't be growing broccoli next year," he said, crouching to snuggle Daisy.

"Why? It looks like it's doing well."

"Sniff the air and tell me what you smell."

I took a deep whiff, then winced. "Uh...farts?"

"Exactly. One of the neighbors is not happy."

"Like who?"

He pointed down the street. "Madeline DuBois. She's been over a few times. The last time she came to make jokes about my smelly yard, she brought a bottle of wine." He shook his head. "Weird."

I raised an eyebrow. "She brought *wine*? Simon, what planet are you living on? She's got the hots for you."

"Her?" He looked genuinely surprised.

"Yeah. Her. She even thought your man-bun was sexy. Why'd you cut it off?"

"Got tired of dealing with it."

"So, back to Ms. DuBois. She's gorgeous, don't you think? Got a killer figure, too. Reminds me of Pamela Anderson, back in the day."

The edges of his eyes crinkled as he smiled. "Not my type. But I did hire her son, Ethan, to pull weeds. Nice kid." He straightened up. "One of these days, I need to get a dog. Maybe you can advise me."

"Daisy came from the shelter. Hard to believe she wasn't wanted. That's the only place I will get a pet buddy."

"Then it's a date. I'll need to go shopping for supplies, too, and could use your expertise on that as well. I've never had a dog."

"You're going to love having a canine companion. Let me know when you're ready. There are several shelters on the Central Coast, so we should be able to get you hooked up with a new love."

He grinned. "I am ready for a new love."

Daisy was getting antsy, so we said our goodbyes and moved along.

After hearing about the two new deaths at the park, I decided to walk over and see what was going on. Maybe I'd run into Hank and get an update.

On the way, we passed Peggy and Antonio's house. Antonio was outside, waxing his Porsche with his back to the street. I pulled my hat lower, took out my phone, and pretended to scroll —but I was actually using the camera and snapped a few photos. Don't ask me why; I just did. Maybe it's the PI in me. Ha.

The For Sale sign was gone. I was surprised that Antonio wasn't gone, too.

The park was unusually quiet—no doubt due to the two recent deaths. Murders. A couple of police cars were parked at the curb, and officers were walking through the encampment, appearing to ask questions. I was surprised not to see our local reporter on the scene. Maybe Megan Martinez had moved on to other stories.

I circled the block toward the spot where Hank had been camped the last time I was there. He wasn't there—but then I spotted him up ahead, walking the perimeter with a serious look on his face.

"Hank!" I called.

He turned, waved, and we met halfway, settling onto a bench with a metal plaque honoring some long-lost local citizen.

"I saw the news this morning," I said. "How're you holding up, Hank?"

He hung his head, slowly shaking it. "I dunno." He sighed. "You would think that the people here would be suspicious of anyone offering food. But a lot of these people..." He shrugged. "Well, you know."

I touched his arm. "I'm so sorry. Did you know the people who died?"

"No, except in passing. Did that Realtor ever remember who gave her the bagel?"

"Not that I've heard."

"We had four dudes patrolling all day yesterday and today,

too." He glanced away. "There's one now." Hank petted Daisy while we watched the senior, silver-haired, black man slowly conduct his surveillance.

"He walks like he is in a lot of pain," I said.

"Joe is. In many ways. Not just physical. That old guy is a Vietnam vet. Coast Guard."

"The Coast Guard? In Vietnam?"

"They were patrolling up and down the Mekong Delta, bringing in supplies. Surveilling. Rescuing soldiers. They played a critical part in that war and had thousands of casualties, yet most people didn't realize they were there. Joe was just a kid then. Like most soldiers."

Hank scratched behind Daisy's ears. "Joe's a quiet man. Worked at Lockheed down south until they shut down the plant he worked at. Then he and his wife opened a burger joint. Their teenage boys worked there, too. They were doing well until his wife and kids were all shot at gunpoint during a robbery. Joe was the only one who survived because he was making a bank deposit at the time of the robbery. Now we're his family." He raised a hand. "Hey, Joe. What do ya know?"

Joe nodded with a thumbs-up. "Still aboveground." He slowly moved past.

I shook my head, feeling a deep sorrow for Joe. "I cannot begin to imagine suffering a loss like that."

Daisy placed a paw on Hank's knee—her not-so-subtle way of saying, *Keep scratching*.

"Wish I had a dog," he said. "But this ain't no life for them. A lot of the people here have them, but they have enough trouble feedin' themselves, let alone a dog. If the dog gets sick, they don't have the cash to go to a vet. So they dump 'em at a shelter."

"I've always wondered about that," I said. "Especially when I see people on street corners with signs saying 'Hungry' and have two or three dogs lying beside them. Just the other day, I saw a young woman panhandling at a stop sign with three huge dogs.

That's expensive. Feeding this girl alone," I patted Daisy's head—"is practically a second mortgage. She eats like a horse."

Hank glanced at me, thoughtful. "I've been thinking about that vet who needs a kidney. You know, when I was at your office and his mother came in."

"Alex Brownstadt. Really nice guy. He's an elementary school teacher."

"Any news on that situation?"

I shook my head. "I am a fountain of no information, aren't I?"

"That's okay, Katy. I know you care, and that says a lot."

I stood. "Good talking to you, Hank. I promised Daisy this is a girl's day, so I'd better get back at it."

We continued our trek, winding around the park, then headed back toward home. My leg was throbbing a bit, so I told Daisy we'd get cozy on the couch and watch *Animal Planet*.

I debated on passing by Peggy's again, but it was the shortest route home, and not only was my leg grumbling, but my stomach was too. I glanced up the street and was relieved to see that Antonio was not outside buffing his red sports car. Still, I crossed to the other side, just in case.

As I neared Peggy's house, shouting erupted from inside. They were really going at it. The inhabitants of the vintage two-story I was passing slammed their front windows shut. I wondered how often they had to do that.

CHAPTER THIRTY-NINE

SUNDAY • OCTOBER 4

Posted by Katy McKenna

"I read your blog," said Sam over the phone. "Eric is coming over for lunch and dessert. Whatcha going to serve him? Or does it matter? You could just move straight to dessert."

"I was thinking PB&J sandwiches, carrot sticks, and a banana."

"You ate that every day during elementary school."

"I still do, because it's good. But only with orange marmalade."

"So gross. No, really. What are you making?"

"Vegan lemon pasta."

"Vegan?"

"I got the recipe from Maxie. She can't do dairy right now because of her colitis. She got the recipe from a site called *Nora Cooks*. If she says it's really good, then that's good enough for me."

"Save some for me. And, you know, you can always reheat it. If things get heated up and it cools off."

"Flowers for my lady." Eric stepped over the front door threshold and kissed my hand like Prince Charming, then reached into his pocket and gave Daisy a treat. "I brought a bottle of wine. I don't know what we're eating, but you can always save it for another day."

"This is perfect. I love pinot grigio. We're having lemon pasta and salad. This will be delicious with it."

In the kitchen, he poured us each a glass of wine. Just before we clinked them, I shared a tradition my sister, Emily, taught me. Maintaining deep eye contact while toasting and sipping is said to bring good luck. What I didn't tell him is, according to lore, if you break eye contact during the toast, you'll suffer seven years of bad sex! But Emily may have been joking about that.

Soooo... Staring intently at each other, we clinked, sipped, then got a little silly and entwined our arms and sipped again, which led to giggles, which led to kisses, which led to...dessert before lunch.

A balmy summer-like breeze stirred the leaves of the California Pepper tree, and birds chirped nearby as we savored our warmed-up pasta on the patio. The picnic table was set with the flowers Eric had brought, and colorful dishes I'd bought years ago from Pier 1, back before those stores closed. An old song that Ruby has often played for me drifted into my mind. The band was Seals and Crofts, and the song was "Summer Breeze." *Summer breeze makes me feel fine...*

The day was absolute perfection. I felt euphoric as Eric poured us another glass of pinot grigio. I lifted my glass, ready to enjoy another sip of that crisp, chilled wine, when a familiar voice floated over the fence.

Josh.

He was scolding his housesitting cousin about the state of the backyard.

Eric caught the shift in my mood. "You okay?"

"Oh. Yes. More than all right. I'm great. Really great." I stood. "Ready for seconds?"

"You mean thirds?" Eric laughed, patting his stomach. "It's delicious, but I'm stuffed. Can't believe it's vegan."

"I'm going to get a tiny bit more." I grabbed my plate and dashed for the kitchen. At the sink, I washed my hands and then clutched the edge of the counter, willing myself not to freak out. But it was too late. I was freaking out.

I haven't kept up with my yoga lessons, but one thing that stuck with me was the breathing exercises. Taking a long, shaky breath, I counted to ten, held it for another ten, and then slowly exhaled through my mouth. I repeated the process five times before serving myself some more pasta and heading back to Eric.

Chuckling, Eric said, "Sounds like your neighbor is unhappy with his tenant."

"It's his cousin. He's housesitting and living rent-free in exchange for keeping things up. He's a college student. Good kid." Answering Eric left me feeling breathless and a bit faint.

He eyed my plate. "Do you mind if I steal a bite?"

"Be my guest. And if you like, you can take some home with you. Your mother might enjoy it."

He checked his watch and sighed. "Speaking of Mom, I gotta get going. Her caregiver wants to leave at four, and it's nearly that now."

I felt sick as I filled a container with pasta for Eric. At the door, my heart twisted in an odd mixture of desire, heartache, and confusion as we kissed goodbye. The truly odd thing was, I felt guilty. Like, I was cheating on Josh with Eric.

After I watched him drive away, I locked the front door. With Daisy at my heels, I retreated to my bedroom, drew the drapes against the late afternoon sun, and curled up in bed with my girl—and the rest of the pinot grigio. Moments later, Tabitha leapt up beside us, her purr engine roaring as she kneaded the top blanket.

I grabbed the remote, flicked on the TV, and scrolled through Netflix, looking for a silly sitcom to distract my aching heart.

Then there was a knock at the door.

My pulse jumped. I checked the Ring Cam on my phone.

Josh.

Daisy wriggled, ready to rush to the door, but I shushed her, turned off my phone, slipped on my Bluetooth headphones, and took a swig of wine straight from the bottle.

CHAPTER FORTY

WEDNESDAY • OCTOBER 7
Posted by Katy McKenna

Monday, October 5: Part One

Yesterday morning, I was a nervous wreck, sneaking around the house with the curtains drawn, terrified that Josh might spot me through the windows. The problem was that if he was still next door, there was a good chance he'd see me backing out of the garage to go to work. And if that happened, he'd probably run over to say hi—maybe even with his wife, Nicole, at his side.

Stepping onto my front porch, I hid behind the curtain of trumpet vine cascading from the eaves. Peeking through the leaves, I spotted his car sitting in the driveway. I darted back inside, debating whether to call in sick. But that wouldn't be fair to Maxie. We had a client coming in this morning, and who knew what else was on the agenda? I couldn't act like a fourteen-year-old. Well, I could. And I was. But I shouldn't.

I took a shower, dressed business casual, spent a little extra time on my makeup in case he did see me, had a second cup of coffee, and weighed my options. I finally decided to sneak out, walk a few blocks, and call an Uber.

"Daisy, I have to leave you home today. But your auto feeder will give you lunch, so you'll be fine."

She was fine until the word "lunch" and then pranced around like it was Christmas morning.

"No, not now. Later." I kissed her head, gave her a cookie, and slipped out the door. Before descending the steps, I peeked through the vine screen again. All was clear, so I cut across the yard, dashed around the property line bushes, and speed-walked down the street. When I was around the corner and out of sight, I breathed a sigh of relief and continued to Maiden Lane Park before calling an Uber. While I waited on the sidewalk, I saw Hank and waved. He joined me, looking jovial.

"You seem pretty chipper," I said.

"I am."

I waited for him to elaborate, but he kept grinning—a stark contrast to the Hank I knew. Usually, his expression was a scowl.

I wondered if he was high. "Okay, I give. What's up?"

"Glad you asked. I'm headin' to the hospital to inquire about donating a kidney to your client. That Alex Brownstadt you told me about."

I know my eyes were probably bugging out. "Really? That's wonderful. But are you sure? This is a big deal, a life-changing deal, you know, and you don't even know him."

"I do know, and I've given it a lot of thought. I've done the research, and unlike those medical TV dramas, it's usually a long process: medical and mental evaluations, testing, things like that. But I need to do this. Who knows if I'll be lucky enough to be a match? So I don't want his mother to know until I do the preliminary work. I don't want to get their hopes up and then the whole thing tanks. But I do know that if I am a match, I am ready to do it. I don't drink. Don't do drugs, except an occasional joint. I'm in pretty good shape. And despite what many may think of someone living my lifestyle, I am reasonably mentally sound if you don't count the PTSD."

"I have thought about it, too. But you are way ahead of me."

My Uber pulled up. I opened the door, greeted the driver, and said to Hank, "Hop in—I'll give you a ride to the hospital."

He frowned. "Why are you taking an Uber? And why have it pick you up here instead of your house?"

I filled him in during the drive, and the more I told, the more like a dope I felt.

———

Maxie also arrived at work in an Uber. Her VW bug had bugged out and was in the shop. In the afternoon, we closed the office early and hopped into our respective rent-a-rides.

I didn't want to risk arriving at my house, spotting Josh outside, and then try to explain to my driver why I was hiding on the floor in the backseat. So I had her drop me off at the park instead. It's only three blocks from home, and it would feel good to stretch my legs.

I was nearing Peggy's house when I noticed a new For Sale sign out front. I stopped to take a quick look. "Cal Borden—Realtor." A balding, older man with a flat nose and a sunny gap-toothed smile.

I took a photo of the sign to show the gang and started to move on when I heard a blood-curdling scream. Not like the screams I heard the other day, which were clearly coming from a heated argument. This was like a death scream.

I froze, debating whether to call the police, but everything had gone quiet. I did a slow 360 to see if any neighbors were reacting. Nothing. Doors shut. No one peeking through their curtains. Heart pounding, I took a cautious step forward, then another scream rang out just as I reached the edge of the driveway.

I decided to knock on the door, and if anything seemed amiss, I'd scram and call the cops. I climbed the steps, and staying as far from the door as possible, I stretched my arm and rang the bell, then stepped to the side. Just in case a maniac answered with a gun.

Another horrible scream echoed from inside. I was ready to run when the door opened. It was Antonio. He looked stiff, serious, unnatural. Was he packing a gun behind his back?

"What do you want?" he said, sounding robotic.

"I was passing by and heard screams. I just wanted to make sure everyone's all right."

He blinked several times, then said, "We are fine." Blink, blink. "It was the TV." Blink. Blink. "I will turn down the sound." Blink. Blink.

"Are your eyes okay? My dad has dry eyes, and he blinks—"

A gun appeared, held by a ruby-ringed, feminine hand. It jabbed Antonio in the side.

"I told you not to try anything funny," said a familiar voice behind him.

Mayor Kay Nelson stepped into view, shoved him aside, and smiled at me like we were old friends. "Come in, Katy. I just made a fresh pot of coffee. Or do you prefer tea?"

"Uh, no thanks." I stepped back and turned to bolt, but her next words stopped me cold.

"It's not an invitation. Get in here."

I glanced around, hoping someone was nearby. No such luck. I weighed my options. Would she shoot me? Maybe. Probably. But at least I'd be outside where someone would find me if they heard the shot.

But all I could see was the gun. In her hand. Waving between me and Antonio. So, good judgment did not prevail. I stepped inside.

"Shut the door and lock it," she said.

I did as ordered.

"Sit on the couch. Both of you."

We sat on either side of Peggy. She was clutching a gold-fringed throw pillow to her belly, rocking and moaning. Her face was ashen, despite the thick smear of red blush on her cheeks.

I glanced down and saw blood soaking through the side of the pillow pressed against her stomach.

I asked the obvious. "Did you shoot her?"

The mayor nodded, then jabbed the gun barrel into Peggy's shoulder. "We had a deal. A simple one." She leaned into Peggy's face and shouted, "And you couldn't even do that right."

She shifted the gun to Antonio's forehead. He crumbled into sobs. Then the mayor swung the gun at me. "Your only fault is being too nosy. And I'm sorry about that. The chief has spoken highly of you. She will be sad about this. But there's nothing I can do about it."

"I don't understand," I said, shaking my head. "I have no idea what's going on here."

"I'll tell you what's going on," she said, pointing a finger at Antonio. "This guy got my granddaughter pregnant."

"She's pregnant? I didn't know," he stammered.

"Was." She glanced at Peggy. "Your wife tried to kill Kerry and succeeded in killing your unborn baby."

"No!" Peggy gasped. "I didn't know about the baby."

Antonio turned to her, face contorted in fury. "I could kill you for that."

"No need," said Kay. "Here's the thing. And you're going to love this." She chuckled. "No. On second thought, you probably won't." She tapped a finger against her cheek. "Let me see if I can get this straight. You already know that I'm Kerry's grandmother. But before my daughter, Jennifer, had Kerry...there was another unplanned pregnancy." She paused, glaring at us.

"Jenny got herself pregnant in her sophomore year in high school. She was only fifteen. Way too young to be a mother. So, she gave that baby up for adoption. A baby boy." Kay sighed. "Jenny's smart as a whip. But apparently not smart enough to grasp the concept of birth control."

Another pause. Another dagger-glare.

"Freshman year at Stanford, she got pregnant. Again. This time, she wouldn't give up the baby. A girl. Kerry. So, I raised her. Jenny had med school and a future ahead of her—she couldn't manage that with a baby on her hip. So, I stepped in."

"And here's where life really went off the rails," Kay said, her voice quieter now. "When Jenny was in her thirties, she married a nice guy, and Kerry—who was a young teenager by then—moved in with them. One big, happy family." She exhaled slowly. "But Jenny had no idea how hard that was for me."

Her hand trembled slightly as she brushed hair from her face.

"Kerry was like a daughter to me. My own daughter. I couldn't have loved her more if I'd given birth to her myself. But I knew she needed to be with her real mother. To get to know her. Still, it nearly broke me." Her eyes swept over us. "Then Jenny and her husband had a baby."

Kay gave a dry laugh. "Motherhood, nursing, hormones—all of it—stirred something in Jenny. Guilt. Regret. She started thinking about the baby boy she'd given up back in high school. She worried he hadn't ended up in a good home. So she started searching for him."

She shook her head with a wry half-smile. "Anyway, she found him. Right here in town. He was doing well, going to community college, and had a nice family. So Jen decided the right thing to do was to leave him alone and not make contact."

I turned to look at Antonio. Did he get it? Did he realize what she was saying?

Kay's sharp eyes caught mine. "Looks like you've figured it out. Care to say it out loud?"

I shook my head. "It's not my place."

"You're right. Too bad you didn't think of that when you rang the doorbell." She sighed, gazing intently at Antonio. "You are the little boy who was given up for adoption."

Antonio's face twisted in confusion. "I was adopted?"

Kay snapped, "Oh, for God's sake, they didn't tell you?"

"No!" Antonio cried, making me feel sorry for him.

Kay concluded with, "My granddaughter, Kerry, has been fornicating with my grandson. Do you know what they call that?" Back to me. "Katy, you tell him."

"Please, I can't."

She cocked the gun. "Tell him!"

"Incest," I whispered.

"I can't hear you."

"INCEST!"

Antonio sobbed, "But we didn't know."

Kay shouted, "Your wife knew!"

"No!" Peggy gasped, looking like she might pass out at any moment. "All I knew was they were having an affair—because you came to my office and told me, Kay. But I didn't know about a baby. And I didn't know she was your granddaughter until the other day at the hospital. And I definitely didn't know any of this other stuff!"

"And yet," Kay said, voice cold and steady, "you tried to kill her with that bagel."

Peggy vehemently shook her head. "No. Not kill her. Just make her sick. Make her go away. I, I didn't put any of that other stuff in it that was on the news. The, uh, lycine."

Kay said, "Xylazine?"

"Yeah. That stuff. Just enough fentanyl to make her sick."

Forgetting I had a gun pointed at me, I blurted, "But Kerry said she doesn't remember who gave her the bagel. She was your Realtor. She would've recognized you."

Peggy shook her head. "No. Antonio was the one she dealt with. He handles all our business affairs. I just signed some papers at her office. She walked in as I was walking out. We made brief eye contact, smiled politely—that's it. I didn't even know who she was until the For Sale sign went up. And I sure didn't know she was already sleeping with my husband."

I turned and glared at the mayor. "Now what?"

"Now, we all go downstairs. To the basement."

"She can't make it down any stairs," I said, nodding toward Peggy. "She needs to go to the hospital."

"My grandson can help her get down there." Kay waved the gun. "Now move. I've got a fundraiser dinner to get to."

Trying to buy time, I asked, "Who's the fundraiser for?"

She grabbed her purse and a Greazie's burger bag from the coffee table. "The homeless," she said with a smirk. "Ironic, isn't it?"

———

That's all for now. I know that's a lot to take in or even understand. It's too crazy. I will continue this post tomorrow.

CHAPTER FORTY-ONE

THURSDAY • OCTOBER 8
Posted by Katy McKenna

Monday, October 5: Part Two

The dark, dingy basement was packed with the kind of clutter only several decades could build—boxes, dated furniture, rolled-up rugs, plastic toys, and piles of old magazines yellowing with age. The sort of forgotten things you'd expect in a house that hadn't changed hands in over forty-five years. Zillow showed the last sale was sometime in the 1970s, so Peggy must've inherited the place, junk and all.

Kay dropped the Greazie's burger bag onto a chipped, vintage gold-trimmed vanity. "Well, I guess I won't be needing these now," she muttered. Then, snapping to attention, barked, "Both of you —in the corner. Now."

She turned to Antonio. "Tony! Hope you don't mind me calling you that. Pull those chairs out from under that godawful oak table."

The legs screeched across the cement floor as he dragged the heavy-looking armed dining chairs away from the table.

"God, I can't believe I owned chairs like that," Kay muttered. "The 1980s—everything was mauve and oak." She waved the gun like a traffic controller on the tarmac. "Set them a few feet apart."

I racked my brain for a way out. If Antonio and I rushed her, she might only get one shot off—at me or him. Or she might miss both of us. But the longer this dragged on, the worse our chances became. I stole a glance at him. His eyes were locked on his grandmother—the mayor.

"Tony!" said Kay. "Grab those extension cords over there on those boxes and untangle them."

I followed her gaze to a grimy, cobweb-draped pile of cords. My stomach sank. I knew exactly what was coming.

She pointed at Peggy, who I was still holding upright. "You, lucky lady, get first dibs. Sit."

Peggy collapsed into a chair with a groan. "I think I'm dying."

"Not quite yet." Kay checked her watch. "Tony, hurry up with those cords. I need to get home and change."

He yanked a long, black cord free from the jumble.

"Tie your wifey up first."

His hands trembled as he knelt in front of Peggy, securing her wrists and ankles. "I'm sorry," he whispered. "I never meant to hurt you."

"I still love you, Antonio," Peggy murmured. "I just couldn't bear to lose you."

"Famous last words," Kay muttered. Then she turned her weapon on me. "Your turn. Pick a chair."

It was now or never. I had to make a move. I shuffled toward an oak chair, eyeing its weight. If I could lift it, I might have a shot. I made as if to sit, then lunged, heaving the chair up to swing it at Kay. But it was heavier than I thought. My balance wobbled, and I crashed to the floor with the chair on top of me.

"Well," Kay said. "That didn't go well, did it? I oughta kill you right now. Tony, help the idiot up. Then tie her up tight."

He did as told, getting me upright while Kay kept the barrel of the gun pressed into the back of his head. Moments later, I was bound to the chair.

Kay tugged the cord wrapped around my wrists and the chair, checking the knots. Apparently satisfied, she stood back. "Okay, Tony. Your turn. Here's how this goes. Sit, tie your feet to the chair legs, and wrap one hand to the armrest. I'll handle the other."

She raised the gun. "And if you so much as twitch wrong, the gun goes bang. Got that?"

Her voice darkened. "And if you don't think I'll do it, think about this—if I get caught, my political career, my reputation, my standing in the community? Over. Dead. So yeah, I'd rather you three be dead than me." She paused, then smiled coldly. "Oh, wait. You are all going to be dead. And I'm walking away. Free and clear."

"How?" I thought that if I talked to her, Antonio might catch on and use the distraction to his advantage.

"Originally, I was going to feed you those burgers and let nature take its course. But with Peggy bleeding all over the place, that will raise too many questions. So, I'm going to burn this old fire trap down."

"You're going to kill your grandson? How can you do that? He is just as connected to you as Kerry is."

She glanced at Antonio, who was fake tying his feet to the chair. At least, I thought it was fake.

"I don't have a choice," she said quietly.

"Yes, you do. We all have choices, and if you do this, you will regret it until the day you die. And Kerry will be heartbroken. Her beloved grandmother will be in prison for triple homicide."

"I don't plan to get caught."

"But you will," I pushed on. "And when you do, Kerry's business will go under. No one will want to work with the grand-daughter of a murderer."

"I won't get caught. Everything is going exactly as I planned. The vagrants are already leaving. A few more deaths, and the rest will scatter. I don't care where they go, as long as it's not in my town."

"So you're the one who's been drugging the homeless?" I asked.

"How clever of you. You figured it out."

"But how did you do it without being recognized?"

Kay let out a dark laugh. "You'll love this. My benevolent grandson here told Kerry he was bringing burgers to the home-less. She thought it was sweet and told me, though she conve-niently left out the part where they were sleeping together. So I followed his lead. Started leaving bags of burgers at picnic tables. Six or seven at a time. Except...one in each batch was poisoned with a deadly dose of fentanyl and xylazine."

I flicked my eyes toward Antonio. He gave the slightest nod. "But someone might have seen you."

She smirked. "Not when I dressed as a shabby derelict. I fit right in."

"But how can you be so cold-blooded that you would murder your own grandson?"

She kept her icy gaze on me. "My troubles began with him and will end with him. I once had a happy marriage and family life. When my daughter got knocked up with him, my husband wanted us to keep the baby and raise him as our own. But my business was thriving, and I didn't want to stay home and raise another kid. And he sure wasn't going to do it. So I arranged a closed adoption." She tilted her head. "And my husband divorced me soon after."

I didn't know how much longer I could keep her talking, but I had to try. "And yet you wound up raising another of your daugh-ter's kids, anyway."

Antonio finally rose from the chair, using the advantage I'd given him.

She nodded. "I did. And look where that got me."

"But you love Kerry, right?"

"Yes. But—"

The doorbell rang. It wasn't loud in the basement, but we all heard it, and I screamed, "Help! Help! Down here! She's got a gun!"

"You stupid bitch!" Kay hissed, slamming a sweaty hand over my mouth. The gun barrel cracked into the side of my head. My neck twisted sharply, and something snapped.

The scrape of chair legs echoed behind me.

Kay spun around just as Antonio swung his chair at her. The gun fired. He crumpled to the floor, a bullet hole in his chest, his eyes wide and locked on mine.

She collapsed, unconscious—but for how long?

With my neck twisted painfully to the side and the throb from the gun barrel blow to my head roaring to life, I struggled furiously against my stiff restraints. Antonio and Peggy watched, both barely clinging to life. I yanked and twisted my arms, the rough electric extension cords digging into my skin until it was raw and bloody. That damn Antonio had tied me well.

An idea struck me. When I'm near my cell phone and say, "Hey, Nova," the virtual assistant always responds. I can ask her for directions, ask questions like how many teaspoons in a quart, and tell her to call people in my contacts. But my phone was in my purse, upstairs on the couch. I tried anyway. "HEY, NOVA!! CALL 911!!" There was no way of knowing if she heard me or not, although it was highly doubtful. I screamed again, the effort sending bolts of pain shooting through my skull and down my neck.

A groan from the floor caught my attention. Kay was stirring, trying to sit up. I was shocked. Antonio had slammed her hard with the chair, and I thought she would be out for hours. Or if I were lucky, forever. Blood seeped from a deep gash on her head, drizzling a terrifying web design over her face. And the way her left arm and hand hung, it looked like a bone was close to popping through her sunbed tan.

"You probably shouldn't be moving," I said.

She muttered, "Why would you care?"

"You need to get to a hospital. You're in bad shape. Untie me so I can help you."

"You don't look so good yourself, and I don't need your help." She let out a low moan as she sank back down.

Peggy was slumped over in her chair, unconscious. Antonio lay in a pool of blood, his glazed eyes fixed on nothing.

Groaning through clenched teeth, Kay pushed herself up again on one trembling arm to a sitting position. "You might be the only one still alive when this house goes up in flames." She added with a twisted smile, "Fun fact: in a fire, body fat acts like fuel. It doesn't burn—it melts. But hey, silver lining...the smoke will probably get you first." She staggered to her feet, swaying, and grabbed the back of my chair to steady herself. "Duty calls."

"You won't get away with it, you know."

She moved away from me. "Want to place a bet on it? Oh, wait. You can't."

"First off, I work for a private investigation firm and was supposed to be back in the office about an hour ago." I wasn't, but she didn't know that. "No doubt my boss has tried to reach me, because I always call when I'm running late. When I didn't answer, she would have tracked me on GPS. In my line of work, things can get dangerous fast, so that's normal protocol." I was making this up as I rattled on. "When she sees where I am, she'll know I'm in trouble and will alert the police chief, who, as you know, is a friend of mine." While I talked, I was still trying to get loose from my restraints without her noticing. It always looks so easy in the cop shows. "I would not be surprised if there isn't a squad car heading over at this very moment."

"Where's your phone?" she whimpered.

"In my purse. Upstairs. But it's too late. You, Madam Mayor, will be dragged out of here in cuffs and will headline this evening's news. If I were you, I'd get out of here now while you still can."

Sounding stronger, she said, "I think you're blowing hot air. I know how the wheels turn, and they won't be looking for you until you've been missing for a couple of days." She scanned the room. "You know what? Starting the fire down here makes the most sense. By the time anyone notices, it'll be too late."

Kay's eyes swept the dim basement until they fixed on a stack of old newspapers piled on top of a battered trunk. She hobbled toward them, her feet dragging across the dusty, gritty floor. "These'll do nicely," she murmured.

With her good hand, she crushed several sheets against her thigh, the paper crackling sharply in the silence, then scattered them around my feet.

"Better start saying your prayers," she said, her voice low and cold.

"Why are you doing this?" My voice cracked, and tears spilled down my cheeks. "I've never done anything mean to you. I voted for you!"

I didn't.

She was spreading paper everywhere, lining them up so the fire would flow into all the furniture, rugs, knick-knacks, and cardboard boxes around the room.

"Fire needs oxygen to burn fast, so I'll crack that window over there that faces the backyard. I doubt anyone will notice the smoke until it's too late." She winced with pain as she cranked the rusty window open. "God, my head hurts."

The mayor returned to me and pulled a cigarette lighter out of her purse. "I know I shouldn't smoke, but for once, I'm glad I do." She held the lighter to a corner of a newspaper, and it lit instantly, burned for a moment, and smoldered out in a curl of smoke.

"I need an accelerant." She inspected the nooks and crannies of the basement and found nothing that would do the job. "Be right back. I'm sure the garage will have what I need. Now, don't you go anywhere."

My back was to the stairs, but as soon as I heard the upstairs door close, I went to work again, wrestling the cords holding me tied to the chairs. I used every ounce of strength I could muster because I was going to be toast if I didn't get out of this. I didn't care if I broke bones to get free.

During my struggle, Peggy came to, lifting her head, bleary-eyed and dazed.

"Peggy! I'm trying to get loose so we can get out of here. You try, too!"

"Can't." Blood trickled from the corner of her mouth.

Still struggling, I heard the door at the top of the stairs creak open.

"Got it!" Kay sang out as she descended the wooden stairs, one slow step at a time. "Paint thinner!" She wedged the container against her stomach with her injured arm, and with a shout of agony, she unscrewed the lid and waved the can under my nose. "Take a whiff of that!"

The intense chemical smell flooded my nose, and I thought I would die at that very second.

She doused the paper and trickled the remaining liquid onto the nearby raggedy rugs. And that's when I realized I was not getting out of this alive.

Kay stood before me, looking triumphant and completely off her rocker as she extracted the yellow lighter from her pants pocket. She was about to flick her Bic when I said, "Aren't you afraid this basement will explode with you in it? The air is filled with fumes."

"If she does, we're all dead," said a familiar growl from behind me. "And I ain't ready to die today."

Hank barreled down the stairs, darted past me, slammed into Kay, and sent her crashing to the floor. The lighter flew from her hand. In one swift move, he planted a knee into her back, pinning her down as she shrieked in pain. He reached over and freed my hands, then yanked the cord from the chair and wrapped it around her wrists, tightening it as she thrashed and screamed.

"You have no idea who I am!" Kay shrieked. "I'll have you arrested and locked up for life!"

Hank laughed. "Good luck with that, Madam Mayor."

He untied my ankles from the chair legs. I scrambled to Peggy and worked at the knots, my shaky fingers slick with blood. As soon as the cords loosened, she sank to the floor. That's when I saw her stomach. The bullet had slammed into her close to where I figured her belly button was. It was hard to tell through her billowy, blood-stained blouse. Her eyes opened wide in terror.

"It's okay, Peggy. She can't hurt us anymore."

I crouched beside Kay while Hank checked Antonio. After a long pause, he shook his head. "He's gone."

"Should we try CPR?"

"It's too late for that."

Peggy wailed a gut-wrenching scream. "No! No! He can't be dead."

"I'm calling the cops and paramedics," Hank said. "Then we're getting out of here."

"What about Peggy and the mayor?"

"The paramedics can deal with those two." He nodded at Peggy. "She's in bad shape but will probably recover."

"What about the mayor?" I said. "What if she tries to get away?"

"Where's she gonna go?"

CHAPTER FORTY-TWO

Posted by Katy McKenna

Monday, October 5: Part Three

You're probably wondering why Hank showed up to save me. I asked him the same thing while we sat on the front porch steps, waiting for the police and EMTs.

"I happened to see you get out of the Uber at the same spot where we caught one this morning. I figured you were still trying to avoid your old boyfriend. Then you stopped in front of this house, went up to the porch, and rang the bell.

"It wasn't any of my business what you were doin', but I was curious. Then I saw you go inside. I've seen the guy who lives here. He often brings burgers to the people in the park, but lately I've been wondering if he's the one poisoning them." He shrugged. "Although he always sits with the people, eats one too, and seems friendly. But the dude has a mean streak. He beat up Teddy pretty good when he found him sleeping in his car. I don't know what the hell Teddy was thinking, but..." He shrugged again. "Anyway, it didn't sit well with me that you'd gone into his house."

"But it was quite a while before you showed up."

"I was debating," he admitted. "It wasn't my place to interfere, but I couldn't just walk away either. So I kept an eye out. When you didn't come out, I got a bad feeling. You know—intuition. I've learned to trust my gut. I walked down the street and stood at the front walk, still debating. Finally, I rang the bell, figuring they might call the cops on me just for standing on their porch. And then I heard someone scream for help."

"That was me—screaming for Nova to call the police."

"Nova? Who's that?"

I laughed and immediately winced. "Don't make me laugh. My neck and head are killing me. But yeah. My phone was in my purse up in the living room, so she didn't hear me."

He shook his head, looking dumbfounded. "Your phone will call the police for you?"

"Yeah. You yell, 'Hey, Nova! Call 911!' Even if the phone is locked, it will respond. Nova is the virtual assistant built into the phone."

"Good to know."

———

I wound up sharing an ambulance ride with Mayor Nelson to the ER. She was securely strapped down, so I wasn't worried about her trying to kill me again. Peggy, who was in critical condition, was taken in a second ambulance.

Most of the ride—and the emergency room—are a blur now. I know they scanned me and said I had a mild concussion and needed a few (more) stitches. No serious damage to my neck, just a severely wrenched muscle that hurts like hell. The nurse strapped a collar around my neck and handed me a welcome dose of pain pills.

Mom and Pop came to my rescue and took me home. They wanted me to stay at their house, but that meant packing up berserko Daisy. So, Mom insisted on spending the night with me instead.

About an hour later, Ruby and Samantha showed up bearing dinner and goodies.

We watched the six o'clock local news—and guess what? I'm in the news again.

But this time, the lead story was: "Homeless man saves local crime fighter—and takes down the mayor."

Me. Local crime fighter.

EPILOGUE

TUESDAY · OCTOBER 27
Posted by Katy McKenna

Catch-up time!

I haven't blogged for a while. Been really busy!

I'm sure you're all wondering about our illustrious mayor, Kay Nelson. What a messy, tragic story—for so many people.

She was arrested on suspicion of I don't even know how many vagrant murders, plus the murder of her grandson, Antonio, and the attempted murders of Peggy and me.

And get this—she's pleading not guilty.

At some point, there'll be a long, drawn-out trial that'll probably get way too much airtime on the news stations and every trashy tabloid show out there. And yes, that also means I'll have to testify. Really not looking forward to that.

I feel awful for Kerry. And—I can't believe I'm saying this—I feel a little sorry for Peggy, too. She's in serious trouble for nearly killing Kerry.

As things unfold, I'll continue to blog about it. Stay tuned.

Update on the murder of Theodore "Teddy" Herbert Hastings III: I've asked Angela several times whether his killer has been caught, and the answer is still no. She's doubtful it will ever happen. She told me that in the United States, about half of all murder cases go unsolved—and the clearance rate for murders of homeless individuals is even lower.

Now, for some good news!

Hank is a kidney donor match for Alex Brownstadt! Can you believe it? What are the odds—and so quickly, too.

If Hank hadn't overheard that conversation at the office, none of this would be happening. Ruby called it "serendipity." It means the occurrence of events by chance in a happy or beneficial way, often resulting in good fortune or lucky discoveries.

The Brownstadts don't know yet. We have an appointment with them tomorrow to share the good news, and Hank wants to be there to meet Alex in person.

It's wild to think that someone I once would've walked past without a second glance—just another faceless homeless man—is now my friend. A kind, decent man who's been through more than most of us could ever imagine.

This entire experience has significantly altered my perception of people on street corners holding signs. I used to avoid eye contact, always assuming the worst—drugs, mental illness, danger.

But the truth is, everyone has a story. Like Teddy. He was a good man, too.

I've got more good news! No, I'm not getting married—although Eric has been hanging around quite a bit.

I do feel a little bad that he found out about my near incineration on the news, but honestly, that first night, and the day after, I was in no shape to call anyone. Thank goodness for pain meds and doggy/kitty cuddles!

Simon's also been visiting a lot. And no, not that kind of visiting. He's working on a new project, and I'm very excited about it. Fingers crossed; government bureaucracy doesn't strangle it before it even starts. Here's the scoop: Simon plans to buy a large parcel of unincorporated land outside the city limits and build an off-grid, solar-powered, self-sustaining community for unhoused individuals who qualify to live there.

In other words: no thugs, no drugs, no criminal records, and no active addictions. People in recovery will be welcome, depending on how long it has been since their last use. Everyone accepted will help build the community from the ground up and work together to sustain it. We're talking a big bunkhouse, several tiny homes, wells, a large-scale atmospheric water generator, an eco-friendly sewage system that recycles gray water, composting, and gardens to grow non-GMO organic food. There will be a dining hall that also serves as a meeting space for activities such as all-denominational church services and educational programs.

Plus, a unisex barber shop coordinated by my mom, and a 24-hour security team led by my retired police officer dad. Ben has offered his services on the legal end of things.

In the future, there will be a farmstand to sell produce grown on the commune, along with an apiary—that's beekeeping, for those like me who had no clue. The bees will also help pollinate the crops.

The first residents? Homeless veterans struggling with PTSD, and retired military dogs also battling PTSD. One of the future goals is to adopt and train shelter dogs to become PTSD support companions.

If this plan gets the green light, we—Simon, Hank, Pop, Mom, Walter, Maxie, and me—will begin interviewing the folks currently living in Maiden Lane Park who qualify to help build the community. I've already spoken with Angie Yaeger, and she's on board. She'll be with us when we pitch it to the town council.

But honestly—how can the city say no? This project won't use a single tax dollar. Simon's footing the initial bill, and it won't impact any existing neighborhoods. And get this—Hank will run the community alongside Simon.

This could be the start of something big.

AFTERWORD

Dear Readers,

Writing this series is a labor of love, and much of it is borrowed from my own experiences.

My grandpa lived in the VA home in Yountville—long before Napa Valley became the trendy wine country destination it is today. The town's also home to the world-renowned restaurant, The French Laundry.

Grandpa served in both World War I and World War II. When I was in grade school, we were pen pals, and my family often made the drive from our hometown of Redwood City, California, to visit him. Our lovable brown-and-white Chihuahua, Bambi, always came along for the ride. She was a big hit with all the old soldiers. These days, we'd probably call her a therapy dog.

Like Maxie, I also have ulcerative colitis. I was first diagnosed in fifth grade, and as a kid, it was incredibly embarrassing. I often skipped lunch because I knew I'd end up sick in the bathroom—which, of course, led to a lot of hurtful teasing. Boy, do I have some mortifying stories! Thankfully, my close friends understood and supported me.

Both my mother and grandmother died from colon cancer, so I'm religious about getting those oh-so-fun colonoscopies!

Here's a little story regarding Katy watching an old episode of *Moonlighting* during a stakeout. Back when the show was still airing, my best friend and I were on a girls' trip to Los Angeles.

One night, after a fun evening at The Comedy Store, we were walking back to our car along Sunset Boulevard. A sleek, sporty black car pulled up beside us, stopped at the curb, and rolled down the passenger window. The driver leaned across the seat and said, "Ladies, it's not safe to be walking around this late at night. Want a ride to your car?" And then I saw him. Behind the wheel —Bruce Willis. Be still my heart!

I've learned a lot about our homeless population while writing this book. While I can't fix the problem, I've found small ways to help. I now carry portioned bags of kibble for their dogs and keep a stash of umbrellas in my car for rainy days when I see someone sitting on a bench, soaked to the skin. The grateful look on their face always makes my day.

Thanks for coming along on this journey with Katy—and with me. I'm so glad you're here. I'm already hard at work on the next book in the series!

With Love,
Pam

ABOUT THE AUTHOR

I live on the Central Coast of California with my husband, Mike, and our furry canine kids—also known as my office companions and writing inspirations.

Mike and I have been partners in the restaurant business for decades. We own Klondike Pizza restaurants and are fortunate to have wonderful, caring managers who keep me busy with fun projects, along with energetic young crews who help me stay connected to their world.

After more than 37 years in business, we're deeply rooted in our community and grateful for the opportunity to give back through fundraisers that support local children, animal shelters, and a nearby farm sanctuary.

When I'm not at the keyboard, you'll probably find me working in the garden, reading a good book, strumming my guitar, doing Pilates, binge-watching TV shows, or being silly with our grandkids.

EMMA and MAGGIE

To visit my Website and Blog-

although I hardly ever blog! I wonder why?
Pamela Frost Dennis

For links to more:
linktr.ee/pamelafrostdennis

ALSO BY PAMELA FROST DENNIS

DEAD GIRLS DON'T BLOG

Book #1 in the Murder Blog Mysteries

Katy McKenna's life takes a dramatic turn when she stumbles upon a newspaper story about the upcoming parole hearing for one of the men who raped and murdered her high school friend, sixteen years ago. Fearing he could soon be set free to prey on other innocent young girls, Katy sets out to make sure this doesn't happen, not realizing she might not survive to blog about it.

BETTER DEAD THAN WED

Book #2 in the Murder Blog Mysteries

Katy McKenna has had enough near-death experiences and heartache to last a lifetime. Now all she wants to do is get her career back on track, find a nice guy, and live happily-ever-after. But when she hears about a man maliciously exposing innocent young women to HIV, she is compelled to put her plans on hold to stop him.

Meanwhile, Katy's mother is forced to reveal a shattering childhood trauma that has come back to haunt her; her obnoxious baby sister is moving in, and her scuzzy was-band is stalking her.

And she's beginning to wonder why every rotten person she has recently heard about has suddenly dropped dead. Is it divine providence? Or is it murder?

COINS AND CADAVERS

Book #3 in the Murder Blog Mysteries

While battling a furry vermin invasion in the spooky attic of her old house, Katy discovers a vintage wooden chest hidden behind a wall.

Although everyone assures her the box is legally hers, its incredible contents compel Katy to search for the rightful owner.

Meanwhile, she takes a temp job assisting her hunky P.I. neighbor, Josh Draper. The assignment: Trap a sleazy wife-cheater. Something Katy knows about all too well from personal experience. During a cozy stakeout in Draper's two-seater, things get awkward as the sizzling tension builds. Who will make the first move?

Since she's already been searching online for past owners of her home, Grandma Ruby asks Katy to use her sleuthing skills to discover what happened to her great-great-grandfather, a bigamist. Katy's quest leads her to find an extended family she never knew existed.

Family secrets are revealed, for better or worse....

Romance blossoms, for better or worse....

And Katy's good intentions lead her into

a terrifying dilemma she may not survive.

WAS IT MURDER?

Book #4 in the Murder Blog Mysteries

Nothing bad ever happens in the peaceful English village of Bridleford—except for murder, that is.

A dear family member has met an untimely end. Now Katy and Grandma Ruby must travel to the Cotswolds of England to sort out legal matters. When they arrive, they're overwhelmed by the friendly villagers who offer help and moral support.

However, when Katy and Ruby become the target of vandals, they realize that not everyone in town is pleased about their presence. *Is murder next on the list?*

WHILE SHE SLUMBERED

Book # 5 in the Murder Blog Mysteries

With her boyfriend, Josh, in Los Angeles caring for his dying ex, a heartbroken Katy turns to blogging and visits with her elderly neighbor, Nina.

When Nina's niece, mystery writer Donna, arrives, Nina is thrilled—at first. Within two days, she confides to Katy, "This visit can't end soon enough."

Soon after, Katy finds herself blocked at the door by Donna, who insists Nina is "too sick" to see anyone. Suspicion takes hold. Is Nina really ill, or is her overbearing niece crafting a deadly plot of her own? Katy is determined to get past the gatekeeper—and protect her friend.

————

Pamela is in her backyard office

working on book #7.